Hallmark
PUBLISHING

CINDI MADSEN

COUNTRY HEARTS

Print ISBN: 978-1-947892-66-8
eBook ISBN: 978-1-947892-67-5

www.hallmarkpublishing.com

TABLE OF CONTENTS

To my smarty-pants son, Brody,
who read one of the classroom scenes and told me
"Mom, I like this. I'm going to read this
whole book when you're done."

CHAPTER ONE

This is what I get for saying I wanted an adventure.

"Wanted" sounded much better than "no other alternatives."

When whisperings of budget cuts became a reality, the principal of the school Jemma had worked at for three years had called her into his office. He told her that the administration was sorry, but they had to lay her off. Considering her limited options, she'd had to smother her panic, roll with the punches, and take a risk.

As she sat in the living room of the cottage she'd been renting for all of a day, she experienced a pinch of loneliness. Add her worries about the raging storm outside, and she struggled to maintain the optimism she'd kept a tight grip on since taking the temporary teaching position. In a tiny Colorado town she'd never heard of before finding the job posting, no less.

The truth was, she did need something new. A bit of a shakeup to get her out of her funk. While she could handle a classroom full of kids like nobody's business—partially because she understood occasionally losing focus and the importance of making learning fun—she was working on taking control and being less of a hot mess in her personal life. On being bolder and having the courage to meet new people and take more chances.

Surely seizing the opportunity to live somewhere besides the city where she'd grown up would help with that, even if it was a forced sort of help.

A crack of thunder vibrated the window panes, and a little shriek escaped. Since she'd nearly spilled her tea, Jemma set her favorite extra-large mug on the coffee table and tightened her fuzzy fleece blanket around herself. *It's an adventure. It's an adventure.*

When people said they wanted an adventure, usually exotic locations or rollercoasters came to mind. Bungee jumping. That kind of thing. Whereas she shuddered at the idea of trusting a rickety man-made machine or flinging herself off a bridge. What if something went wrong? Did people really trust a cord to catch them? Because she certainly didn't.

It wasn't that she was the type of person to need her entire life mapped out or for everything to go according to plan. No, as a third-grade teacher, she'd forever be disappointed if she let curve balls get to her. If there was one thing you couldn't plan for, it was what would pop out of a kid's mouth next. But she needed to be more organized and less idealistic, and the next time she was in a relationship, she wouldn't be the only one aware it was happening.

How could I have been so clueless? Why didn't I confirm we were dating instead of hanging out?

It definitely would've saved her a lot of frustration and sorrow. It made her feel delusional to mourn the loss of a boyfriend who'd turned out to only be a friend. Especially since in the beginning, she'd passed up a more-secure position to stay at the school where Simon worked so they could grow that friendship into more.

Maybe I should just give up on guys altogether and embrace the idea of being single forever.

The wind outside picked up speed, rattling the shutters on the window, and her heart rate kicked up a few notches. She glanced at the large black-and-white bunny at her side. "You'll protect me, won't you, Señor Fluffypants?"

Her former students had helped her name him, settling on Señor Fluffypants because of the black patch of fur over his nose that looked like a moustache. She'd had him since he could fit in her palm, but he'd grown into a four-pound snuggly floofball.

At the next grumbling burp of thunder, he jumped off the cushion next to her and rushed under the couch. So much for her knight in fluffy armor.

No need to be scared. Surely this house would've blown away long ago if it was that fragile.

Or maybe the years of decay will catch up now that I've decided to move in.

With its cheery blue trim and shutters, and the faint remains of vines crawling across the white exterior, the country cottage had looked so idyllic. Like she could spend her weekends curled up on the couch with her tea and a book and get lost for a few hours.

Now she felt lost in the way that she didn't know anyone, her bunny had abandoned her, and she couldn't concentrate on her book with the storm raging outside. Who knew thunder could be that loud?

The sky lit up outside, a streak of lightning making the world bright before it went dark again.

Man, I wish I could call up Randa and beg her to come over. Her fellow teacher had started out as Jemma's mentor, but they'd quickly become best friends. When Jemma had freaked out over being fired and asked how on earth she was supposed to pay her student loans and bills, Randa had talked her down from the ledge. She'd reminded Jemma of all the times they'd tried new activities—like the time Randa had convinced her to eat at the new Indian food restaurant and Jemma had found a new spicy dish to love, tingling lips and all. Or how they'd accidentally made a wrong turn and ended up completely lost but laughing until they were crying.

They called their mishaps adventures, and because of those adventures, they'd tried out more interesting restaurants and had funny stories to tell in the teachers' lounge and at parties.

With that in mind, Jemma had pulled up her bootstraps and cast a wide net as she'd searched for a new position. Even with good references and Randa's connections, no one was hiring—not mid-year, when most contracts were already filled.

But then Jemma had found a listing to cover for a third-grade teacher on maternity leave. She'd applied on a whim, and when Principal Alvarez had called for an interview and they'd hit it off, Jemma had become convinced this was the position for her.

And when she'd experienced a bit of trepidation over moving to the small town of Haven Lake where she didn't know anyone, she'd told herself it'd been a while since she'd had a real adventure and that she was going to embrace this one.

She lifted her phone and pulled up her dictionary app— she was always puzzled when people were surprised she used it so often. Why wouldn't you take advantage of having a dictionary at your fingertips?

Thanks to being in the middle of nowhere, it took forever for her phone to spit out the definition.

ad·ven·ture *noun*
an unusual and exciting, typically hazardous experience or activity

"Wait. Typically hazardous?" Jemma's voice pitched higher. "Why didn't I read this definition *before* moving here? Señor Fluffypants, did you know about this?"

Her bunny stuck his furry head out from under the couch, but the loud bang on the door made him skitter back underneath. It also made Jemma jump enough that she dropped her phone. She stared at the wooden door as if she had X-ray vision.

Who'd come knocking when she didn't know anyone yet? Especially in this storm?

The loud rapping noise came again, and there was something odd about it. It sounded low and almost...metallic?

Jemma gripped her phone in case she needed to call the cops—who knew how long it would take them to get all the way out here?—and padded across the room. There wasn't a peephole because of course there wasn't.

She swung open the door, and a large horse snout darted inside.

She fell back on her bum, her mind struggling to make sense of the image in front of her as her tailbone throbbed from the impact. The falling sleet around the white horse served as a dreary background, and the creature whinnied, the sound even louder than the raging storm.

"I'm not sure what you want," she said, because this had been a weird day and she might as well cap it off by talking to a horse.

The horse stomped a foot, the metallic cling of its shoes making her go *ah, that was why the knock sounded like that.* It didn't magically tell her why there was a horse on her porch, though.

Just how backwoods was this town?

Jemma pushed to her feet and cautiously approached the horse.

The cold air was rushing in, making her wish for the blanket she'd left on the couch, but when the horse sniffed her hand, she couldn't bring herself to pull away and slam the door in its face. He—or she—was beautiful. White, all except the black nose and gray speckles across its face. Sleek and muscular, with a long, snowy mane blowing in the wind.

Out of the corner of her eye, Jemma caught movement, and a dark figure materialized as whoever it was strode closer. More details stood out as he stepped into the pool of light the open door sent across the porch.

Male, tall, strong jaw, and cowboy hat.

Jemma reached up and smoothed a hand down her hair, sure it was messy from all the unpacking and furniture rearranging.

"I'm sorry," he said, sliding a bridle on to the horse's large head. "I tried to catch him, but he was off and running before I could get out the door."

Their eyes met for a brief second, and an unfamiliar swirl went through Jemma's gut.

Mr. Cowboy ran his hand down the horse's neck as he secured a rope to the bridle with his other hand. "I'm assuming you're the person who's renting Mrs. Klein's cottage."

"That or I broke in before the horse could beat me to it," she said.

Mr. Cowboy laughed, and the swirl in her gut grew stronger. He tugged the rope and pulled the horse a few feet back so its hooves were no longer breeching the line between the doorway and her living room floor. "I'm Wyatt Langford. I live just yonder."

Yonder? People actually said yonder? "Jemma Monroe."

Wyatt reached up and adjusted the tan cowboy hat on his head, seemingly unbothered by the sleet dripping onto his long coat. "Anyway, Mrs. Klein used to feed Casper carrots, and he's not getting the message that she doesn't live here anymore. Or that he's *supposed* to stay in the barn, especially on cold nights." Wyatt used his grip on the reins to twist the horse's face toward his. "If I didn't know any better, I'd swear you're trying to make sure I catch my death. Then who'd feed you, huh? Did you think about that?"

She smiled at the affectionate way he "scolded" his horse. It was a tactic she sometimes used in her classroom.

"Anyway, we'll get out of your hair."

A bolt of lightning flashed across the sky, followed closely by a rumble of thunder, and they both glanced toward the heavens as the horse clomped back a couple of anxious steps.

"I didn't realize lightning and thunder could accompany snow," Jemma said. "Or sleet or slush or whatever this is."

Wyatt tipped his head toward the right, and she caught a glimpse of sandy-blond hair. "It's the lake effect. We had an unseasonably warm day for winter, but then a cold front came in off the lake. Once they clash, you get crazy weather like this. I hope you're prepared for lots of snow. This is just the beginning, and one of the milder storms at that."

She wanted to say she'd dealt with snow before, but the fact of the matter was she'd never dealt with it very well. She didn't like that it interfered with her preferred choice of foot-wear, or how the floors were always muddy. But it was regularly cleared by snowplows, and life went on. Still, something about his warning made her think about that "hazardous" part of an adventure.

Then again, judging by the pair on her porch, maybe it wouldn't all be hazardous. "Would you like to come in for a bit? You could warm up and we could cha—"

"Sorry, I've got to get back. Nice meeting you," he said, tipping his hat, but what she heard was *I'm done talking to you.*

He led the horse down the porch steps, and she closed the door.

A shiver racked her body, and she rushed back to the couch and wrapped herself with the discarded blanket. Like earlier when she'd heard the knock, she glanced at the door, and her mind conjured the image of the cowboy and his horse walking away.

She'd hoped for a slightly warmer welcome, both temperament and temperature-wise.

All her worries rose up again, and she told herself that she just needed to settle in, first into her cottage and her routine and, in two more days, into her new job.

Sure, maybe this adventure didn't feel quite as fun without her usual copilot. But with any luck, there would be other people who'd take time to get to know her and chat.

Even if it clearly wouldn't be the cowboy next door.

CHAPTER TWO

"BAILEY RAE!" WYATT'S FOOTSTEPS ECHOED through the living room as he burst inside, stomping snow off his boots and doing his best not to track in mud, which was a losing battle 'round these parts, no matter the season. "We're gonna be late!"

With the grass dried up and buried under snow, wintertime meant all the animals needed to be fed first thing in the morning, the harvesting machinery needed tuning up as soon as he could get to it, and the cows were getting nice and fat, ready to have babies come spring.

Although, there were a few heifers he was already watching, because a handful of calves inevitably came before expected, usually during a horrible snowstorm.

Each season seemed busier than the last, work piling up faster than he could get to it, and there was always so much to be done. Since there hadn't been school for the past two and a half weeks as they'd celebrated Christmas and New Year's, Bailey had fallen into old habits of staying up late and sleeping in. He'd woken her up before heading to the barn, and to try to gauge where his eight-year-old daughter was in her getting-ready routine, he glanced at the table.

At least the dirty bowl, the cereal box, and the carton

of milk she'd left out yet again meant she'd eaten breakfast. "You've got to put away the milk, or it'll go bad."

It wasn't the first time he'd reminded her, and he highly doubted it'd be the last.

Bailey Rae rushed into the room, one strap of her backpack in place, her blond curls sticking up in every direction. *Dang it. I forgot to braid it last night.* Evidently they were both out of practice on the school routine.

When he'd pictured his life as a father, he never would've guessed there'd be so much shopping for clothes and learning how to style hair. But once his ex-wife had decided she wanted a city life—a *single* one—his list of daddy duties had doubled.

"Sorry about the milk, Daddy." His daughter looped her arm through the other strap of her backpack. "I was just trying to put together the perfect outfit."

"And you've succeeded," he said, eyeing her zebra-print shirt, rainbow-striped skirt, and heart leggings. Plus the sparkly pink cowboy boots she never went anywhere without. He'd thought she might outgrow wearing all the colors and prints at once, but the fashionista was strong with this one.

As strong as her cowgirl side, and for as young as she was, she was actually a lot of help.

After she woke up and did some primping, that was. But since she worked hard, both on the ranch and at school, acing her homework and tests to the point they'd put her in a few advance classes, he was glad she remained a kid in some areas.

Wyatt motioned her closer, swiping his hands on his jeans before gathering her hair and wrestling the strands into a semi-tangled ponytail. Braiding it before bed helped tame the frizz and kept out the snarls, but sometimes you just had to make do.

If they didn't hurry, she was going to be late, so he decided to forgo trying to find anything in her messy room and pulled a rubber band out of the junk drawer.

"Do you think my new teacher will be nice?" Bailey Rae asked, wincing as he secured the band.

"I'm sure they will be." Anna Lau, the teacher she'd had the first half of the year, had started her maternity leave shortly before Christmas break, so the school had hired another teacher to fill in for the first couple of months of the year.

He'd gotten an email about it, but he'd been in a hurry and had meant to look at it later. Only, five hundred other more pressing things had come up and he'd forgotten, and this was why he was forever behind. "Do you have your lunch?"

Bailey Rae lifted her unicorn lunchbox and turned around so Wyatt could slide it into her matching backpack.

He eyed the thin hoodie draped over her arm. "You need a warmer coat than that."

She let her head roll back, and her lower lip came out in a pout. "But my big coat ruins the outfit."

Wyatt crossed his arms and gave her the hard stare. "Remember our agreement about leggings?" He didn't want to say he'd lost the battle, but more that they'd compromised. He wouldn't keep insisting on warmer jeans if she'd wear a heavy coat, plus gloves.

"Fine," she said, slipping off her backpack and pulling on her puffy pink winter coat before struggling into her backpack for the second time.

"It's important to be prepared. You don't want to go out in bad weather without a coat. What if the truck got a flat tire? Or the battery died? Then you'd need to hike, and you'd risk gettin' frostbite, all for fashion."

It was part of his job to prepare her for the world. To teach her how to be self-sufficient and plan for every scenario. This world could be a bumpy place, and while he didn't want her to lose her free spirit, he didn't have much patience for failing to be prepared. For not practicing caution. When you worked around machinery and big animals, you *had* to be cautious, or the consequences could be life-changing, possibly deadly.

Bailey Rae blinked her big brown eyes at him—eyes she'd gotten from her mother. "Well, I'd just have you carry me, then I'd be warm and it'd help you stay warm too. Win-win." An over-the-top grin spread across her face, and he shook his head but lost the battle to hold back his own smile.

His precocious daughter quickly closed her lips, as if she remembered she was no longer smiling big enough for her teeth to show. He'd tried to talk to her about it, but she'd clamped up and told him it was "nothing" over and over. Now her used-to-be signature grin only made rare appearances and disappeared way too quickly.

Inwardly Wyatt sighed, wishing he could figure out why. Another thing they didn't have time for, so he gestured toward the door. "In the truck, smarty pants."

The cold air slapped his skin as they rushed down the steps and climbed into the truck. He'd left it running, so the cab was at least toasty.

Wyatt pulled out of the driveway and headed down the winding dirt road that led to the highway into town.

His phone chimed with a text, and he dug it out of his snap-button shirt pocket and automatically handed it to Bailey Rae.

"It's Aunt Lori, asking if you need her to pick me up after school. She also says she has leftover stew and wondered if we wanted some."

"Tell her—"

"'Yes to the stew,'" Bailey Rae said as she texted, "and thanks, but since she has a new teacher, I'm taking her to get a treat after school.' And sent."

"Sounds like you've got it." Not what he would've said, though, because his sister had enough to do without providing them dinner. Lori often helped with rides and meals and things like birthday parties. She also treated Bailey Rae to the occasional spa day, where she'd come home with glittery nails in every color. But since Lori had had another baby a couple of months ago, she was plenty busy herself, and he didn't like having to bother her. But it'd be a shame to let stew go to waste, and he'd save her a trip by picking it up on his way home from town, after he'd dropped off Bailey Rae.

As they neared the end of the snow-covered dirt road, he spotted a cherry-red vehicle. The back end spun left to right instead of the tires propelling the tiny car forward.

"You're gonna get stuck in the bar pit," he said, although the driver was too far away to hear.

The back end slid and, sure enough, the car drifted off the road and into the small burrow that helped water and melted snow drain.

Wyatt slowed, easing the brake pedal to the floor as he downshifted.

Spatters of white flipped off the uselessly spinning tires of the red car. Did the driver really think slamming on the gas would magically fix the messy predicament?

The door to the car opened, and the woman who'd moved into the cottage next door stepped out. She struggled to get up the slight incline but finally made it up to the level part of the road.

Is she wearing high-heeled boots?

Her dark hair was curled and cascading around her shoulders, a stark contrast to the red coat that looked about as thick as the hoodie Bailey Rae had tried to wear. She rounded the car, headed back down the slight incline, and shoved against the trunk, as if that'd actually move her car.

Unless she was the Hulk, that vehicle wasn't going to budge.

"Stay here," Wyatt said to Bailey Rae as he threw the truck in park.

"Way ahead of you. I don't want to freeze my nose off or get my outfit all snowy. And yeah, yeah, I'd deal with it for survival purposes if I had to."

Jemma probably had the same plan with her fancy outfit, and therein was the problem with not dressing for the weather—she was asking for frostbite for sure.

She spun to face him as he climbed out of the truck.

At first she squinted at him, but then her forehead smoothed. "Oh. Hi again." Her cheeks and nose were pink, and a puff of white escaped her mouth as she gave a long exhale. "I, uh, seem to be stuck."

"And getting more so by the second."

She frowned at him, so clearly that was the wrong thing to say. Still, he couldn't seem to get a hold of his mouth.

"What are you thinking, wearin' those shoes when there's this much snow on the ground?"

Her frown deepened. "I just wanted to look nice. I'm not clueless—I wore snow boots to shovel my sidewalk, but I figured once I got going, I'd make it into town and..." She glanced at her car again, and her dangly silver earring got stuck in her scarf. She went cross-eyed while removing it with her too-thin gloves. "Don't they plow these roads?"

"Way out here?" he asked with a laugh. "The town barely maintains the main roads. You're going to need snow tires and possibly chains, especially on that little car. I warned you there'd be a lot of snow."

"'A lot' is such a vague term. One I underestimated." She took a step, slipped, and worked to steady herself on the car. "I really need to get into town. It's my first day. I can't be late."

"Late" was something he was going to know too much about here pretty quickly, but it wasn't like he'd leave her stranded. He headed to his truck and grabbed a shovel out of the back.

Jemma waved, a big smile on her face, and while he was confused for a second about what he'd done to get that kind of reaction, he realized the wave was meant for Bailey Rae. She'd leaned so close to the windshield that the tip of her nose was pressed against the fogged-up glass.

As Wyatt neared, Jemma's smile wavered. She hugged her arms around herself and stomped, he assumed in an attempt to get warm.

"You can climb into the truck with my daughter if you'd like. The heater's cranked nice and high."

"Oh, I…" The longing glance she aimed at the truck gave her away, although he could tell she was about to politely decline.

"I've got this. It'd actually be better if I didn't have to worry about where you're standing."

"Okay. I guess just holler if you need my help."

Fat chance, but at least he managed to keep those words from coming out of his mouth. He didn't want to be mean, despite the fact that this entire situation could've been easily avoided.

Jemma picked her way over to the truck in those absurd shoes, opened the creaky door, and then he got to work digging around her tires so he could get on with his overbooked day.

"Hello," Jemma said to the adorable blond girl once she could get her teeth to stop chattering. "Sorry for the delay."

"It's okay." Her knee went to bouncing, pulling Jemma's attention to the rainbow-colored skirt and heart leggings. "I'm sorta nervous 'bout today, anyway."

Jemma's stomach drifted up near her ribcage as she fretted over her first day at a new school, where she wouldn't have Randa down the hall in case she needed backup. Where she didn't know *anyone*. "Me too."

The little girl gave her outfit a once-over. "You look nice. I love the bright red, and those earrings are supercool. Someday I'm going to wear the big, dangly ones, but Daddy says I have to wait till I'm older. And when I ask, 'But how old?' he always just says, 'Older.'"

Jemma bit back her laugh and decided to focus on the compliment part. "Thank you." She smoothed a hand down the skirt of her black-and-white striped dress, where her more conservative white leggings filled the gap between the end of it and the start of her knee-high boots. "I'm afraid that I went with looks over warmth, and now I'm paying for it."

"Story of my life," the little girl said with a dramatic sigh, and this time Jemma did laugh. She was an explosion of colors and styles. If Jemma tried something so bold, she'd look ridiculous, but this girl made it work.

"Well, you do look fabulous. I'm Jemma, by the way."

"Bailey. My family mostly uses my first and middle name, so I go by Bailey Rae as well. You can call me either one."

Jemma's gaze drifted to her car as Wyatt climbed inside,

the shovel he'd been using sticking up out of the ground next to her back tires. "Does this happen a lot? People getting stuck out here?"

"No one 'sides us really lives out here anymore. Mrs. Klein hardly ever went anywhere before she moved to Arizona. But don't worry, my dad will get you unstuck."

Sure enough, her car lurched forward, and Wyatt drove it up the slight hill until the front two tires were on the paved road.

Currently it was about as white as the rest of the world, although there weren't as many snow drifts as on this tiny dirt road.

Jemma twisted in the seat, her knee lightly knocking into the steering wheel. "It was nice meeting you, Bailey. I live next door now, in Mrs. Klein's cottage, so I'm sure we'll be seeing more of each other."

Bailey nodded and sat back in her seat, and Jemma sucked in a breath to prepare for the cold before opening the door. Her boots slid in the snow, and she cursed herself for wearing them. If she was late for her very first day, her outfit wouldn't be nearly as impressive. And judging from the disapproving way Wyatt had eyed her footwear, he certainly wasn't impressed.

She smothered her offense and focused on what was important. "Thank you for your help."

"Sure thing. Now, what you're gonna wanna do is keep your momentum going, but not too fast. Just turn into the back end if you start to lose control."

Right. She'd totally do that. Her hesitation must've showed, because he asked, "Think you can manage to get into town from here?"

"I hope so." It was more honest than she meant to be,

but she was realizing she didn't know much about driving in snow like this. That she *was* unprepared.

The nerves she'd tamped down drifted up again, making her worry if she was also unprepared for a whole new classroom dynamic. What if her usual tricks didn't work on country kids?

When in doubt, fake it till you make it. With that in mind, she lifted her chin. "I got it, thank you."

"Okay, well, I'll be behind you if you need me."

That fact added more pressure, although it was also semi-reassuring. At least she wouldn't be stuck for hours, but she didn't want him to have to stop again. To delay him even more.

Since he didn't seem to be big on conversation, and her toes and fingers were going numb, she climbed into her warm car. The tires slid a bit as she pulled on to the main road, but she managed to keep the car straight. The closer they got to town, the better the roads were.

Once they hit Main Street, Jemma desperately wanted to stop at the cute coffee shop with the welcoming white-and-blue awning to get a morning pick-me-up, but she'd spent every spare minute she had dealing with the snow. Instead of pulling off the road, she simply gave a pining glance to the vinyl cup of joe on the window and drove on to the old brick elementary school, pulling around to the side of the building with the teachers' lounge.

Unfortunately, there'd be no time to lounge or meet her coworkers, but she did need to check in with the principal before rushing to her class to meet her new students.

CHAPTER THREE

"I'M USUALLY EARLY, I PROMISE," Jemma said to Camilla Alvarez, the principal she'd interviewed with to get the job.

They'd also met yesterday so she could at least halfway set up the classroom in the way that worked for her. While she was forever running behind, when it came to her job, she worked to be not just on time but early, and she hated going into a classroom without time to collect herself. Kids sensed fear, and she'd wanted to have a few minutes to settle in before her first student showed up.

Thanks to getting stuck, there were probably already several kids in the room, getting unrulier by the second.

"Don't worry about it. You missed the bell by mere seconds." For such a short person, Camilla walked remarkably fast. She swiped a strand of wavy, dark hair behind her ear, showing off more of her flawless bronze completion, and gave Jemma a reassuring, dimpled smile. "Snowy days always cause a few delays. One of our aides is watching the class now, so take a deep breath, and we'll get you officially introduced."

Vaguely, she heard the woman at the front office greet whoever had come in through the main double doors.

"Sorry we're late," a deep male voice said, one she swore

she'd heard about fifteen minutes ago. "We had to pull our city-slicker neighbor out of the snow bank."

Jemma stepped into full view and, sure enough, there was the cowboy next door and his much-friendlier little girl.

Bailey waved at her. "Hey! My dad was just talking about you."

Wyatt's eyes met hers. The cordial smile on his face faltered, but he didn't exactly rush to say he was sorry.

"Thanks again for your help," she said, her words coming out slightly clipped. "As I mentioned, I underestimated the snow. And the lack of snowplows." And a whole mess of things.

It was like her new neighbor was chivalrous, but surly. Not exactly friendly, yet not exactly unfriendly.

"Bailey is one of your students." Camilla squatted slightly to address the girl, and it showed how preoccupied Jemma had been earlier that she hadn't asked Bailey what grade she was in. "Do you want to help me introduce Miss Monroe to everyone?"

Bailey's face lit up. "I'd be happy to, 'specially since we already met this morning. She lives right next to me." She turned to Jemma. "I'm so glad you're nice. Our last teacher was pretty nice, and I was worried we'd get one of the mean teachers. Like..." She grimaced and lowered her voice. "I'd better not say."

"Probably a good idea," Wyatt said, placing a hand on her shoulder and giving her an affectionate squeeze, and Jemma noticed he wasn't wearing a wedding ring. Thanks to her single status, she checked on reflex, but she was also in the habit of cataloguing details about her students' parents that would help her be more sensitive to their family situation.

While the two interactions she'd had with the man were hardly ideal ways to meet the parent of one of her students,

Jemma told herself not to freak out. After all, she'd never been one to do things the conventional way.

Wyatt tipped his hat at her. "Nice to meet you again, Miss Monroe."

"You, too, Mr., um…" She blanked on his last name, and her face heated up as she searched her memory. All that would come was Wyatt, and she should probably go more formal now that she knew he was the father of one of her students.

"Langford."

"Right. Sorry. I'm meeting so many new people and…" She trailed off, trying not to be discouraged about how rough this entire morning was going.

"No worries." Wyatt bent next to Bailey. "Okay, have a good day. Love you."

"Love you too. Don't forget that this counts as a first day because I have a new teacher, so that means I get a treat after school."

He chuckled. "How could I forget when you've already reminded me twice this morning?"

Bailey flung out her arms. "I just like to be sure when treats are involved."

Jemma couldn't help smiling at that. She felt the same way about treats.

"Then I'm reminding you to eat the carrot sticks I packed in your lunch," he said, and Bailey wrinkled her nose. He straightened, his gaze drifting to Jemma. "Good luck, city-slicker neighbor."

If he hadn't said it lightly, with a hint of teasing, she might be offended. "I'm sure I'll see you around, cowboy neighbor."

He smiled, a genuine smile that highlighted his chiseled features and made something stir in her gut. Surely not butterflies, because that was a bad idea. But it was just what she needed to lift her chin, gather her wits, and turn to the principal, who was beaming in a way that made her immediately feel nervous again.

"Let's do this."

Wyatt cast one last glance toward his daughter as she started down the hall of the very same school he'd attended back in the day, her outfit a bright splash in the drab hallway. She practically skipped everywhere she went, and she darted toward her classroom, Principal Camilla Alvarez—who he went to school with back in the day—and Jemma Monroe behind her.

Those ridiculous high-heeled boots snagged his attention again. While he maintained the opinion she should've been more prepared for the weather, he regretted his remark about having to pull her out of the snowbank. It hadn't set him back all that long, and obviously she was out of her element.

So that's Bailey Rae's new teacher.

He'd expected someone older. Matronly. Jemma wasn't either of those things. She was stylish, probably in her mid-twenties, and she had a nice smile, which was something he definitely shouldn't notice.

Usually he didn't notice much about women—hadn't really looked twice since his ex had left him, Bailey Rae, and their simple life together behind.

I wonder how long a woman like Jemma will even last in Haven Lake.

Quickly, he told himself that it was dangerous to give the woman much thought.

She lived next door and was his daughter's teacher, and that was all there was to it.

Anything else might get him into trouble, and his life didn't allow time for anything else anyway.

But there was nothing wrong with being glad he'd have some entertainment as he watched his new neighbor adjust to small-town life.

CHAPTER FOUR

A COUPLE OF HOURS INTO THE day, and it was going rather well. Jemma was quickly learning names and, overall, they were really good kids. Naturally, they were testing the boundaries, but she held firm, showing them the line.

The kids who fought hardest against boundaries often needed them the most, but she'd learned that as long as she reinforced that line, no budging, they'd eventually respect it. Be better for it, even.

After she'd told a story about hailing a taxi in the pouring rain to get to a concert, one kid replied with, "You're not from around here, are you?"

Which led to telling them how she was from Denver.

Sometimes, lessons required kids to stay on task, but in her opinion, curious minds were a good thing, one she liked to foster and reward. She turned the discussion into a state geography lesson, adding fun facts about the city. How it was the state capital and that a miner had founded it back in the day and named it after the Kansas Territorial Governor James W. Denver to gain his good graces.

After the bumpy morning, it was nice to feel like she was getting her groove back.

"Okay, so now let's open our science workbooks."

"Miss... What was your name again?" Chase, a kid with buzzed blond hair and a twangy accent asked. The kid looked like a miniature cowboy, one ready to hop on a horse at any moment. Earlier, when he'd walked up to sharpen his pencil, she'd heard a slight *ching, ching, ching* and had seen that he had spurs on his boots.

"Miss Monroe." She straightened, just in case she had to give him a gentle chiding to stay focused.

Whispers traveled across the classroom in a wave, the chittering growing louder as Jemma wondered what had set them all off at once. There were snickers and squeaks, and a couple of students stood and began backing up.

"Come on, guys, we need to quiet down and focus. Later we'll do something fun, but you have to behave. Look at how quietly Tyler's sitting." Praising students who behaved had proven far more motivating than yelling at students who weren't.

Although, Tyler's eyes were growing more round by the second.

"Okay, but Miss Monroe," Chase said, "you might wanna look up."

Trepidation crept across her skin, and she slowly tipped up her head.

And screamed.

A giant yellow-and-white snake slithered in the empty air, its back half still in the heater vent.

Jemma backpedaled until her thighs hit her desk. She knocked it across the floor a few inches, the legs screeching against the tile. She heard her cup of pens and pencils spill but didn't take her eyes off the creature hanging from the ceiling.

Her heart was beating too fast and her throat went bone-dry. The snake was coming down, and the students were growing louder, several of them standing and rushing toward the opposite end of the classroom.

The side with the door.

The side she'd rather be on.

Okay, keep it together. You've got to be strong for your students, regardless of how badly you want to run screaming.

She licked her lips, trying to figure out how to deal with a snake and coming up blank—it wasn't exactly in the teacher handbook.

Chase's spurs made their light *ching*ing noise as he headed toward the dangling serpent instead of away from it. "You want me to get it?"

"It might be dangerous," Jemma said. "I'll just...call someone." She reached for the phone on her desk, her gaze remaining on the snake and its flickering forked tongue.

Chase put his fists on his hips as he studied it. "It's just a corn snake—it's the rattlers you've gotta be careful of. But they give you a warning rattle so you'll leave them alone."

"I'd leave them alone without the rattle," she murmured. Now that she was giving the reptile a closer look, she realized Chase was right. It was a corn snake, and she vaguely recalled learning about them in science class.

They weren't poisonous.

Didn't make it less creeptastic, but a little more comforting.

Chase looked at her, silently asking permission, and she nodded.

He stepped up on a chair and grabbed the snake, right by the neck and in the middle. Goose bumps broke out across her skin, and a few of the girls made noises that varied from disgust to admiration—the admiration was undoubtedly for the boy who'd wrangled the snake, not the actual serpent.

As icked out as Jemma was, she still tried to use the experience as a science lesson. "Who can tell me what snakes eat?" Her voice wavered slightly, but she'd managed to sound calm and semi-collected.

"Mice!" someone called out, and she repressed another shudder. This morning she'd considered the snow a pain, and now she'd rather think about anything besides creepy-crawlies.

"Yep."

"Can we find him a mouse and watch him eat it?" Kylie M. asked.

This time, Jemma couldn't repress her shudder, despite finding it funny that one of the quietest, sweetest-looking female student in her class was so excited about the prospect. "I think we'd better find where he belongs and make sure he gets back there safely."

A couple of phone calls revealed that the fifth-grade teacher had a snake—one who'd gone missing after someone had forgotten to put the top back on his terrarium after feeding him.

Three days ago.

Apparently they'd also bumped the terrarium, which had put the snake's stick against the wall, and Mrs. Russell had been hoping he'd show up somewhere.

Lucky me. I'm so glad he chose my *classroom.*

Jemma told Mrs. Russell that her pet would be returned shortly. Since Chase had been brave enough to catch the thing, she let him walk it down the hall as she played lookout in the doorway.

Once he'd returned to the classroom, she assigned the kids to read section twenty in their workbook so they could discuss it in a few minutes.

She flopped down at her desk, and her heart slowly returned to beating at a normal pace. But her mind was still racing.

Where in the heck have I moved that snakes falling from the ceiling seems like a fairly normal occurrence?

"Okay, time to pack up for the day. Gather your belongings and line up at the door." Jemma stood, and everyone rushed forward at once. She held up her hands. "In an orderly fashion, or everyone will have to sit back down."

She should've added that first. Man, how did she get so rusty?

She labeled each row and called them forward to line up. The bell rang, and she opened the door, wishing each of her students a good day as they exited to meet older siblings or parents or file over to the bus.

One of the parents stepped up to introduce herself, a strawberry-blond, chubby-cheeked baby on her hip. "Hello, I'm Chase Matthews' mom, Wendy."

"Oh, hello. Jemma Monroe. Your son was a *huge* help today."

Wendy's eyebrows arched up, and Jemma wondered why she was so surprised. Sure, Chase had trouble sitting still, but he was respectful enough and had totally saved her with the snake. Her heart always went out to kids who thought they were trouble because adults kept telling them they were, and honestly, she couldn't help but like funny kids who marched to the beat of their own drum. Probably because she'd been like them back in her elementary school days.

Fortunately, she'd had a few teachers who'd seen through the fidgeting and random outbursts of information that had nothing to do with the subject they'd been discussing.

Jemma quickly relayed the story about the snake to Wendy Matthews. Pride radiated from Chase as he puffed out his chest, an ear-to-ear grin plastered on his face.

"I don't know how I would've gotten through the day without him," Jemma added, completely sincere. If it'd been up to her to grab that snake, she'd still be working up the courage.

"Oh, I'm so glad to hear that. He's real helpful around the house, and so good with his sister." Wendy ran her hand over her son's head, and a mushy sensation flooded Jemma's chest. "I meant to talk to you about his spurs, but we were running late this morning. He got them for Christmas, and it's all I can do to get him to take them off to sleep. I told him if they were too distracting, or if he got into trouble, he wouldn't be able to wear them anymore."

"It makes me feel better to know I have a cowboy-slash-snake wrangler in class," Jemma said, and then she wished him and his mom goodbye.

Bailey was last in line, patiently waiting for Jemma to finish her conversation.

She turned her full attention to the girl with the awesome sense of style and cheery attitude. "Thanks again for helping introduce me to the class."

"You did a good job today," Bailey said, all matter-of-fact. "I think this is going to work out nicely."

Jemma laughed. The girl was definitely advanced for her age, in speech and, as she'd found out earlier today, in reading. "Why, thank you. That's high praise." Praise she wasn't sure Bailey's dad would agree with. And why did she keep thinking about Wyatt Langford?

After he'd seemed so huffy while digging her car out, she'd been set to avoid him at all costs. She'd renewed that goal when she'd overheard him talking about her.

But that last interaction, where he'd smiled at her, two grooves showing up in his cheeks as he'd wished her good luck and had added that teasing "city-slicker neighbor," made it hard to want to permanently avoid the guy.

She wondered about Bailey's mom. Maybe her parents were one of those couples who lived together and didn't think they needed a marriage certificate and rings to make it official. To each their own, but once she found her one and only, she wanted a certificate and a ring and to shout it from the rooftops.

"What treat are you gonna get for making it through your first day?" Bailey asked her, bringing her back to the here and now.

"I haven't had much time to think about it. Any suggestions?"

"Havenly Brew is just down the street, and it has these ginormous chocolate chip chocolate muffins." Bailey made a circle with her hands, demonstrating how big. Then her arms dropped down by her sides. "That's what I'm getting."

"Mmm, that sounds amazing. I might have to stop by and try one for myself."

Bailey nodded and readjusted her backpack. "You should. I'd better go. My dad is probably waiting, and he's not the most patient."

Jemma pressed her lips together to keep from laughing. No, he didn't seem to be the most patient, although his love for his daughter was palpable, and that also made it hard to stay frustrated over his brusque manners.

Of course, she'd been accused of being a "chatty Cathy" before, so she understood that not everyone liked to make small talk as much as she did. Luckily, she was often surrounded by kids, and many of them were *amazing* at small talk.

"See you tomorrow," Jemma called out as Bailey headed away from her.

With every one of her students off for the day, she turned and walked back inside her classroom. All in all, it had been a good day.

While the occasional teacher had mentioned her high heels at her old school, the entire staff here had gathered around at lunch to ask how she wore those "torture devices" all day—well, that and to tease her about the snake incident.

She'd made a joke that her heels weren't the best for pushing cars out of the snow, and everyone had laughed. It had made her morning with the snow and unexpected serpentine visitor seem less disastrous.

She spent a few minutes straightening and setting up for tomorrow. She needed to plan her lesson, but now that Bailey had mentioned the chocolate muffin, her stomach grumbled every time food came to mind. She could use some coffee to ensure she had the extra energy she'd need.

Plus, she hoped the more time she gave the sun to melt the roads, the easier it'd be to get back to her cottage. It wasn't like there'd been an abundance of places to rent in this tiny town, but now she was rethinking her decision to be on the outskirts. How much snow could one place get?

Probably enough that I shouldn't tempt fate with that question.

On her way out of her classroom, she ran into Camilla. "How'd it go?" the woman asked as they continued down the mostly empty hallway. "I mean besides the snake incident, which ¡qué susto! I would've lost my mind."

Jemma threw a hand to her chest, right over the spot where her heart was beginning to thump quicker at the mere memory of that forked tongue and beady eyes. "Oh, I screamed. Considered passing out."

Her earring got hooked on her scarf again. She was going to have to remember not to wear this combination. "Other than that, things went pretty well. And again, I'm sorry about this morning. Tomorrow I'm going to leave even earlier."

Not that it would do much good if she ended up stuck and had to wait for Wyatt and Bailey to come dig her out, but she was going to stick with optimism.

Camilla waved a hand through the air. "Seriously, don't worry about it. I'm sure our tiny town is quite a change from what you're used to."

Jemma nodded. "Admittedly, I was thrown off for the second time today when Chase Matthews told me a story about watching a cow give birth, but what was even funnier was how the rest of the class nodded like it was completely normal. Then a few added stories of their own about animal births, everything from cats to horses."

Camilla laughed—she had a nice laugh too, one that set you at ease and made you happy at the same time. "Oh, yes. Small towns and farming communities have their own unique stories. I'm sure you've heard they're famous for everyone being in everyone's business and how fast news travels as well."

"On movies and in TV, yes."

"Good. Then let's get right to it." A gleam lit Camilla's brown eyes as she leaned in and lowered her voice. "What's up with you and Wyatt Langford?"

CHAPTER FIVE

Wyatt scraped his boots the best he could on the mat outside of the coffee shop before pulling open the door so Bailey Rae could bound inside.

He'd had to swing by Tractor Supply first so he could get a part ordered before the store closed for the day. In there, his dirt-caked jeans and boots fit in well enough, but April, the woman who owned the coffee shop, probably wouldn't appreciate it if he dragged in mud.

Although, with all the snow now slushy and melting, the floors were probably a bit of a mess already.

While there were droplets of melted snow here and there, there wasn't much mud. Or maybe the cherry wood floors simply hid it well. The exposed brick wall gave the place a warm feel, but he'd never really understood the pale-blue counters and blue and yellow mismatched chairs set around square tables. It took a lot of effort to match but not match on purpose.

As usual, the place was fairly packed, a mix of regulars and the after-school crowd filling all but a couple of tables.

In general, he didn't stop by the shops in town as much as most people did. He simply didn't have time. Owning a ranch meant his work was never done, and adding in things like homework, school programs, and the dance classes Bailey Rae took every Sunday afternoon meant he was forever behind.

The scent of coffee beans and freshly baked pastries hit him, and his mouth watered.

He had no problem admitting his skills in the kitchen were lacking, so he understood his daughter's desire to stop for a treat *he* hadn't made.

Thank goodness his sister sometimes took pity on him between taking care of her own family, or he and Bailes would probably have the same boring meal every single night. He'd grabbed the leftover stew from her earlier today and was more excited than usual for dinner, but he'd also told Lori that she now had two tiny kids to take care of and she didn't need to worry about them. Helping with rides was more than enough, and if he ever caught up on work, he'd find a way to repay the many favors he owed his sister.

Sleep was overrated, anyway.

April gave them her signature welcoming smile, and it widened even more as she peered down at his colorful princess. "Why look at you, Miss Bailey Rae. I absolutely adore your outfit."

Bailey Rae popped out a hip and struck a pose. He had no earthly idea where she'd learned that from. "Thank you! I worked so hard on it." She moved closer to the register, her eyes scanning the glass case with the pastries and desserts. "I'm here for—"

"Lemme guess. A chocolate muffin."

Bailey Rae vehemently nodded, a close-lipped smile on her face.

Over the summer, she'd lost her front teeth. They'd grown in by the beginning of the school year, but a month in, she'd asked if her adult teeth looked funny. If they were too big for her mouth and if they stuck out too far.

He'd told her he loved her smile, but a week or so later he'd noticed she fought smiling with teeth. If April and chocolate muffins couldn't get it out of her, he didn't know what would.

He suspected some of the kids might've teased her about her slight overbite, and he hated that kids always poked at others' insecurities. Once again he wondered if he should bring it up, but every time he did, she clammed up more, her almost smile turned into a melancholy pout that lasted longer each time.

I wish she'd believe me instead of them.

His sister always accused him of worrying too much, but he didn't think it was possible to dial it back with the girl who brought sunshine into his life. His daughter was what kept him going, and he'd do just about anything for her.

"What about you?" April asked, addressing him.

"I'll have one of the chocolate muffins too. And a regular coffee, black."

"Ooh, and can I have one of the Italian sodas?" Bailey Rae bounced on her toes and pressed her hands in prayer position. *"Pleeeease?"*

Played like the sucker I am. "Fine."

She clapped and ordered the Bohemian Raspberry— extra-large. In other words, she'd be begging for him to pull over to use the bathroom halfway home.

The bell over the door jingled, and Wyatt automatically glanced back.

And froze.

Jemma walked in and shook snowflakes from her dark hair. He looked past her, out the large window facing the street. It was hard to make out much besides the back of the giant coffee cup design stuck to the glass, but he could see a few white flurries. They must've begun falling a few minutes ago, but the snow didn't seem to be sticking to the ground yet.

His gaze accidently drifted to Jemma for a quick second before he forced it forward.

April leaned to one side, peering around him. "That must be our new elementary teacher," she said, excitement filling her words.

The woman loved knowing the who's who of town and what everyone was up to at all times. People always joked that she dealt in coffee beans and gossip, which was another reason he sometimes avoided the shop. He'd rather people not know his business.

Wyatt quickly schooled his features. No letting her know that he was acquainted with the new woman in town.

"She's actually my teacher," Bailey Rae said, back to bouncing on the balls of her feet. "She's so, *so* nice." She spun around and waved, nice and big. "Miss Monroe! Hi!"

April leaned closer, her stomach hitting the cash register as she raised an eyebrow. "So it's *Miss*, is it? Been a while since a single woman moved into town."

Wyatt didn't reply. It'd only give the coffee shop owner ideas, no matter what he said or how he said it.

Jemma hesitated at the door, her expression saying she wasn't sure if she should hang back until he was done ordering. That last moment in the hallway popped into his head. It was okay to be neighborly, right?

If anything, it was part of his *duty* as her neighbor. Not to mention his daughter was already waving her over and asking if she'd come to try the chocolate muffin.

"Make that three muffins," he said to April, focusing on pulling the bills out of his wallet so no one could misread anything in his expression. "Plus whatever Miss Monroe wants to drink."

The click of her heeled boots filled the air. "Oh, no, that's o—"

"I insist."

She smiled at him, the blue, blue eyes he somehow hadn't noticed earlier cutting right through his defenses, and a sensation he hadn't felt in years stirred in his gut. "Thank you. But I should be the one treating you for your help this morning."

April was practically salivating behind the cash register, her gaze volleying between the two of them as if she was a spectator at a tennis match.

Wyatt cleared his throat. "So? What do you want to drink?"

Jemma stepped up next to him, and when her perfume hit him, he quickly exhaled. She tapped a white-tipped fingernail to glossy lips, glancing from the giant menu chalkboard with all the funky-named drinks to April. "So many options. What's your specialty?"

"Well, the drink of the week is Frappe the Snowman. It's a white chocolate Frappuccino with carrot cake spice, and another secret ingredient—your next drink's on me if you guess it right."

"That sounds delightful. I'll have that."

The woman uses words like "delightful" and goes for the fancy drinks. Why am I not surprised?

"What?" she asked him, her hands going to her hips in classic teacher stance—he'd been a bit rambunctious growing up and had seen that stern expression too many times. "Why are you looking at me like that?"

"No reason. Just wondering if you were going to have some coffee with your whip cream and sugar."

"Just enough to keep me going while I plan tomorrow's lesson. Let me guess. You drink it boring and black so you can prove you're tough as nails."

"I've got nothing to prove. I just don't see the point in ordering drinks masquerading as coffee."

One eyebrow arched, and he told himself not to focus on those blue eyes. "It's called self-care."

"Don't you mean sugar coma?"

"I can whip out my dictionary if you want me to, and we can see which definition is closer."

Part of him wanted to tell her to go ahead. He was enjoying their exchange more than he should, especially since he'd started it to prove to himself that she was one of those fancy women who cared about the finer things in life.

But April was studying them too closely—already calculating a plan that involved matchmaking efforts, no doubt. Everyone in town seemed to think he should pair up and settle down, as if he wanted to go down that road again. He'd already made peace with the fact that it'd be just him and Bailey Rae from here on out.

Wyatt fumbled with the wad of bills in his hands and handed them over to April, who got to making the drinks and grabbing the muffins.

Bailey Rae grabbed a few napkins from the area with the straws, condiments, and plastic cutlery. While looking directly at him, Jemma grabbed a couple of packets of cream and sugar, her features heavy on the *you can't tell me what to do.*

His daughter turned to her teacher. "You should sit by us. Then you can tell me if you like the muffin."

"Oh, I should get to planning," Jemma said as he said, "I'm sure she's busy, and we should get home anyway."

They exchanged a glance. Well, at least they were on the same page. It was one thing for people in town to go getting ideas, but he didn't want Bailey Rae to get too attached, either.

Wyatt asked April to change their part of the order to go, and after they'd divvied up the drinks and muffins, Jemma lightly placed her hand on Bailey Rae's shoulder. "I'll see you tomorrow in class. And I'll have a special guest with me."

Bailey Rae's eyes widened with excitement. "Who?"

"You'll have to come to class and see. But what I can say is that he's super cute, and you won't want to miss meeting him."

For the briefest, weirdest moment, Wyatt wondered if maybe she had a boyfriend. The pinch of dismay he experienced was another reason it was best for them not to get too involved with their neighbor.

Good thing that on the outskirts of town, "next-door neighbor" meant they still had about a quarter of a mile between them.

As long as Jemma didn't get stuck in the snow again, he should only have to have minimal interactions with her. The occasional school drop-off and pick-up, and that was it, and he was going to make sure it stayed that way.

The instant the barista had handed Wyatt his order, he'd rushed Bailey out of the coffee shop, almost as if he couldn't get away from her fast enough.

Sheesh, what did I say?

And just when she'd concluded maybe he wasn't as gruff as she'd originally thought. It was nice of him to buy her coffee and muffin, even if he'd mocked her drink choice.

"Don't take it personally," the auburn-haired woman behind the cash register said. "My goodness, I seem to have forgotten my manners." She wiped her hands on her pale-blue-and-yellow-floral apron before extending one. "I'm April Copeland, and this here's my little slice of heaven, also known as Havenly Brew Coffee Shop."

"Jemma Monroe," she said as she shook her hand. "I'm the new third-grade teacher—well, I'm filling in for a while, anyway—and I adore coffee and I'm already in love with your charming coffee shop."

The words April had said before they'd made their introductions caught up to Jemma's brain. "Don't take what personally?"

"Wyatt. He's a bit…" April's pale blue eyes rolled to the ceiling, as if she'd find answers there, and Jemma decided to help fill in the blank.

"Grumpy? Laconic?" *The weirdest mix of rude and polite?*

April tipped her head one way and then the other, the overhead lights highlighting the smattering of freckles across her cheeks and nose. "I was going to say overwhelmed and always in a hurry, what with taking care of his ranch and being a single father. He's never been much of a talker, but after his wife left him, he says even less."

Jemma did her best not to react to that. After all, Camilla had mentioned as much when they'd spoken after school. The principal also declared there'd been "a vibe" between them, and Jemma had assured the woman she was imagining things and there was no vibe.

So why did she feel disappointed that he'd rushed out so quickly?

This is what you do. You overthink minor interactions and turn them into something they're not.

Remember how you're thinking more logically about men now?

Wyatt Langford was wrong for her on a lot of levels. Not

only did she have no clue about cowboys or what to discuss with a guy like that, he'd also made it rather clear he considered her ridiculous.

On top of that, she didn't know how long she'd be here. Between teaching and her online classes to finish her Masters in education, she was plenty busy. Her long-term goal involved eventually going into administration, where she could implement changes without needing permission from people who totally didn't get her and make a bigger difference.

Part of her had wanted to give up on that goal once she'd been laid off. How could she change things when she couldn't even hold on to her job? But she'd reminded herself it'd been about the budget, not her skills. Besides, she'd put in the time and was so close to earning her Masters, which would bump up her salary, as well as widen the job pool and make her more attractive to prospective employers.

Back to the cowboy issue, though, she'd also never date a student's father. It muddled things too much. Confused the kids, and then how awkward would parent-teacher conference be?

"Jemma? Are you still with me?"

Dang it, she'd gotten lost in her thoughts again, the day-dreamer kid she used to be taking over since she was out of practice reining that side of her in. She toyed with the straw of her drink. "He's my neighbor and I have his daughter in my class, so it's no big deal. I meet all kinds of different parents."

"Probably not ones who are as nice to look at," April said with a sly smile that practically begged her to spill her secrets.

Knowing better than to comment, Jemma took a sip of her Frappe the Snowman. "This is amazing, by the way. Is the secret ingredient…?" She focused on the flavors dancing on her tongue. "Marshmallow?"

"Nope."

Another gulp. "Cinnamon?"

"Yes, but that's not the secret one. It's part of the carrot cake spice."

With April properly distracted from talking about Wyatt's nice looks, Jemma decided she'd simply enjoy the delightsome combination. "I'm going to go set up at a table and see how well it pairs with my muffin. Thanks again."

She carried everything over to a table in the corner and bit into her muffin, which was as delicious as Bailey had claimed. After planning out tomorrow's lesson, she packed up her laptop and lesson planner. She'd have to complete her online coursework at home, slow Wi-Fi or not, because the snow was starting to stick and the sun was starting to dip.

Once Jemma climbed in her car and hit the road they hadn't bothered plowing, she cursed herself for not leaving sooner. The tires slipped on the patches that had halfway melted before refreezing, and she held her breath as her rapid pulse throbbed behind her temples.

For a couple of terrifying seconds, she was sure she was going to slide right off the road and end up stuck all over again. Obviously, driving in the snow was going to take a mixture of practice and prayer.

One thing was for sure, though—if her car slid off the road again, there was *no way* she was going to ask Wyatt Langford for help.

She'd simply risk frostbite and hike home, too-thin coat and heeled boots notwithstanding.

Some might call that pride, but she liked to think of it as self-preservation.

As soon as she pulled up in front of her new/old place, she let out a sigh of relief, her shoulders sagging as her lungs deflated.

"I made it," she said aloud, forgetting for a moment that Señor Fluffypants hadn't taken the trip with her today. Evidently she talked to her bunny more than she realized, which didn't make her feel semi-crazy at all.

After turning the heater to high and soaking up every second of heat she could, she shut off her car and rushed down the sidewalk, the heels of her boots digging in enough to keep her from falling, although the soles were slippery.

With her hand trembling from the cold, it took two times to get the key in the lock so she could open the door and hurry inside.

Her laptop bag hit the coffee table with a *clunk* and she shed her coat, then immediately decided to pull it back on. The cottage was drafty, and the old vents that ran along the floor didn't put out nearly enough heat.

With her first workday officially behind her, she scrolled through her contacts, tapped on Randa's name, and hit the FaceTime button. After years of waving in the hallways and lunch breaks spent mostly together, it'd seemed weird to be in school without her comforting presence.

Her friend's familiar face and long, curly, dirty-blond hair flickered on the screen for all of two seconds before the feed froze. The green eyes and tan skin from spending all summer in the sun pixelated into gray nothingness, and her words came out spotty and garbled.

One frustrating minute of that was all Jemma could take, so she gave up on the FaceTime option and simply hit the phone button.

"Hey," Randa said, and at least her voice came through perfectly clear, although Jemma would miss her exaggerated facial expressions. The girl never stood a chance at lying—she was more tell-it-like-it-is anyway—and she could get students excited about anything by injecting enthusiasm into her voice and delicate features. "How's the country?"

"Snowy and cold, and so far, everyone seems nice. Except my neighbor. Although that's not exactly true. He's nice but in a grumpy, begrudging way."

"Explain." See? Straightforward and good at rolling with the punches.

"They don't plow the roads out by where I live. I have to make it seven miles before I hit clear roads, and I know that doesn't sound like a lot, but when you have to go super slow and end up sliding off into a snowbank, it's forever."

"Oh my gosh, you wrecked? Are you okay?"

"More like I gently slid into a tiny ditch and got super stuck. Totally fine, except my pride. I was trying to push my car back onto the road, and along comes my cowboy neighbor—we have to take the same tiny dirt road to get to the main road. Anyway, he takes one look at me and frowns at my boots—"

"The cute black ones with the killer heel?"

"Those are the ones." The fact that Randa knew her *and* her shoe collection so well made it easier to picture her on the other end of the line, regardless of being unable to get the video chat to work. "He sort of scolded me for wearing them. It's not like I thought I'd be pushing my car in the snow this morning when I got dressed. I just wanted to look nice for my first day."

"Naturally. Nice and tall too, although for the record, you're tall enough as it is."

"Wyatt's taller, even in the heels."

Randa *hmm*ed.

"No *hmm*ing. It was merely an observation."

"Is this Wyatt guy cute?"

Jemma flopped onto the couch and bent to unzip her boots. "I hardly see how that matters."

"That means yes."

Her mind automatically recalled the guy, tall and broad, the tan cowboy hat covering his head. "Okay, he's cute, but his daughter is in my class. She's a total sweetheart. And he did buy me a muffin and a coffee to make up for it. I just…"

Now she wasn't sure why she'd brought him up. She quickly launched into the story about her unexpected—and unwelcome—snake visitor, which had Randa laughing so hard she was gasping for air.

"I'm seriously cry-laughing. As well as picturing a one-room schoolhouse like in *Anne of Green Gables*, where you have kids of all ages in one room and they write on slates."

"Oh, I didn't even tell you about the horse that knocked on my door the first night I'd moved into the cottage."

"Stop," Randa said through more laughter.

"I'm also pretty sure I passed a llama farm, but I was too scared to look too closely because I didn't want to slide off the road again. As I already mentioned, I wasn't wearing the shoes for it. But I swear there were llamas."

"Maybe you're in a Disney movie. If the animals start talking, you'll know for sure."

Jemma laughed, enjoying the camaraderie and missing her friend. While there were nice people and it'd turned out to be a pretty good day overall, she just wasn't sure she belonged in Haven Lake.

At least it's only temporary.

CHAPTER SIX

"THIS IS SEÑOR FLUFFYPANTS. HE'S a black-and-white Holland Lop, and he's three years old." Jemma hefted the chubby bunny out of his wire kennel and invited the students to come closer. They asked questions about his floppy ears, and she explained that lop breeds have that type of ears, and how way back in the day, they made this breed by combining a couple of others.

"Does he eat carrots, like Bugs Bunny?" Brody asked.

"Good question. He eats some alfalfa-based pellets to make sure he gets all his vitamins, but he also gets carrots for treats sometimes. I bet your parents talk to you about getting your vitamins, don't they?"

Several of them nodded.

"My grandpa grows alfalfa," Chase added proudly.

It was nice that so many of the kids had been around a variety of animals, because they all seemed to know how to carefully pet her bunny, and while Señor Fluffypants had grown accustomed to noisy classrooms, he was always calmer when the students were calm as well.

After making sure everyone had gotten a turn to pet the bunny, Jemma instructed her students to have a seat.

Bailey gave Señor Fluffypants's head one last pat as she

whispered, "We have lots of animals on the ranch, but no tame bunnies. Just the wild ones that are scared of people. I really like your bunny—he's super-duper fluffy and cute."

"Thank you. By the way, you were right about the muffin. It was delicious." Affection wove through Jemma as they shared a moment, and then it was time to launch into the math portion of their lesson, which wasn't nearly as well-received as the bunny had been.

But a few minutes in, the kids settled down and got into the groove of things.

By the end of her second day, Jemma decided she could mark it off as a total success.

Right as she was getting ready to give herself a big red check, Camilla came in. She gave her a smile that was more of a grimace. "So, um, don't freak out, but I forgot to tell you that the third-graders do a Valentine's Day play."

Despite the instructions, Jemma's lungs constricted. She'd never done a play before, not anything bigger than minor skits in her classroom. "Wait. *I'm* in charge of it?"

Camilla stepped farther into the room, bringing her thumbnail up between her teeth. "You and the music teacher. The third grade puts it on every year, and most of the town comes. I totally blanked until Mrs. Hembolt asked me about it. We usually start prepping for it as soon as everyone returns from Christmas break."

"Is there a script?" Jemma wasn't sure she had the skills to make up a play from scratch. Everyone underestimated how much work productions like that were, but she'd helped Randa out with last year's fifth grade production, and by the end, the staff and students were exhausted. It was a huge undertaking that required volunteers and a lot of extra hours.

"Mrs. Hembolt's gathered several, and we have a handful in the library we can choose from. Do you have time for a quick meeting with her? I'll stick around to help you pick as well if you'd like me to."

"Yes, please." So maybe she'd been thrown a curveball, but at least she was part of a solid team.

Thirty minutes and ten scripts later, they'd picked a cute, funny play called "Cupid Goes Crazy." It was mostly about kindness and friendship and loving people even if they were different from you. Seeing the script and picturing her students in the roles, the audience grinning up at them, took the edge off her panic and left her cautiously excited.

Mrs. Hembolt clapped her hands and bounced in her chair. The woman had thick glasses that made her eyes look abnormally large and a halo of curly white hair. She'd also burst into song twice as they'd been sorting through plays. "This is going to be absolutely adorable! I can't wait to dive in."

As they were packing up, Camilla turned to Jemma. "Before I forget, I keep meaning to talk to you about something…"

Jemma's stomach bottomed out. Was the principal unhappy with her job performance? Had she received parental complaints? Surely there wasn't another play or event. Too many of Jemma's plates were spinning out of control already.

"Several of the other teachers and I take a country dance aerobics class," Camilla continued, "and we're always looking for people to join." She wrapped her arm around Mrs. Hembolt's shoulders. "Aren't we, Dorothy?"

Dorothy nodded so fast her glasses slid down her nose. "Oh, it's good fun. You simply must come!"

"You simply must." A hint of mischief danced in the curve of the smile Camilla aimed at her. Jemma was beginning to think the principal's side hustle was talking people into things. "Every Thursday night, so show up at the dance hall tomorrow a few minutes before six."

The panic Jemma had barely ridded herself of seized her once again as the two women stared at her. Country dancing? Seriously? Not only was she more of an alt- and rock-and-roll girl, she also had iffy coordination, became self-conscious in the spotlight, and only danced in the privacy of her own house.

Now she was almost wishing the conversation was about her work performance. "Sounds...intriguing, but I don't know how to country dance."

"That's why you go to a class where you can learn, silly," Camilla said. "We go for fun and for exercise, to get to know one another outside of the classroom, and to support each other and the new dance instructor. All perks of living in a tight-knit community."

Perks? Jemma considered reading alone in the quiet of the cottage a perk. She also didn't want her coworkers to get to know her while she was flailing about, making a fool of herself.

Her apprehension must've been written on her face, because Camilla dropped the arm she had around Mrs. Hembolt and gently squeezed Jemma's shoulder. "Come on. At least give it the ol' elementary-school try."

"Don't you mean college try?" *Good job, Jemma. Correct your boss, who's just reaching out and doing her best to include you and make you feel welcome.*

Camilla's smile widened. "No, I mean elementary school. Kids are more open to trying new things."

Open. Trying new things.

In other words, this fit in with her goals and was included in the adventure she was supposed to be having.

Which is how she found herself battling her inner coward, forcing herself to step out of her comfort zone, and saying yes.

The rumble of an engine had Wyatt perking up his ears. For one illogical moment, he thought maybe it was his new neighbor dropping by, but as the sound grew louder, he heard the deep growl of a diesel pickup truck.

He grabbed his coat and slung it on as he pushed through the front door. *Of course it's the person I called. Why on earth would it would be Jemma Monroe?*

Maybe the real question was why did she keep popping into his brain? How did it even have room for anything that didn't include work?

It was just because he regretted being so short with her that day she'd gotten stuck. So not how you were supposed to treat your neighbor or your kid's teacher.

Yep, that's the only reason. It definitely wasn't that retort she'd made about drinking his coffee black to prove he was tough as nails, or how she'd made that joke calling her froufrou drink self-care.

And that's more than enough thinking about that.

Wyatt zipped up his wool-lined coat as he rushed over to where Dempsey Lyons had parked, right in front of the used-to-be-red barn.

"Sorry it took me so long to get out here," Dempsey said while climbing out of his truck, big black medical bag in hand. He had on blue scrubs, which meant he'd rushed over as soon as his clinic had closed for the day.

The only vet in a town full of a lot of pets and livestock, Dempsey was busy from first thing in the morning to early evening and, in some emergency cases, late at night. Since

Wyatt understood that all too well, he hated to call up his friend and add to his long list of work, but when it came to his horse, he'd rather be safe than sorry.

The hinges creaked a bit as Wyatt opened the heavy wooden side door to the barn. "I just appreciate you taking time out of your busy schedule."

"Anytime. I'm serious, man." Dempsey stepped inside, blinking against the bright lights and then clapping Wyatt on the shoulder. "Truth be told, it's good to see you. It's been way too long."

"It has," he agreed. A lifetime ago they'd played ball together, both football and basketball, although Dempsey had shone on the field as quarterback, whereas Wyatt had been more at home on the court.

Around most people, Wyatt often stood back, stayed quiet, and observed. But he and Dempsey had known each other forever. He was also the guy who'd shown up after his marriage had fallen apart and had helped him sort out the pieces. He'd seen him at his best and worst, and an odd sort of relief flowed through him at the idea of not having to watch everything he did or said.

Not having to worry it'd somehow get back to his daughter.

"Since we're clearly never going to catch up on work anytime soon," Dempsey said, "we should schedule time to hang anyway."

"Are you saying this doesn't count as a quality hangout?" Wyatt joked as he led his friend to the stall where his bay mare, Zora, rested on her side. She stood at their approach, her right front leg lifted a couple of inches off the ground.

Wyatt ran his hand down her neck to keep her as calm as possible. "As I mentioned over the phone, she stepped in a hole and rolled a bit." He jerked his chin at the leg she wasn't putting her weight on. "By the time I walked her back to the barn, it looked swollen. I don't think it's broken, but wanted to make sure that it wasn't, or that something else wasn't going on."

Dempsey let the horse sniff him and began soothingly talking to Zora while Wyatt gripped the bridle. She was used to people and hadn't needed to be restrained before, but he wanted to be ready, just in case.

After another minute or so of the two of them calmly talking to and rubbing down the horse, Dempsey bent to check out the leg. "How's Bailey Rae these days?"

"As big a handful as ever, but just as sweet as the day is long."

"She's getting so big," Dempsey said. "What is she now? Six? Seven?"

"Eight. Almost nine."

His friend looked up at him like he expected Wyatt was pulling *his* leg. "Seriously? It's been that long since I held that squeaky pink baby burrito in my arms?"

The image of their younger selves hit him, how Dempsey had held Bailey Rae like a football he'd wanted to protect and hand off at the same time. Over the years, he'd gotten used to being around her and kids in general, and last summer he'd attempted to teach her to throw the perfect spiral pass. She mostly humored the guy she referred to as Uncle Dempsey, because the girl couldn't care less about sports and didn't have a competitive bone in her body.

Wyatt leaned a hip against the post nearest him. "Yeah, hate to break it to you, but we're getting old."

Dark strands of hair fell in Dempsey's face, and he raked them back into place. "Speak for yourself." He gently ran his hand down the horse's leg as he glanced at Wyatt. "Pretty soon, you're going to have to deal with things like dating and driving."

"Hey, now," Wyatt said, fake sternness in his voice. "Don't go tryin' to give me gray hairs just so I'll look older."

They shared a laugh, and Wyatt scuffed his boot on the hay covered floor. "Since we're asking the tough questions tonight, are you and that woman from Colorado Springs still going strong?"

Dempsey shook his head. "Nah. I'm too busy for a relationship, especially one with almost two hours' distance between us. Despite the fact that she only works part time, she didn't want to have to drive here where—" he made air quotes, "—there's nothing to even do."

A tight band formed around Wyatt's chest as that comment hit too close to home. Not just because of his ex-wife, Andrea, but because he was thinking of Jemma again, and how she was a city girl through and through.

Dempsey reached into his bag and started digging. "It's a minor sprain, the tendon bowing just the tiniest bit. Still, the better we secure it and the less she moves it, the quicker it'll heal."

His friend pulled out a couple of hot-pink...braces? "Fetlock boot. All I've got on me is pink."

"I'm sure Bailey Rae will be thrilled," Wyatt said with a chuckle. "The only thing I care about is that Zora is able to feel better and heal." He patted her side. She'd been with him through a lot and was the horse he counted on most. While he tried to play it cool, he constantly worried about all of his animals. But especially this one.

"I'll put one on her other leg as well, since she'll start putting more weight on that side and we don't want her to end up straining it. The boot will keep her leg stable, but she'll need to stay in her stall for a while. I'll administer a painkiller and an anti-inflammatory and give you both to use over the next few days, but she should be back to normal in a few weeks to a month."

Once Dempsey had put on the boots and given the horse the medication, he backed out of the stall and closed the door. He wiped his hands on his scrubs and dug his phone out of his pocket. "I'll set it in my calendar to come check on her in two weeks."

"You don't have to do that. I can bring her in or just shoot you a picture so you don't have to drive out here after a long hard day."

"I know, but I'm gonna, and I might as well drag you out for a drink afterward." He turned the phone screen toward Wyatt to show it'd been inputted in his calendar. "It's high time someone reminded you how to kick back and have a little fun."

"I'm afraid I'm a lost cause on that front."

"I'll be the judge of that. Besides, you can't keep shutting out the townsfolk who've been here for you since forever. Or by the time you get those gray hairs, you'll be the bitter old man everyone's afraid of."

Dempsey punched his arm in a joking way, but Wyatt could tell he wasn't completely kidding. Perhaps he'd done a better job hermitting than he'd originally thought. For a while it was because he hadn't wanted to talk about his divorce and had been completely overwhelmed at being in charge of everything, including his then six-year-old daughter, and then it sort of became habit.

But as his friend pointed out, his being busy wasn't ever going to change.

He just wasn't sure he'd be able to change from the harsher, loner guy he'd become, either.

CHAPTER SEVEN

THERE'D BEEN SEVERAL TIMES JEMMA had wondered how she'd gotten herself into situations, but this one took the cake.

Mmm. I wish they had cake. I haven't had cake in forever.

Of course, if she was going to eat that—or keep eating muffins and drinking sugary drinks of joy from Havenly Brew—exercise was important.

As she stood near the back of the dance hall on Thursday afternoon, she wasn't sure this kind of exercise was for her. There was country music playing lightly in the background and women of all ages surrounded her, chatting and stretching.

Dorothy Hembolt, the music teacher who was helping with the Valentine's Day play, was up front, wearing a red gingham skirt that must've been from the square-dancing glory days she'd mentioned as they were choosing a play.

She had to be in her sixties, and yet she was down on the ground stretching, legs spread wide, her white bloomers matching the lace on her flared skirt.

April was also up near the front, wearing worn boots and a large blingy buckle, and a few other women had cowboy hats on. Mrs. Russell, the fifth-grade teacher with the escapee snake, and Mrs. Glynn, the first-grade teacher, waved at her from their positions in the middle row.

While Jemma was enjoying getting to know her fellow teachers, she was still going to stay in the back of the spacious room, where fewer people could bear witness to her dance moves. Or more like dance blunders. She'd been told that a lot of town events were held in the wooden-floored hall, and she glanced around, thinking surely there was a back exit she could sneak out of without anyone noticing.

Camilla walked over and bumped her shoulder into Jemma's. "Wipe that skeptical, scared look off your face. This class is a blast, and the teacher is awesome. Essie's originally from Puerto Rico but moved to the States when she was in high school. She danced professionally for about a decade. Fortunately, she found her way to Haven Lake about six months ago, and we're lucky to have her.

"Since we want to keep her here and help her build the dance studio she's been talking about—which would bring in more people from the other tiny towns surrounding us and be great for the local businesses—everyone's vowed to make sure her dance and aerobic classes are well attended."

Jemma nodded, because what else could she do? "I'm not saying I don't want to take an aerobics class, but country dancing? That's like learning to walk all over again. Maybe I should wait till the jazz class, because check it out..." She flared her fingers and wiggled them in the air. "Jazz hands!"

"That just means you've already got jazz down," Camilla said with a laugh. "Which means—" she did a lasso type move over her head as she took on a twang that sent Jemma's trepidation from a seven to a ten, "—country dancin'!"

Jemma felt the blood drain from her face, and her internal organs were going into full-blown freak-out mode.

"You know how important the arts are, yet schools are forever cutting them," Camilla continued.

Another reason Jemma wanted to go into administration, although she knew keeping and retaining more arts would be a never-ending fight.

"Besides—"Camilla smacked her hips—"these were meant for the *Jarabe Tapatío* and not so much for line dancing, but you don't see me complaining."

"What is the *Jarabe Tapatío*, how hard is it, and does it require listening to country music?"

"Most people refer to it as the Mexican hat dance. It originated as a courtship dance and I'd say semi-difficult to learn. It has a lot of footwork and arm motions. Once you get those down. it's fairly easy, but we'd need a mariachi band and big colorful skirts to lift and twirl, so it's out. Plus, this is only my third class, so I'm about your same level."

Before Jemma could argue that she was sure that wasn't true, a petite woman with bronze skin and a thick head of dark, springy curls walked up to the front.

"Hello, everyone, and welcome to country dancing aerobics." Bright-pink lips accented a grin so wide that Jemma smiled back despite her nerves. Their instructor's enthusiasm radiated from her, and she promised thirty minutes of dancing that wouldn't even feel like exercise.

"And I'm so excited to see we have a new student."

Everyone turned to Jemma and beamed. Over the past few days she'd slowly started getting used to how everyone she passed waved or stopped to introduce themselves and say hello. Had begun to like it, in fact.

Right now, though, she was sort of missing her anonymity.

"I'm Essie, and you are…?"

"Jemma. I've never done any country dancing before, so I'm nervous."

"No worries. This is a judgment-free zone, and we're all just here to have a good time and burn some calories. *Bienvenido,* Jemma."

With that, Essie instructed everyone to get into place, adding a clap that made them immediately scramble to hop to.

Jemma took a few steps away from Camilla and a couple of steps back from the rest of the people so she wouldn't accidentally kick or smack into anyone. The door in the back right corner, flush with the wall, caught her eye. *There's the emergency exit I've been searching for.*

But the time to flee had obviously passed so, ready or not, she was about to learn how to country dance.

They started out clapping as they stepped side to side. *Okay, this I can handle.*

Essie demonstrated the move they were about to do, something she called the country swing. It involved swinging your arms as you swayed your hips. Camilla smiled at Jemma and she returned the gesture, thinking maybe she'd actually be okay.

"And now that we're warmed up," Essie called, "we're going to increase the tempo!"

The beat of the music increased, and Jemma struggled to keep up with the grapevine stutter step move, followed by a stomp, kick ball change move. They were supposed to repeat the sequence eight times, and during the first three she bumped into Camilla, cursing her earlier naïve confidence.

Instead of moving away for her own safety, Camilla simply called out the moves, demonstrating and counting to the beat. By the last count of eight, she'd done it!

But then a stream of new steps was thrown her way.

During an extra-complicated move, Jemma looked to Camilla, but the woman simply shrugged and whispered that she still hadn't figured out this one and always went the wrong way. So they laughed and did their best and made up a few moves on their own.

Thirty minutes later, Jemma braced her hands on her knees, fighting the urge to fall to the floor as she gasped for breath.

Essie had walked past a few times, always encouraging her and helping demonstrate a few of the moves she'd struggled with, and as everyone was completing the last of their stretches, she returned to check on Jemma. "You okay?"

"I'm…" *Out of breath. Exhausted. About to die.* "Fine."

"See! So fun, you didn't even know you were working out."

Not exactly how Jemma felt, but it had been more fun than expected. Definitely a workout, though, and she wanted to check her phone and see if it had truly only been thirty minutes, because it felt like longer.

Man, I'm out of shape.

Essie flashed that exuberant smile again. "I use a lot of the same basic moves in each routine, so each class will get easier and easier. Pretty soon, you'll be a pro."

Jemma had similarly assured her students of that kind of thing before, and as they learned about new subjects and began to understand, it did get easier. *Pro* seemed like a stretch, and she often advised her class not to set such extreme goals that they ended up being discouraging instead of encouraging.

Camilla asked their firecracker dance teacher a question in Spanish and she responded, their words blurring together. Jemma had always meant to learn more Spanish than the classes she'd taken in college, but they were speaking faster than she could follow, only a familiar-sounding word she couldn't recall the meaning of here and there.

After I finish my Masters, I'll pick it back up and work on trying to become fluent. A couple of the students in her class spoke both English and Spanish, and she wanted to be able to understand them as best as she could, whichever language they preferred.

She straightened and blew out her breath. Most of the other women were gathering their things, and as soon as she could walk on her Jell-O legs without them giving out on her, she'd do the same.

Essie turned to her, placing a hand on her shoulder. "See you next week!"

Before Jemma could respond with a "maybe," Camilla wrapped her arm around her shoulders and said, "You definitely will!"

Wyatt had just settled into his well-worn recliner on Friday night when the knock came at the door. He glanced at the clock, thinking it was late for company. Bailey Rae had just gone to bed, and he was exhausted from scraping stalls, repairing fence, and chopping and stacking wood so they'd be plenty prepared for the next storm.

Maybe an hour of kicking back and watching television was too much to ask. He pushed to his feet with a groan—a mama cow had charged him this morning when he'd simply been trying to help her premature calf, the first one of the season and born just on the border of being big enough to survive. But he understood the parental protective vibe, and he should've remembered she was one of the most defensive of the herd.

Now he had a physical reminder so he wouldn't forget.

He swung open the door, surprised to see Jemma on the other side, his escape-artist horse by her side. Unlike her usual fancy duds, she was wearing a puffy coat over sweatpants and tennis shoes. The wind swirled the dark ends of her ponytail around her pinkened cheeks.

She ran her hand down Casper's pale neck. "I believe this belongs to you."

Wyatt gaped at the two of them. "I didn't even see him leave—and I triple-secured that gate this afternoon."

"Are you too smart for your own good?" Jemma asked in a soft, cooing voice, and Wyatt nearly nodded. But of course, she was talking to his horse, who nickered and nudged her arm until she renewed her petting.

"Too spoiled is more like it. I told Mrs. Klein repeatedly that if she was going to keep feeding him, he was going to keep showing up."

"Well, I did let him share a meal with Señor Fluffypants, so…"

Wyatt cocked his head, trying to make sense out of her words. "Señor Fluffypants?"

"My bunny—they both like carrots, after all, and after his initial shock and wariness, he's decided that Casper is all right."

Wyatt felt his mouth stretch into a smile, wide enough it strained his lips and cheeks a bit, thanks to too long of disuse. "You have a bunny named Señor Fluffypants? Why doesn't that surprise me?"

"First of all, my students named him. And second of all, because I'm awesome and I have an equally awesome pet, and don't act like you're not jealous."

"It's pretty hard not to be when your bunny probably stays put and I'm stuck with the Houdini version of a horse."

"Maybe it's because you named him after a ghost. I bet he goes incorporeal and walks right through the gate. *That's* why nothing can keep him in."

With a shake of his head and more of that smiling he was unaccustomed to, he reached for the troublemaker.

The traitor nuzzled Jemma instead.

She giggled and snuggled Casper back, and no wonder the horse had followed her over, despite the fact that she didn't have a bridle or a lead rope.

Then Wyatt noticed her chattering teeth and how red the tip of her nose had become. How inconsiderate of him to stand in the doorway and banter with her without letting her step inside to warm up. "Come in. You're freezing."

"No, I'm fine," she said, a rattle of teeth biting off the words. "Okay, that's a lie. I'm freezing. But in my defense, it's so freaking cold here. How do you stand it?"

"A fire helps."

Awe flooded her features, her eyes going cartoonishly wide. "You have a real live fire?"

He ushered her inside and pointed her toward the crackling flames. "I'll put Casper in his pen, *quadruple* secure the gate, and be right back."

The jolt from icy air that hit him as soon as he stepped outside was just what he needed. Not that he regretted asking Jemma inside to warm up—it was the least he could do. But he'd been a little too comfortable standing there, admiring the pink coloring her cheeks and the way her big blue eyes sparkled as she lightly teased him.

Not to mention that joke about his horse being a ghost, as if she'd finally solved the mystery.

With the cold startling him fully awake and kickstarting his brain, he was remembering all the reasons why he and Jemma needed to stick to neighborly and nothing more.

A few more minutes of frigid night air, and he could go back inside and keep things on the friendly side. No thinking about how pretty she was, or how every time she laughed or gave a quick comeback, his heart picked up an extra beat.

Jemma eyed the pictures on the large wooden mantel as she stretched her fingers closer to the dancing flames inside the stone fireplace. Frames in a mix of wood and silver displayed smiling pictures of Bailey through the years. Including a few from when she was a baby, and Jemma studied the woman holding the tiny bundle.

Bailey was a perfect combination of her mom and dad, the same pert little nose and big brown eyes as her mom and the honey-colored hair and slightly indented chin from her dad.

The other pictures showed her through various stages. Kindergarten, first grade, second…and assumedly her third-grade picture, which was different from the rest in more ways than just her looking a year older.

A burst of cold air accompanied the opening of the front door. She hoped it wasn't rude to mention the difference in pictures, but she cared about Bailey and was curious about her in general. She was so bubbly, but she didn't seem to be as social with the other children in her class. Especially the girls. "Bailey's not smiling in her latest picture."

Wyatt's forehead crinkled.

"I couldn't help but notice," she said, gesturing to the last frame in the line of pictures.

"Ah. That. She lost her two front teeth over the summer, but they were mostly grown in by the time picture day came around. Ever since they came in, she stopped smiling as wide as she used to. I suspect one or more of her classmates said something about them being big or her slight overbite."

Jemma sighed. "Most of the kids are good kids. I'm not sure why they poke at each other so much. I think it's because they're all changing and they feel insecure and don't know how to handle it, so they poke at other people. It gets worse in junior high."

"Something to look forward to," Wyatt mumbled.

"Sorry to be the bearer of bad news, but aren't you a fan of being properly prepared?" She probably shouldn't have added that last part, but she couldn't help it.

One corner of his mouth kicked up, making the worry she'd crossed a line evaporate. "Funny."

"I thought so."

He jerked his chin toward the fireplace. "Don't you have one of these at your place?"

Jemma bit her lip. "Well, there wasn't a switch." She could see Wyatt opening his mouth to say something condescending that would ruin how nice it was to talk to him and warm up by the fire, and hurried to cut it off. "Don't worry, once I couldn't find one, I realized it was an old-school fireplace that I'd have to start. But there were only a few logs, and I tried to light it three times. I never could get it to fully catch."

"You don't know how to start a fire?"

The incredulousness in his voice pricked her defenses. "I've never started one before. I wasn't in…Fire Starters of America or whatever."

"We prefer Pyros of America," he said, and a laugh burst out of her.

She covered her mouth with her hand, glancing down the hallway where she assumed Bailey was sleeping. When she turned back, she noticed how close Wyatt was. How the flames danced in his hazel eyes, and that a tiny swing of her arm would make her skin brush his.

Her pulse quickened, and her throat went dry.

He grinned at her, and a mutinous flutter traveled through her belly. Tenderness softened his expression, and she thought that she'd rather deal with the gruffness. The tenderness was making every cell in her body misfire.

"Come on. I'll show you." Wyatt kneeled by the fire and pointed to the corner that wasn't lit anymore—the black logs were only partially burned. He detailed how to stack the wood in a crisscross pattern, talked about kindling, and then extended a match her way. "Care to do the honors?"

With him right by her side, she was already feeling rather toasty, and she was pretty sure it was more than the fire. The firelight lit his features with a soft glow, showing off the strong line of his jaw and the dusting of stubble across it.

She struck the match and touched it to the kindling.

Both Camilla and the coffee shop owner had made it clear they thought she should go for the cowboy, and this kinder, softer version tempted her to take their advice. It went beyond him being nice to look at, or that she could tell he really was a gentleman deep down.

Compassion had coated his words as he'd explained how to build a fire, the same gentle care she witnessed every time he talked to his daughter.

If only there weren't a dozen reasons that crossing lines would be a bad idea.

"See how it's catching?" he asked, and she reluctantly looked away from his face. "Now you can lean closer and blow. Not too hard, or it'll go out. Just a little encouraging wind."

"Maybe you can talk to Mother Nature about the encouraging wind. She keeps sending the kind that rattles my windows, and that first night I was here, I was sure the roof was going to blow right off."

"Not sure she'd listen to me, but if it makes you feel better, that roof's about as old as I am, and it hasn't gone anywhere." His eyebrows drew together. "Come to think of it, it probably needs replacing. Do you have any leaks?"

"Not so far, but you're not doing a very good job of comforting me." Her lungs tightened a pinch, her fears about her old house rising to the surface. "It was like two seconds of calm before you stirred the worry pot."

"The worry pot?"

"*That's* the part you're focusing on?" Her voice pitched higher. Now she was wondering how long it'd be before the roof sprung a leak, and what was she supposed to do then? Sure, she could call her landlord, but the older lady lived far away and, she assumed, without a lot of means for roof repair.

Jemma's salary couldn't cover luxuries like that, either.

Wyatt placed his hand on her shoulder, and her inner storm immediately calmed. "Hey. The roof will be fine. That's just where my mind goes. Preventative maintenance and what needs done. Normally my brain likes to focus on that kind of worrisome stuff as soon as my head hits the pillow. That way I can't sleep."

"I've had that problem before as well." Her words came out slightly breathy, matching the skidding of her pulse. Then there was the way all her blood rushed to the spot where his hand warmed her shoulder. "Admittedly I'm sort of a fly-by-the-seat-of-my-pants, attack-troubles-as-they-come girl, but I'm sort of out of my league out here. It's like learning how to adult all over again, when I thought I was doing a fairly decent job of it already."

He chuckled, and her stomach crawled up, up, up. "I know

what you mean. And I was too hard on you that day you got stuck in the snow. I was in a hurry, and patience isn't my strong suit. I think I'm a tad rusty at dealing with people—I'm better with animals."

"Well, I'm learning snow preparedness is one of the chinks in my armor, but I'm getting better at driving on the slick roads, and hey, at least now I also know how to start a fire." She glanced at the way the orange-and-yellow blaze had caught and spread before returning her gaze to the guy next to her. "And I don't believe you on that last part. I've seen the way you are with Bailey."

The love that crept into his features made him that much more attractive, while serving as a reminder why she shouldn't focus on his attractiveness.

"Bailey's different," he said. "She's like pure sunshine, you know. All those colors and the bouncy, never-ending energy. It's impossible not to feel happy around her."

Affection warmed her chest as she recalled her interactions with his daughter—pure sunshine was the perfect way to describe her. "She's a great kid. And I love how she has her own sense of style. I should hire her as my wardrobe consultant."

They shared another smile, and Jemma's self-preservation mechanism kicked in. If she stayed here much longer, her brain might take a backseat to the glowy goodness flooding her insides.

Then she might forget all the complications and make a mess. She was sticking with the exciting part of the adventure and avoiding the hazards.

Her knees creaked as she straightened, her thighs burning after being squatted down for so long—some of that was definitely from yesterday's country dancing class and all those squat-and-kicking moves. "Thank you for letting me warm up and for the lesson on building a fire."

"Thanks for bringing back my horse. Need a ride home?"

A ride would be nice. But then she might do that forgetting thing, the way she'd forgotten how cold it was until she'd been halfway here with his horse, thinking it was a farther walk than she'd realized. The way light traveled through darkness could be so misleading.

Jemma waved a hand through the air. "I'll be fine. It's just a quick jog." Not that she'd be jogging it, but then again, maybe it would be good motivation to try jogging.

"Just take my truck. I'll come get it tomorrow morning."

"No need. Being on my own is something I do have experience in." As she reminded herself whenever she landed in a difficult situation, she was a strong, independent woman. Her parents had been on the older side when they'd had her, and by the time she'd reached high school, she'd helped around the house and had done most of her paperwork and college applications herself. So she was used to diving headfirst into the unknown and getting things done.

Sometimes it'd be nice to have help, but she couldn't learn to rely on it.

Wyatt pressed his mouth into a firm line. He seemed to be having some kind of internal struggle. "At least text me and tell me you got in safe? Or I'll never be able to sleep."

She supposed that was a sensible request. She dug her phone out of her coat pocket and typed in his name, then extended it so he could enter his number.

Their fingers brushed as he returned it to her, and a tingle coursed up her arm and settled at the base of her neck.

He walked her to the door, swung it open, and gripped the wooden frame. "Good night, Jemma."

The tender way he said her name caused more fluttering

and tingling. She hated to go, more than because of the cold breeze nipping at her skin, but again, that was all the more reason to.

"Good night, Wyatt."

CHAPTER EIGHT

"M ISS MONROE, WHY DON'T YOU have a husband?"
No surprise, the question came from Chase—
the kid seemed to be filled from the bottom to the top with
questions. And stories about working on the farm with his
grandpa.

After talking to his mom again, Jemma had made a deal
with him that he could wear his cowboy hat along with his
spurs on certain days as a reward, and since the hat was a
couple of sizes too big, it wobbled slightly every time he
looked up or down.

Idly she wondered if Wyatt had been like that growing
up, and she couldn't help smiling at the thought of him as a
little rambunctious cowboy.

"Well?" Chase asked, and now every set of eyes was on
her, curiosity swimming in the depths. To make it fair, hats
were a reward for everyone who'd hit the highest two colors
on the behavior chart, so several of the students had them on.

Jemma sat on the edge of her desk and crossed one ankle
over the other. "I guess I just haven't met the right person
yet."

"I'll be your boyfriend," Luis, one of her shyest students,
said.

"I appreciate that, Luis, but I need a boyfriend my own age. Someday. Right now, teaching you guys keeps me plenty busy."

"But what about when you go home?" Sydney asked from her seat in the first row.

"I have Señor Fluffypants."

One of the girls glanced at the bunny, happily sleeping away in his kennel, her forehead all scrunched up. "But he doesn't talk very much."

"Which is nice, honestly. No one interrupts my TV shows or asks me a question when I'm trying to read a book." Half true. While he didn't disturb her reading time, sometimes her bunny *was* too quiet. He always listened, but he didn't say much back.

"My sister always talks *so loud* during my show. And at the dinner table." This from Parker, the boy who'd decided to wear a Raiders hat, which seemed to be quite the controversy among the other football fans. He smacked his palm to his face and sighed as he dragged it down. "She never stops talking, and it makes me *so tired*."

Jemma stifled a laugh. She didn't want him thinking she was laughing *at* him, but it wasn't the first time one of her male students said something about how much girls talked.

"Sounds lonely," Bailey said, a sad note to her voice.

A twinge Jemma didn't expect tugged in the center of her chest. Sometimes it was lonely, in spite of assuring herself she was fine—and she was. But occasionally she longed for someone to come home to. To cuddle up with and talk to about her day, whether it was good or bad.

The last thing she wanted was for her class to worry about her, so she pulled out a smile. "Luckily, I have all of you to talk to." It was one reason why she'd been drawn to teaching, especially this age group. She got to be part of molding these malleable minds, often before the world seeped in and jaded them.

Their obvious concern made her fondness for them grow even more. Something often happened in adulthood, where people forgot to slow down and thank each other for the little things. Forgot to tell each other how much they cared.

One of the hardest things about teaching was seeing kids who were sad or had trouble at home. It always made her feel so helpless, and about the only thing she could do was make sure they knew how much she adored them. "You guys make me happy. I constantly tell Señor Fluffypants about how I have the best class ever."

They all seemed placated by that, and she instructed them to get out their colored pencils. "We've got twenty minutes to finish our solar system drawings, and then we'll go to the music room so we can practice the songs for the play."

They'd read through it yesterday, and today they were learning songs. "Tomorrow, you'll get your assigned parts so you can start memorizing your lines."

Art time was always popular, even with her students who struggled through other subjects. Now that she'd been teaching them for a full week, she was also getting to know the students better and becoming more comfortable with her daily routine—including the part of it that involved watching the weather, scraping the sidewalk, and maneuvering snowy roads. She'd learned to wear her snow boots until she reached the school parking lot, and then she'd change into the fun type of footwear that earned befuddled frowns from Wyatt.

Not that she'd seen him since the night he'd taught her to build a fire.

So that she wouldn't focus too much on her misbehaving thoughts—seriously, why did they drift to him so often?— she walked around the classroom. She peered over shoulders, complimenting the students and admiring how detailed, yet varied, their drawings were.

Jemma paused next to Bailey, who had on an opalescent pink hat with closed eyelashes and a unicorn horn. Hat day was quickly becoming as much of a reward for her as it was for her students.

No surprise, Bailey's solar system had more colors than most, and Jemma opened her mouth to say she liked the star outline of a horse that looked to be running around Saturn's ring.

Bailey set down her purple pencil and pressed her lips together, like she was deep in thought.

Jemma almost walked on so as to not disturb her, but then Bailey said, "My dad's not married, either."

Her mouth opened and closed, but Jemma wasn't sure how to respond. In the end, she went with a noncommittal *hmm.*

"Sometimes I worry that he gets lonely."

Jemma smoothed a hand down Bailey's thick, curly pony-tail. "Oh, honey, I wouldn't worry about that. He has you."

The tension in the girl's shoulders loosened. "Yeah, that's true. And I talk a lot. Once he told me that his ears were tired, and I told him that sometimes my ears get tired, but my mouth *never* gets tired."

A laugh slipped out this time, but Bailey giggled too.

Then it was time to put away their supplies and head to the music room.

As Jemma walked her class down the hall, she decided that in spite of having no idea what the future had in store, this was a good experience, one she'd needed. It made that whole mess of having Simon tell her he only liked her *as a friend* in the midst of losing her job feel further away.

She was also starting to like the quirkiness of this town and its people, and how different each day felt.

For the first time since her arrival in Haven Lake, she thought she'd definitely made the right decision by jumping into the adventure of coming here.

Wyatt pulled up to the elementary school, getting lucky and finding a parking spot fairly close to the main entrance.

He was a few minutes early, and he considered climbing out of his truck, walking up the grassy hill and standing near the classroom door Bailey would come skipping out of. He rarely arrived with enough time to do so, but the primary problem with that idea was why he wanted to.

He hadn't seen Jemma in four days, since the night she'd returned his horse. He'd replayed their moments in front of the fireplace far too often.

The long list of reasons why he shouldn't be thinking about the woman ran through his head again: she was a born-and-raised, bona-fide city girl; she was his daughter's teacher; and he didn't have time to date anyway.

It'd be a lot easier to ignore the flicker of interest if it wasn't the first time he'd experienced that sensation since Andrea had left. He needed to remember that flickers turned into flames that could burn you, and a big no thanks on that.

Still, Jemma was new in town, and he wanted to know if she'd figured out her fireplace, and he really should make sure she wasn't freezing every night in her house. After all, it was the neighborly thing to do. The *very least* he could do after being so short with her that day she'd gotten stuck in the snow, even though he had apologized the other night.

Just because being prepared and self-sufficient had been

hammered into him from an early age didn't mean he had to be so impatient when other people hadn't had the same lecture. Since his conversation with Dempsey, he'd contmplated the "grumpy" thing, and had decided he'd work on not blocking everyone out.

Might as well start now.

The door to his beat-up feed truck creaked as he pushed it open and then slammed it closed. He had to hip-check the door in order to get it to fully shut, but his other truck was in need of a new alternator and currently in pieces in his oversized mechanic garage.

People did a double take as he walked past, as if he were the Boo Radley of the town. He'd been in the coffee shop a week ago, so he wasn't sure why they all gaped as if they'd forgotten what he looked like.

Clearly this had been what his best friend had been talking about, so he worked to put a smile on his face, regardless of how weird it felt to walk around grinning like a loon for no reason.

"Wyatt?"

He spun at the familiar voice. His sister stood there, his brand-new niece wrapped up in the fabric carrier draped around her chest, his chunky two-year-old nephew on her hip. "Lori. What are you doing here? Did I miss you enrolling my prodigy cowboy in school early?"

He bumped fists with his two-year-old nephew, Logan. "When are you going to come ride the tractor with me?"

"Tractor! Tractor!"

"Thanks for that," Lori said, her smile saying she was teasing but the words coming out with a hint of exhaustion.

"It's just nice he still gets excited. Nowadays if I ask Bailey Rae, she sighs and tells me that her outfit isn't meant for farm work."

"Well, her outfits rarely are. I guess we should trade for a night. Logan can ride a tractor, and Bailey Rae can go shopping with me."

Logan reached his chubby hands toward Wyatt, and he took him from his sister. He didn't know how she carried them both. His nephew was built like a linebacker, all solid and compact, and he was struggling slightly with not being the baby anymore.

His niece fussed from inside of the draped fabric, making grunting, squeaky noises, and Lori swayed back and forth. "As for why I'm here, my neighbor had an appointment that ran late, so I'm picking up her son. He's also obsessed with tractors and four-wheelers."

"Sounds like my kind of kid." Wyatt tossed Logan a couple of inches in the air, grinning back at him as he giggled. "For a second, I wondered if I'd asked you to pick up Bailey Rae and then forgot about it."

"No, but if you ever need me to…"

"Thanks, but you've got plenty on your plate." His sister's husband was a nice guy, more into accounting than ranch work. He also traveled quite a lot for his job, and despite how much that left Lori to do by herself, she still volunteered to help neighbors and friends all the time. She had a heart of gold, one he didn't want to take advantage of, and he could never repay her for the countless times she'd helped out since he'd transitioned to single parenthood.

The bell rang, and kids streamed out of the classrooms in a steady flow. Wyatt stepped closer to the door Bailey would exit, his heart thumping faster as he anticipated seeing Jemma.

Every day when he asked his daughter how school was, it was Miss Monroe this and Miss Monroe that, which was yet another reason it was hard to avoid thinking about Jemma.

Clearly his daughter was smitten with her new teacher, and while her other teacher was good, Bailey Rae was more excited for school these days. And heaven help the person who brought up the upcoming Valentine's Day play, because she could talk about it for hours, ignoring any and all attempts to change the subject, and keep on going till she fell into bed.

"More than anything in the world, I want to play Cupid," she'd said last night as he was tucking her in. One thing he'd learned was that "more than anything in the world" lasted anywhere from a day to a year.

He'd finally gotten the covers snug when she'd sat up. "I don't care if he's typically a boy. Daddy, you know I can shoot love arrows as good if not better. I'm a much better shot than the boys in my class."

Wyatt hoped she wasn't bragging too much about that during class, but he couldn't help experiencing pride over it. While she was so over tractor rides, his bow and arrow lessons had stuck.

As usual, she was the last one out of the classroom, and of course she'd hung back in the doorway to talk to her teacher. Jemma's eyes met his across the space, and the smile that curved her lips made him forget what he'd been thinking.

"Hey." She stepped closer and aimed that killer smile at his nephew. "Who's this cutie?"

"This is my nephew, Logan. That's my sister right..." He turned to find where she'd gone in the crowd and found her looking back at him, a smug twist to her features. Great. He'd definitely hear about this from her later.

Why had he thought meeting his daughter at the door and saying a quick hello to her teacher with a whole bunch of people watching on was a bright idea?

Lori stepped forward and gave a little wave. "Hi. Lori

Gibson. I've heard such good things, and it's nice to finally meet you."

"Aww, the kids here are so sweet. They have the best stories too."

"Actually, I heard a wild story about you on your first day," Lori said. "They said you had to deal with snakes dropping from the ceiling."

Red crept across Jemma's cheeks, but she laughed. "Just one snake, luckily, although he was big enough to count as two or three. I didn't know if I was being pranked or initiated, or if I'd just moved to the backwoods."

"What about a snake?" Wyatt asked, surprised he hadn't heard the story. He glanced at Bailey Rae.

His daughter shrugged. "There was a snake. Chase was on it, so I knew we were safe. But Miss Monroe screamed real loud—like, Mrs. Hembolt opera loud."

Jemma put her hand over her mouth, he suspected to cover a laugh. "I didn't expect it, and it was a giant snake, so yeah, I screamed. What would you do if a snake was suddenly dangling over your head?"

"Help him down, of course," Wyatt said. "Poor thing doesn't have arms or legs."

Jemma shuddered. "It's not right, not the way they move or their forked tongue or…" She shuddered again, and he laughed, wishing he'd been there to see it.

Also wishing the tiniest bit he'd also been the one to take care of the snake and save the day, which was silly, and seriously, where was his head at? He'd obviously lost his mind.

"Well, Bailes, guess we'd better get going." He shifted his nephew to his other hip and placed his hand on his daughter's shoulder. He told himself to get moving, to not ask the question that would lead to more talking and more of Jemma smiling and more of that churning in his gut…

But he couldn't help himself. "Did you, uh, ever get your fireplace figured out?"

The gems in her dangly earrings caught the sunlight as she shook her head. "I haven't had a chance to pick up wood yet, but I hear there's a storm coming this weekend, so I'm going to for sure buy a bundle or two before then."

"Good, good. I'd suggest more like four or five. Just to be safe." He didn't have anything else to say, and now he was noticing that most of the other students and parents had cleared out. Here he was keeping Jemma, and she probably had things to get to. "See you later."

"Later," she said.

Wyatt walked Lori to her van to help her juggle all the kids. Once everyone was loaded and belted inside, she turned to him and gave him a knowing smirk that sent prickling apprehension along his skin. "Now I get it. Why you decided to wait at the door."

"Careful. Little ears..." He tipped his head toward his daughter, but she was pulling funny faces, making the other kids giggle. He lowered his voice. "She's my neighbor and Bailey Rae's teacher. That's it."

"She's also pretty."

"I hadn't noticed."

Lori crossed her arms and arched an eyebrow. "Liar."

She always could read him like a book—growing up, it'd landed him in hot water several times. "Fine, I noticed. Doesn't change anything."

"It's okay to move on."

"I have."

"Okay, but—"

"Leave it alone, Lori. Just because you're happily married doesn't mean we all have to be paired up to be happy. I'm good."

She nodded as if she understood, although he suspected she'd bring it up later. "See you on Sunday for dinner?"

"We'll be there." Wyatt gestured to Bailey Rae that it was time to go, and they waved their goodbyes and headed toward the truck.

He may have also glanced back toward Jemma's classroom door, but that was just out of habit.

CHAPTER NINE

D OROTHY HEMBOLT HAD MORE ENERGY than Jemma had after an Espress-yourself, which was the drink of the week at Havenly Brew. The surprise in that drink was that you wouldn't sleep at night if you had one too late in the day.

"And one, two…" Mrs. Hembolt used her conducting baton to bring the kids in on the count of three. Today was the first time she'd pulled out the skinny wand with the bulbous rosewood handle, which had led to several of the kids asking which Harry Potter house she belonged to.

"The one that gets after kids if they don't focus, listen, and sing as loudly as possible while staying on key," Mrs. Hembolt had said without missing a beat.

Kylie M. had commented that it sounded like Slytherin, and it'd taken every ounce of Jemma's control to keep the laugh that wanted to escape inside. Then she'd cleared her throat and backed up the music teacher, encouraging the kids to pay attention and work on their song for the play.

Each time they practiced it, the song sounded better and better, and on cue, Mrs. Hembolt joined a few bars in, as if she couldn't help herself. No matter how high or low the kids sang, she raised her voice to opera levels, either humming or belting out the words.

Several times in the teachers' lounge, Jemma and the other teachers would be chatting during their lunchtime, and the woman would just burst into song, like life was her very own musical and she was undeniably the star.

"That was marvelous." Mrs. Hembolt tucked her baton under her arm and clapped. "You all are such amazing singers." Sure, she pushed the kids, but she also beamed at them while sincerely praising them, which made them work hard to please her.

Jemma wholeheartedly agreed. There was something incredibly adorable about a group of kids singing about friendship, kindness, and love. The community was going to flip over "Cupid Goes Crazy," she was sure of it.

Mrs. Hembolt pushed her glasses up her nose and lifted a paper. "Now, for the parts..."

Jemma shouldn't play favorites, and she liked to think she didn't too much, but she held her breath, hoping Bailey would get the role she wanted. It'd been all she'd talked about, and Jemma liked the idea of switching it up and having a female cupid.

All week, Bailey had been wearing clothes with hearts on them to prove how committed she'd be to the role.

"Cupid will be played by..." Another readjustment of the glasses. Jemma could hardly take the suspense. "Bailey Rae Langford."

A squeal escaped Bailey as she threw her hands over her mouth, pure joy radiating off her in waves.

Jemma had to fight the urge to go throw her arms around her and congratulate her. Later there'd definitely be a high-five, though.

Mrs. Hembolt continued to rattle off the names and parts. Chase was the second lead, the business person who tried to help Cupid clean up the mess *she* made when she hit wrong target after wrong target, until everyone had been hit with an arrow. Foam arrows for the record, so no one would end up crying instead of being instilled with goodwill.

It was a perfect fit. Chase had charm for days, and he also read above his grade level. Plus, he'd get to run around the stage a lot throughout the play, which would help keep him from getting as antsy.

Man, if we could bottle up that kid's energy, we could sell it and give the energy drink business a run for their money. Jemma had learned that once his fidgeting got to a certain level, he'd been bottled up for too long and it'd burst out of him, usually in the form of something that'd distract the entire class.

So instead of trying to diffuse the situation afterward, she'd watch for signs he was about to blow and give him a task or errand, one that often involved retrieving something from the library or office. Sometimes she simply made everyone get up and do the "get out the wiggles" dance.

The last of the parts were given out, and most of the kids seemed happy with their roles. Mrs. Hembolt handed Jemma a copy of the list as well so she could email parents and let them know their kids needed to work on memorizing their lines over the next three and a half weeks.

Bailey slowed in front of Jemma, who held her hand up for a high five. She smacked Jemma's palm and grinned, teeth and all, totally unguarded in this moment. "I told my dad over and over that this part was what I wanted more than anything in the world, and I got it. I actually got it!"

"You did, and you're going to be such an excellent Cupid."

Lips closed over her teeth, but her grin and excitement remained.

Jemma wanted to tell Bailey how much she liked her smile, but there were too many kids around them, and she didn't want to draw extra attention or make her feel uncomfortable.

"Okay, back to the classroom. Form a line."

They did as instructed, cheerfully chatting as they walked down the hallway. As long as it didn't get too loud, Jemma would rather them get out some of the chatter now so once they reached the classroom, they could dig in.

Camilla was in the middle of the hallway and stepped up to Jemma as she started past. "Do you have everything you need for now to get ready for the play?"

"Yeah, Mrs. Hembolt just gave out parts—I love her energy and spirit, by the way. As long as she's directing and taking care of the music, I can easily handle the rest. I've also blocked off some extra time in class to practice parts."

"Perfect. You just let me know what you need, and I'll do my best to get it." Camilla glanced at her watch. "Hey, so I've got an appointment with a student and his parent here in a minute, but I wanted to see if you wanted to meet at Havenly Brew after school. No business. I just want to take some time to sit and chat."

"That sounds lovely. See you after school."

Once again, it felt like things were lining up here. She still missed Randa and occasionally longed for the amenities the city provided—the slew of take-out options and places to shop, and how she could catch a movie without having to drive forty minutes away.

But she loved the way the school was run here—how the admin knew every single student by name and how passionate the teachers were about their work. Most of the parents were all in too.

At first Jemma had worried she wouldn't have any friends for the six or so weeks she'd be here, covering for their former teacher until she felt ready to come back.

Now she was starting to worry she was already getting too attached, not only to her students, but also to a few of the people in town as well.

As soon as Jemma and Camilla pushed inside Havenly Brew, the sweet scent of the bakery and the bitter scent of the coffee beans hit her. It was one of those smells Jemma wanted to carry home with her so she could pull it out when she needed a mood boost, only then she'd be disappointed at her bare cupboards and empty mug.

"How are you ladies today?" April asked, greeting them warmly as she stacked a new sleeve of cups next to her on the counter. She'd worn her auburn hair curly today, and the contrast of it framing her pale skin made her eyes pop more than usual.

"It's been a pretty good day," Jemma said. "Exhausting, but good." Camilla echoed the sentiment, and then Jemma added, "I just have to tell you how cute you look. I love the curls."

"They're a pain to maintain, but I felt like mixing it up today."

April leaned her forearms on the counter, in the narrow spot between the cash register and glass case of pastries. "You gals came in at the perfect time. Usually I don't reveal my new drink of the week till Sunday, but I decided to unveil it early since the Crowthers just had their baby this morning. A six-and-a-half-pound girl named Joyce, after their grandma, who was also the woman who taught me how to bake and encouraged me to follow my passion."

"Am I ever glad for that," Camilla said, patting April's hand. "I've never had a bad drink here. Even the ones I'm sorta skeptical about turn out to be delicious. What's this new one called?"

April straightened and gestured to the chalkboard that held the weekly special. "It's called Almond Joyce. It's a cherry Frappuccino made with coconut milk and almond flavoring. Then whip cream, of course, pink sprinkles and coconut shavings, and a cherry on top."

"So basically it's like drinking a cupcake?" Jemma asked.

April nodded enthusiastically, and Jemma's taste buds were equally as excited as they imagined that scrumptious-sounding combination hitting her tongue. "Um, yes please."

"I'll take one as well." Camilla batted away Jemma's extended twenty-dollar bill, insisting on paying since she'd done the inviting.

One thing Jemma had learned in her short time here was that there was no fighting the townsfolk's generosity. She leaned her hip on the counter and studied the chalkboard that now had two specials on it, since the Espress-yourself was still there on the bottom. "I'm already excited about when you'll unveil your next drink. How do you come up with all the names and flavors?"

"Oh, they just come to me. I think it helps that I start the day with so much caffeine and sugar."

"Ah, the perfect combination," Jemma added with a smile.

"Exactly." April uncapped the lid to a black Sharpie and scribbled their names on two of the cardboard cups she'd just stacked. "By the way," she asked around the marker lid in her mouth, "have you seen Wyatt lately?"

Camilla turned to Jemma with raised eyebrows, one dimple flashing in her cheek, making it clear she was curious about the answer as well.

As Jemma had told the principal before, she'd read in

books about how quickly word traveled in small towns and the way everyone was in each other's business, but every time she experienced it, it still struck her how different life was here. Back in Denver, she used to frequent a cafe near her downtown apartment complex, and although she'd ordered the same thing every time, the baristas had always asked for her order and her name, no hint of recognition.

Part of it had probably been how big of a hurry she'd always been in. While she didn't so much want to be the topic of gossip, the genuine care behind their gentle interrogations also made it hard to shut them totally down.

"Um, he picked up Bailey from the classroom yesterday." Not today, and Jemma had been slightly disappointed he hadn't been outside the door waiting. Which was silly, especially considering their initial few meetings. He still didn't say much—save that night he'd taught her how to start a fire, and even then, he'd been on the quiet side.

"Look how she went all dreamy." Camilla gave April a conspiratorial nudge with her elbow. "Whatever thoughts she's having about him are definitely good ones."

Jemma wiped her features clean the best she could without a mirror to see which expression she was accidentally giving. "I was thinking about my sugary drink."

"Mm-hmm."

"You both obviously want to play matchmaker—"

"Ooh, good idea," April said, capping one of the frothy pink drinks and sliding it to Camilla. "We should team up."

"So not what I was saying." Jemma sighed, but couldn't help smiling. "You ladies are going to get me or yourselves or that cowboy in trouble. Trouble all around. I teach his daughter and we're on friendly terms, but that's it and that's all it'll ever be."

She should leave it at that, but she couldn't help adding. "I did meet his sister and her kiddos yesterday."

"Oh, yes. Lori's a total sweetheart," April said. "When she had her first baby, I made a blue smoothie called Bubba Blueberry because he was the biggest baby in the county."

"He was a chunk. I barely resisted pinching the cheeks."

The hiss from the whip cream can filled the air, and then April poured on a healthy amount of sprinkles and capped it. She extended it to Jemma, who licked the whip cream that had squirted out the seam and was sliding down toward her hand.

"So, Wyatt and his sister grew up here, right?" she asked, and they nodded. "What about their parents?" She hadn't heard mention of them, and Wyatt was running the ranch alone, but she hadn't wanted to be insensitive and ask.

April wiped her hands on a paper towel. "Raymond Langford passed too young, shortly after Bailey Rae was born. Peggy eventually moved to Florida, where she takes care of her elderly parents."

While Jemma didn't see her parents nearly enough, she hated the thought of them being that far away. Wyatt truly was mostly on his own, and while she didn't like the idea of that, she was even more impressed at how involved he was in Bailey's life. She'd had former students' whose parents were in the same position and had rarely shown up. No doubt it was hard to juggle everything. She didn't blame them for not being able to make it to myriad school events, but she saw the difference it made in kids' lives.

She was about to say that she admired Wyatt, while emphasizing it was only in a friendly way, but she knew when it came to her in-cahoots matchmakers, it would only encourage them more.

Better to change the subject entirely.

She took a sip of her drink and couldn't help the *mmm* that came out. Then an idea popped into her head—there really was something to April's caffeine-and-sugar-jolt theory. "You know, I'd love to serve something pink at the Valentine's Day play. It'd have to be a non-coffee drink, since we probably don't want to caffeinate the children, especially that late at night, but how hard would it be to make a big batch like that?"

April tipped her head from side to side as if she were mentally doing calculations. "Not hard. And I'd happily provide a discount for the school."

"We'll make sure to publicly thank you and tell everyone to come visit the shop, although most of the town probably does that already. As long as this is all okay with you, Camilla."

Camilla licked whip cream off her lip and nodded. "I think it's a great idea. We'll serve it at the end, so the kids are on their way home before the sugar rush hits."

They all shared a laugh, and then Jemma and Camilla took their drinks to a table in the corner.

It wasn't quite changing the curriculum or the way students learned, but it felt good to feel like she was making a difference. To be somewhere her ideas were actually listened to and considered instead of immediately being shut down.

In fact, she was going to consider it step one to making her way toward a job in administration.

CHAPTER TEN

J EMMA LIT THE KINDLING SHE'D stuck between the perfectly stacked wood.

As the flame licked at the wood, she gently blew, and the orange glow spread and fully caught. She pumped her fist, feeling all accomplished. Yesterday she'd had to take snowy roads home, but after some bumpy trial-and-error swerves, she'd successfully pulled her car out of a fishtail.

And now her fire was growing by the second.

I'm practically a country girl now.

With that accomplished, she wandered into the kitchen so she could make some tea, Señor Fluffypants hopping behind her. First she'd make an extra-large mug of ginger peach green tea, and then she'd settle in front of the fire to read and relax. It might not be what most people considered fabulous Saturday night plans, but it was her happy place.

I should probably keep working on being more social.

Then again, she'd put in late hours this week, and she'd had her second country dancing class a couple of nights ago, which totally counted toward being social. While she still winced at the twangy music here and there, Essie had been right. Most of the moves were similar, although there were a few weird ones with names like "wonky feet" and "penguin tail," and she'd thoroughly enjoyed the class.

It helped that everyone was so encouraging, calling out the steps when she faltered. Essie had thrown a complex move at them that had sent Jemma and Camilla stumbling over each other again, and she'd gotten as much exercise laughing as she had dancing.

A gray haze drifted into the kitchen, and she wrinkled her nose as the scent of smoke hit her nostrils. "I guess that's to be expected," she said to Señor Fluffypants. "A little smoke with our fire."

She didn't recall gray clouds filling the air in Wyatt's living room that night they'd been crouched in front of the fireplace, but she'd been distracted by his nearness and his deep voice, no longer impatient but tender.

Tears stung her eyes as more smoke filtered in, and she cupped her warm mug and went to investigate.

The mug slipped from her hands as she stepped into the living room, the ceramic cracking and sending shards and tea across the floor.

One side of her screamed, *no, not my favorite mug!* But she couldn't focus on that right now. She sprinted toward the fireplace, staring in horror as smoke billowed out in belching black clouds. "No, no, no. Why are you doing this?"

Big surprise, the fire didn't answer. She waved a hand through the thick air, her nose burning and her eyes watering. She accidentally sucked in a lungful of smoke and coughed.

Still hacking, she sprinted into the kitchen and opened cupboards until she found a pitcher. She stuck it under the faucet and filled it to the top, chanting for the stream of water to hurry it up already.

Once the pitcher was brimming, she rushed back into the living room as fast as she could without spilling. At least the flames were staying *inside* the fireplace—if only the same could be said for the smoke.

Dousing the wood with the water effectively put out the fire, but black-and-gray clouds continued to inundate the room.

Her cell phone caught her eye. She lifted it, debating for a moment over who to call.

While women occasionally liked to joke about reasons to call in firefighters, there was nothing on fire. In this little town, the fire department was run by volunteers, so the men often had other jobs as well. "Shoot, shoot, shoot. What do I do?"

She didn't have a ton of numbers, but since Wyatt had insisted she text him to let him know she'd arrived safely home, she had his. Bonus, he lived close.

Even better, he'd know what to do, even if he gave her a look like she should be able to take care of it herself.

Finally, she tapped the number, nearly hanging up twice as it rang and rang. Just when she figured she'd have to leave a message, Wyatt's deep voice carried over the line. "Jemma?"

"Um, I have a...situation." She scooped up her bunny and tucked him in close as she walked over and threw open the window, despite the frigid temperature.

"Are you stuck? Where are you at? I'll get my truck and—"

"I started a fire in my fireplace, just like you showed me..."

"Oh. Good job." Clearly he was wondering why she was calling to tell him, as if she were one of her students at show and tell and hoping for a gold star.

"But then my living room started filling with smoke, and I put out the fire, but it's still smoking and—" A sputtered cough burst out of her, making it impossible to finish her sentence.

She didn't have to, though, because Wyatt said, "I'll be right there."

Wyatt cut the engine and launched himself out of the truck before it'd fully rolled to a stop.

The door to the cottage was open, a thick cloud of smoke spilling out of it, and fear rose and squeezed the air out of his lungs.

Jemma had said she'd put out the fire, but that was a lot of smoke.

His boots pounded out a loud rhythm as he rushed up the porch steps and stormed inside. "Jemma?"

She had a blanket up over her nose, and relief washed through him. Because she was safe. That was all. "I promise I did it just like you said, but then I went to make a cup of tea— Oh, I should clean that up."

She squatted in front of a broken mug and began picking up the pieces.

He glanced at the fireplace and batted the hazy air. With the window and door open, it was clearing some, but his eyes and nose still stung, and the urge to cough clutched at his throat.

Covering his nose with his shirt, he walked over to the fireplace and leaned over it, then craned his neck to peer up the chimney. He patted his pocket, pulled out his phone, and turned on the flashlight. Back in the day he used to have to carry a flashlight around, and he had to admit the phone's feature had come in handy more than once.

It also meant he'd dropped his phone in a pile of manure

once, and a cow had stomped on it and broken the screen before he could retrieve it. Life-proof cases weren't quite enough for his lifestyle.

He quickly backed out, wheezing and working on exhaling instead of inhaling. He tugged his shirt down as he spun toward Jemma. "It's clogged. I bet it hasn't been cleaned out in years."

"And that's something you're supposed to do? Clean it out? Or are there… Don't make fun of me, but are chimney sweeps still a thing? Should I call the dude from *Mary Poppins?*"

The fact that she was making a joke made him smile. It also confirmed she was okay. "If you've got the dude from *Mary Poppins*'s phone number, feel free to give him a ring, but if that doesn't work out, Bob's Chimney service is the next town over and they do a good job. Or…"

He was forever behind, and he'd told himself a hundred times to be neighborly without getting in too deep, but he couldn't help but offer. "I've done mine. I can gather the supplies and do what I can to clean it."

"Oh, I don't mind paying someone. Or I could pay you if you…well, 'want to do it' is probably the wrong way to phrase it." She rubbed her hands on her arms. Any second her teeth would start chattering.

"I don't mind. But it's cold and late, and I don't want to leave Bailey Rae at home by herself for too long." The drive over took about a minute, and walking only four or five. Plus, she'd call if she needed him, but still.

"Of course. Go. I shouldn't have called. I just sort of freaked out and I had your number and… I'm your problem neighbor, aren't I?" Her shoulders sagged, and he fought the urge to wrap his hands around her arms and take over rubbing warmth into them.

"Not at all. You just keep things interesting."

She cracked a smile. Then a shiver racked her body.

"Come on," he said, lightly touching her shoulder, and even that was enough to awaken every cell in his body. "We'll go to my place and get you warmed up while the house airs out."

"Oh, I don't want to intrud—"

"I insist."

She nodded, her teeth fully chattering now, and grabbed her coat. Her gaze drifted toward the kitchen. "I put Señor Fluffypants in his cage by the open back door, but I still worry about him breathing in all that smoke."

It took Wyatt a second, but then he recalled her comment about how Señor Fluffypants didn't mind sharing his carrots with Casper. Bailey had also mentioned the bunny, and how the class took turns feeding him while they were at school. "You can grab him. What's one more animal?"

The concern in her features faded, and she rushed into the kitchen and returned a moment later, holding the cage and muttering soothing words to her black-and-white bunny. She was quite the sight, pink pajama pants with hearts on them, ash-flecked hair pulled up in a bun, a smudge of gray on her cheek.

A mushy sensation tumbled through him, taking out one organ after another. Problem neighbor, indeed.

Wyatt opened the passenger door to his truck and helped Jemma inside. Once he was settled behind the wheel, he cranked the heater—although it wasn't very warm yet—and within a couple of minutes, they were pulling up to his front porch.

Since Jemma was just stubborn enough to try to juggle the bunny carrier and climb out of the tall truck, he grabbed the carrier's handle so she wouldn't end up face-planting in a snowbank on her way down, and then they hurried inside to get warm.

Bailey Rae gave a happy squeal over their guests as he explained the situation. "You picked a good night to come over. Tonight's movie-and-s'mores night. Dad said I can pick the movie, but I can't decide."

His daughter held up two DVDs of girly movies he'd seen way too many times and, big surprise, Jemma was familiar and launched into the pros and cons of both.

After settling on one and popping it into the DVD player, Bailey Rae asked if she could hold Señor Fluffypants. She pulled the bunny into her arms and sat between him and Jemma on the couch, a giant grin on her face.

He smiled over her head at Jemma, who immediately returned the gesture.

Most of his weeks were blurs, one day bleeding into another, and regardless of the fact that he'd never call himself caught up, Saturday nights were the exception. They were the nights he reserved for watching a movie with his daughter, and for a little while, nothing else existed.

The same sense of calm he normally experienced on movie nights flowed through him, but every time Jemma and Bailey Rae shared a giggle or talked about how cute an outfit or a hairdo was, the comfort and contentment multiplied.

"Don't you think, Daddy?" Bailey Rae asked after she'd remarked that one of the pairs of shoes looked like something Jemma would wear.

He nodded, as if he paid attention to those things—in Jemma's case, though, he paid more attention than he should.

Jemma spun and put her elbow on the back of the couch. "You should see this little shop in downtown Denver. It's one of my favorite places in the world because they have purses and shoes in every color you could imagine."

Bailey Rae's eyes widened. "I can imagine lots of colors."

"Do they have any sensible footwear?" Wyatt asked.

Jemma defiantly lifted her nose in the air. "Life's too short for sensible footwear."

He'd noticed that while she was shorter without her heels, she still came up to his chin. He also couldn't help noticing how fondly Jemma talked about the big city, making it obvious she missed it.

During the last thirty or so minutes of the movie, the ladies' eyes were glued to the screen, both of them leaning forward like they hadn't already seen how it ended. They also shushed the few comments he'd made, so apparently talking time was over.

They both sighed at the happy ending. Then, with no warning, Bailey Rae shoved the bunny into his hands. "Time for s'mores!" She shot off the couch and sprinted into the kitchen for the supplies.

Wyatt frowned at the furry creature, trying to figure out how to hold it and wondering if it was potty trained. He predicted he'd find out in about three, two...

A laugh sputtered out of Jemma, and he glanced at her. "What?"

"It's just you and that bunny. Don't you own horses and cows? And I swear I saw some chickens when I brought over your horse. Yet you're afraid of a bunny."

"I'm *not* afraid of it." He twisted the pet so its wiggling nose faced him, but continued to hold it away from his body, and Jemma laughed again. "I just don't want it to use the bathroom on me."

"Here." Jemma's fingers brushed his as he handed over the bunny, and a shock of electricity coursed up his arm and settled in his chest. She placed her pet in its carrier and scooted to the edge of the couch. Her eyes met his, and he was suddenly aware of how close she was, and her endlessly blue eyes, and the way her easy smile lit her entire face.

Then he was thinking of how good she was with Bailey Rae.

Of how beautiful she was, with or without makeup. Of how kind and bubbly she was and how he smiled more when she was around.

Of way, way too much.

"Got the stuff." Bailey Rae stepped into the room, her arms filled with a box of graham crackers, a bag of marshmallows, and a Hershey bar. "Miss Monroe, how do you like your marshmallows?"

"Light brown on the outside, melty on the middle."

"Me too, but I always get impatient and burn them." Bailey Rae dumped everything on the side table nearest the fireplace, and Jemma moved next to her. They stuck marshmallows on the metal sticks and extended the ends toward the flames.

Wyatt slowly pushed to his feet and walked over to join them.

As usual, Bailey Rae caught her marshmallow on fire. Then she shrugged and assembled her s'more.

Jemma glanced at him as she rotated her stick. "What about you? I know you said patience wasn't your strong suit, even though you've demonstrated a whole lot of it tonight. With me and that movie."

"I'm better with marshmallows than people."

She looked from him to Bailey Rae, who'd melted chocolate on her lip and chin, and then back at him. "I'm pretty sure that's not true."

"Well, she's easy. Practically raises herself."

"I'm not just talking about her. You've bailed me out of a

mess twice now. I appreciate it. And I enjoyed the movie, so thank you for inviting me."

"Hey, Miss Monroe..."

Jemma turned around and grabbed the graham crackers his daughter had extended her way. "I think it'd be okay if you called me Jemma when we're not at school. Miss Monroe feels so formal."

Wyatt considered objecting. He couldn't get too close to Jemma, and Bailey Rae shouldn't either.

But Bailey Rae nodded and was off and talking before he had a chance to interject. "Cool. So, Jemma, did you know we had our first baby cow last weekend?"

"Aren't they born in the spring? Or is that just my city girl upbringing showing?" She bumped her shoulder into his, and his pulse quickened. He could smell her perfume too, something light and vanilla.

He gave her a quick smile as he got to work building his s'more. "We always have a couple that decide to come early. Usually on the coldest day possible, although I suppose I shouldn't say that, because at least it wasn't during a blizzard."

Jemma's eyes went wide. "What do you do then?"

"Bundle up and go to the barn to see if she needs help."

"The cow?"

"Yep. Occasionally they do, and if I'm not there to help and something goes wrong, we could lose one."

"Whoa. I had no idea it was so intense."

"You should see the baby calves when they first come out," Bailey Rae said. "They're all wobbly and they make this tiny little moo. Since this one's a preemie, his moo sounds kind of like a mew and he's so, so cute. Also, our horse has pink boots right now. When I was talking to her earlier, I told her we matched."

His daughter had always been a bit of an oversharer, but

Jemma didn't seem to mind. She asked a few more questions about when most of the other babies were born.

Mostly spring, with a handful of late ones that showed up in June and were runts for most of the summer. It always impressed him how quickly they caught up to the rest of the calves, though.

"Can we show her the baby calf?" Bailey Rae asked, bouncing on her toes and working on making her second s'more. "If you want to see it, that is. Which trust me, you do."

Wyatt expected her to say no, and he wouldn't blame her because she'd already been too cold plenty of times today, but Jemma said, "I do want to see it. Even if I have to bundle up."

They shoved down the last of their s'mores, put on a variety of coats and gloves and scarves, and made the short trek to the barn. Bailey Rae grabbed Jemma's hand and walked her closer to the pen where the recovering mom and calf were, a mix of black and white.

High-pitched squeaks filled the air, and Wyatt covered his grin with his glove. He never squealed or made cooing noises to the cows, which was probably why the calf wobbled over to the ladies instead.

Then again, his sister always joked he was the bull whisperer because he treated the giant animals like puppies. What could he say? He'd always been better at communicating with dudes. After nearly a decade with Bailey Rae, he was starting to speak female a little better, though.

He checked on a few of the other cows, but they still had some time to go before they'd be having their babies, so nothing was pressing for now. They walked to the other section of the barn, with the stalls where he kept his horses. Jemma stopped to say hello to Casper, who was happy to see her, and then they introduced her to Zora. Wyatt opened his mouth to explain the bowed tendon, but Bailey Rae beat him to it.

"I'm sad I didn't get to talk to Uncle Dempsey when he came over—it's been a long time since I saw him besides waving." She jumped off the gate, landing on the ground with a puff of hay dust. "Oh, and he's not my uncle by blood, but he is my uncle." Her eyebrows scrunched together. "It's kind of hard to explain. You tell her, Dad."

"Oh, I get to talk now," he teased, poking her side and making her giggle. Then he looked at Jemma, who had that easy smile on her face that mixed up his brain and made a mess of his insides. "Dempsey's the town vet, and he's also one of my oldest friends. He's known Bailey Rae since she was just a crying baby."

"Hey, you said I didn't cry that much."

Wyatt ran his hand over his daughter's head. "You didn't. But when you did, man did you go on and on."

She giggled and shrugged. "That's what babies do."

"Then they grow up and get lots more fun," he said, meaning every word. As busy as he was, his daughter could and did lift his spirits. He'd do anything to make her happy, which was why she was in ballet and why he couldn't stop ordering unicorn gifts to surprise her with.

Bailey Rae gave his hand a quick squeeze before returning her attention to Jemma. "So, that's the grand tour of the barn."

"And what a grand tour it was," Jemma said. "Can we swing by and look at the baby cow one more time?"

Bailey Rae led the way, and when they left the barn, she asked if she could ride back to Jemma's house with them. They went into his house to make sure the fire was taken care of, and then Jemma grabbed her bunny carrier and they all piled into the truck.

Once they arrived at the cottage, Wyatt checked that the smoke had mostly cleared and that the heater was working so she'd be warm enough tonight.

"Thanks again for helping me out," Jemma said to him and Bailey Rae. "And for letting me crash your movie night."

"It was so much fun, and you get all the things Dad doesn't. We should totally do it again." Bailey Rae hugged Jemma around the middle. "Goodbye. See you Monday morning."

Jemma squeezed back, and Wyatt watched on, his chest growing tighter and tighter. Earlier tonight he'd felt too many of the mushy emotions, but now the quicksand effect was taking over. He was getting in too deep, the sand coming too close to his head.

Not to mention his daughter and her growing attachment—it was written all over her face. She was happier now, but she'd taken it hard when Andrea had first left. Her own mom hardly checked in, and only made plans to see her a few times a year.

It'd hurt him too, even though he'd known they'd been growing apart and she'd been unhappy out here in the country and with motherhood. But watching his daughter hurt had sliced him right open.

Made him feel helpless.

This was too dangerous. He needed to put a stop to it before it was too late. So he decided he'd help Jemma out with her chimney by cleaning it when both she and his daughter were at school, and then he'd put some much-needed space between them.

CHAPTER ELEVEN

A STRANGE SENSE OF NOSTALGIA HIT Wyatt as he and Dempsey stepped inside the restaurant on Wednesday night.

His friend had shown up as promised, wearing nice jeans and a button-down instead of scrubs. After he'd declared Zora good enough to remove the boots and had told him to give her about fifteen minutes of slow walking for a week or so before riding her, they'd piled into his truck and driven to Crossroads Bar and Grill, where one of their former classmates now ran his family restaurant.

Same way they used to back in high school, since there was only the diner and coffee shop in Haven Lake. Crossroads was in the middle of five small farming communities, making it a hub for all of them. Back in the day, it used to be the place they went to see people—girls, mostly—from other schools.

It'd been where he and Andrea had met up a lot when dating, since it meant they both drove about half an hour instead of either of them having to drive a full one. In a small community, avoiding places with those conflicted-type memories wasn't an option. There were a lot of good memories too, though.

Like the time Dempsey and some guy from another school had argued over who got to choose the music on the jukebox before collectively deciding to play nothing but some cheesy, overly mushy movie soundtrack song *no one* wanted to listen to. By the fifth time it had started up, everyone had been groaning, covering their ears, and begging for mercy.

The multicolored jukebox still sat in its usual corner, and he'd bet money they hadn't updated it in years. Fortunately he was the age now where that sounded nice, because as old as it made him feel to say it, they just didn't make music anymore like they did back then.

His feet felt glued to the entryway, unable to lift and propel him forward when he saw the place was fairly packed, especially for a Wednesday night. "You're right. I think I forgot how to do this."

Dempsey clapped him on the back. "The walking thing, or ordering at a restaurant, or…?"

"Yes," he said with a laugh. It felt weird to be out. Even weirder being thirty minutes away from home. Bailey Rae was with Lori and her kids, so he knew she was in good hands, but it still felt odd going out to eat without her.

Sometimes he longed for a night out with his buddies, but he found he missed his daughter's constant chatter. She filled in all his blank spaces, and he had a whole lot of them.

Nick waved from behind the bar, and that made it easier to head on inside. They exchanged bro-hugs over the beat-up wood surface. "Wyatt Langford in the flesh. When Dempsey told me you'd be with him tonight, I couldn't believe it."

"Actually, you bet me money, so you now owe me five bucks," Dempsey said, and they laughed.

"I have big news," Nick started, but then a customer at the other end waved him over and he lifted a finger. "Give me a minute, and I'll have my sister come out and cover so I can chat with you guys."

He rushed toward the customer, the same way his father used to whenever they'd come in. It made Wyatt realize that out of the three of them, Dempsey was the only one who wasn't following in his father's professional footsteps.

"Been working on a truck?" Dempsey asked, jerking his chin at Wyatt's blackened fingertips and nailbeds. No amount of scrubbing could get out oil when he was working on a vehicle. It took days and a lot of citrus, grease-cutting soap, and usually by then he'd end up elbow deep in a truck or tractor again, so he'd about given up.

But for once, his fingers weren't black from a vehicle.

It was from cleaning out Jemma's chimney.

"A truck. A chimney. Tractors. A bit of it all." That was mostly true too, if he counted the past week.

Once spring hit and multiple cows started having babies on the same day, it'd be a crazy blur, and then summer would come around and it'd be time to start tending to crops and eventually the harvest. Which meant he had to work on his vehicles now.

His phone seemed to burn in his pocket, though, making him want to reread the text Jemma had sent thanking him for taking care of her clogged chimney. He hadn't replied, telling himself it was an open-and-shut conversation, but it was crazy how often he'd wanted to.

Nick walked back to them, still behind the bar. "Want me to grab drinks before I sit down?"

They added burgers and fries to their drink order, and within a couple of minutes, they'd settled at a table in the corner, Nick included.

"So what's this big news?" Dempsey asked.

"Remember Virginia Parsons?"

Wyatt and Dempsey both nodded. She and Nick had dated the summer before she'd gone off to college, and the guy had been mopey for months afterward, constantly saying no other woman compared.

"Well, we ran into each other about four months ago and sort of picked up from where we left off, and…" A wide grin split Nick's face. "Long story short, we're engaged."

Dempsey tipped his drink toward him. "Congrats, man."

"Yeah, congrats," Wyatt added, and they clinked their glasses together.

Their burgers and fries showed up, and Wyatt dug in. It was good not to have the same tired meals he always cooked, and even nicer he hadn't had to make it.

"What about you guys?" Nick picked up a French fry and dragged it through his ketchup. "What's going on in your lives?"

"Work," Wyatt said.

Dempsey nodded. "About the same." He told Nick he was newly single, and then both of Wyatt's friends turned their gaze on him, as if he'd have some grand confession about his dating life.

"Why are you looking at me? I've got work and Bailey Rae. That's it."

Dempsey pivoted in his seat, setting his forearm on the table. "I heard something about you and your neighbor, the new school teacher."

Every muscle in Wyatt's body froze. "Oh, yeah?"

Dempsey cocked his head. "Really? You're not going to spill? I met her briefly in the coffee shop, and we had a funny conversation about her bunny once she found out I was the town vet. She seems nice. Pretty too."

"Nothing to spill. She's my nice neighbor who teaches my daughter." She was also funny and pretty, but he didn't think he could agree with those without his friends seeing how much he'd accidentally let himself like Jemma. He took a bite of his burger. "Why? What did you hear?"

Wyatt squeezed his burger so hard his patty nearly slipped out of his bun. He'd been trying so hard to avoid the rumor mill—for Bailey Rae's sake—and he wasn't sure he wanted to know, but he also needed to know if he had to do damage control.

"Just a lot of people in town saying you two would make a good couple. You know, the usual."

"Yeah, they said that about me and the new dance teacher for a while too," Wyatt said. "With you single now, I'm surprised they're not trying to pair Jemma up with you."

Dempsey shrugged. "I've kept the fact that I'm not still attached on the down-low, although they'll find out soon, no doubt. They tried to pair me with the dance teacher before they attempted it with you."

"Why do they always do that? Pair people up?"

"It comes from a place of love. They think they're helping," Nick said, although with him running the restaurant full-time and the fact that they'd always lived on the far outskirts, it meant he rarely made it to Haven Lake these days.

Or maybe he did. Maybe Wyatt was the one who wasn't in town enough to know.

"Nick's engaged, and I'm still recovering from a fresh breakup." Dempsey twisted to face him, giving him a pointed look. "It's been *years* since you've dated."

About three years if he were counting, which he was trying not to do. "What? You're saying I'm up? Like dating's a baseball game, and I'm supposed to take my turn at bat?"

"I'm saying you might at least want to take a swing. You can't win if you refuse to play."

He got the logic, but he didn't think winning was an option. What his friends didn't understand was what it felt like to be a father and have to experience the same emotions your kid went through.

Didn't understand what it was like telling your daughter that her mom had left. Then, shortly after, that her grandma was also moving away. He understood his mom's need to head to Florida, both to ease her grief over losing Dad and to take care of her elderly parents, but it'd been one more transition period. Another person she loved leaving.

For a while, she'd asked Lori when she was going to move, since everyone else had.

Wyatt shook his head. "I'm not going down that road again."

"Ever?" Nick asked, all shock.

Yep, the man was definitely in love. If he lived in town, he'd probably be pushing him together with Jemma or any other single woman who so much as visited as well. "'Never say never' and all that, but I'm not making the same mistakes. And I always have to think of Bailey Rae and what she needs."

"Speaking of," Nick said, "you should bring Bailey in some time. I haven't seen that girl in way too long. And I want her to meet my fiancée."

From there they talked about summer, when they could get together to grill and catch up, and Wyatt accidentally peeked at his phone and brought up the text from Jemma again, smiling at the rambling stream of sentences of words and wishing—just for a minute or two—that things could be different.

CHAPTER TWELVE

As the students gathered their backpacks and lined up to leave, Chase turned to say something to Bailey, and she beamed at him like he'd lassoed the moon and offered it to her.

Growing up, Jemma had crushed hard and often, so she knew that twitterpated look all too well. These days, she tried to be more careful. It simply hurt too much when feelings were unreciprocated—that was what she'd decided after a wasted year of pining after Simon.

Last weekend, though, she'd slipped, and she may or may not have given Wyatt the same adoring expression when he'd dropped her off Saturday night and made sure she'd be warm enough.

Bailey continued to give Chase a love-struck smile as he turned to his buddies. He mentioned how excited he was to work on the tree house he was building with his dad that weekend.

Oh, Bailey. Be careful.

While Chase was a good kid, there were several girls who'd batted their eyes at him in that same way, and while she felt protective of all her students, she felt extra protective of Bailey.

The chime on her phone went off, and she told her students to line up at the door.

They'd all filed into a nice straight row by the time the bell rang.

One more day in the books, Jemma thought as she opened the door.

She bid farewell to each of her students, and when Bailey walked past, she skimmed her hand along the top of her fabulous curls. "See you tomorrow, Miss Bailey Rae."

The girl affectionately squeezed Jemma's hand, and her heart went all squishy on her. "Tomorrow I get to shoot my arrows, right?"

"Yep. Tomorrow we'll have all the props for the play."

"I can't wait. Also, did you know it's my birthday on Saturday?"

"I saw that in my notes. How about I wish you a happy early birthday today and tomorrow?"

Bailey skipped outside, and Jemma automatically scanned the area, searching for a familiar brown cowboy hat.

Wyatt had texted her on Tuesday around noon to let her know he'd cleaned and tested her chimney, so she was in the clear to start a fire and shouldn't have any more problems with smoke.

She'd sent a rambling thank you message about how much she appreciated it. Then she'd anxiously waited a return text.

And waited some more.

For a reply that *still* hadn't come, two whole days later, and she'd been obsessing about it way too much.

At least being in charge of a large group of children kept her mentally and physically busy, but every day after school as she glanced toward the sea of the parents and offered smiles and waves, her mind went to Wyatt.

She'd thought they'd made progress—that they'd been crossing into at least friend territory—but she'd seen his horse this week more than she'd seen him.

It almost felt like she'd imagined their fun night and the spark between them

Maybe it's for the best.

She sighed and sat at her desk to tend to her large pile of grading. With play preparations and practice taking up a large chunk of her time, she'd gotten behind in other areas, including her online courses.

She could probably get more done if she went home instead of staying at the school, where people often paused in her open doorway to say a quick hello that often turned into more. Her social interactions had hit an all-time high.

But when she got home at the end of the day, she still felt lonely, lonelier than usual.

That was the thing about spending time with other people who were funny and made you feel accepted—it made you miss not having it even more when it went away.

And that's why they call it a crush. In the end, you feel like a bug that someone's stomped on.

Her phone vibrated across her desk, the buzz the only sound since she'd left it on silent mode. When Randa's name flashed across the screen, she quickly swiped to answer.

"How's your country adventure going?" her friend asked. "Any more animal adventures? Should I call in a snake hunter? Are you going to have a YouTube channel soon?"

"Ha-ha. Just sticking to bunnies and horses, mostly, although I did see a teeny-tiny baby calf. Oh, and you should see the play we're doing. It's called 'Cupid Goes Crazy.' We did a gender-swap thing and have one of the girls playing Cupid. She shoots all the wrong people with arrows, and it's so cute and funny how it unfolds, but of course in the end it's about showing kindness and love to everyone. It's seriously the most adorable thing ever."

"Sounds like my kind of show."

Jemma shuffled papers around. "It's going to sell out for sure with the whole town coming," she joked, although she was also sure there'd be a full house. "So if you want tickets, you'd better tell me soon."

"Don't tempt me," Randa said. "I miss you, and I sort of want to see this small town for myself."

"That would be awesome."

"Plus, then I could meet your cowboy neighbor."

A bit of Jemma's excitement leaked out of her, like a balloon without a knot. If it wasn't the people in town, it was her best friend. "He's... We're... He's been quiet this week. Which is fine, because we're just friends—or more like neighbors. And I need to focus."

Now that Randa had mentioned Wyatt, though, it was all Jemma could focus on. She'd been so close to calling her best friend Saturday night to tell her how much fun she'd had with him and Bailey, all because she'd smoked herself out of her own place.

Now she was glad she hadn't. It'd make Randa's questions even more probing, and scrape at the raw part of her that was sad she didn't have more to report.

Headlights cut through the dark, winding down the road at the far end of the ranch. They turned right at the fork in the road, which confirmed it was Jemma. Coming home late.

Not talking to her this week had been harder than Wyatt had ever imagined it'd be.

A soft moo came from his side, and a pink nose nudged

his hand. Thanks to Bailey Rae, their first calf of the season thought he was a puppy.

Wyatt ran his hand down the fuzzy calf's head and neck and gave its side a pat. "Do you think Jemma's getting home late on a Friday night because of work, or because she was out on a date?"

The calf mooed.

Like a totally sane person, he replied. "Yeah, I don't like either option, either. But what am I supposed to do? I decided it was a bad idea." He also wasn't sure if she'd felt the same pull between them that he had.

But again, it didn't matter.

A few minutes later, he could just make out gray puffs of smoke coming out of her chimney and fading into the dark sky. At least he knew that her fireplace worked and she was warm.

Before he'd realized what he was doing, he'd dug his phone out of his pocket. He wanted to text Jemma and ask how she was. He eyed the friendly calf and found it looking right back at him with those dark pupils. Its tongue dangled out of its mouth as it nudged his hand, and now that he had cow slobber on his hands, he was thinking he shouldn't have taken off his gloves.

"Thanks a lot," Wyatt said, wiping his hand on his dust-coated jeans. He wasn't sure if he'd just made his skin cleaner or dirtier.

Because he was a big softy, he grabbed a nearby livestock blanket and secured it around the calf. *Yeah. Bailey Rae's the only reason he acts like a puppy. You keep telling yourself that.*

Eventually he pried himself away, exhausted and ready to call it a day. Or a night. Either way, it'd been a long one.

The porch steps creaked with his weight as he walked up to the front door. He stomped off his boots and batted at the dust, and then decided that was as good as it was going to get—one of the benefits of being the only adult was no one got upset at him for dragging in too much of the outside. With him bringing in dirt and Bailey Rae forever making crafts with glitter, their messes were at least interesting.

The screen door banged closed behind him, and he glanced at his daughter, who was on the couch with her tablet. "What's the homework situation?" he asked.

"Done. Like, forever ago. It was so easy." She tossed her tablet on the cushion next to her and came bounding over, her energy level at about a ten. "Did I tell you I got to shoot arrows today during play practice?"

Only one hundred times. "I bet you loved that."

"Yeah, I did. Miss Monroe kept 'em coming, so I didn't even have to retrieve them, just fire, fire, fire."

The next few minutes were filled with talk of how much his daughter loved her teacher. And his hand automatically sought out his phone again. He had her number. Could be talking to her with a couple of taps.

It's been days. When's this compulsion going to go away?

If anything, the overwhelming urge to call and hear her voice supported his decision to put extra space between them. As did the conversation with Bailey Rae. She clearly adored Jemma, and attempting a relationship with her would mess with that dynamic. The first half of the year had been rough for his daughter, and she was finally back to her happy self.

She seemed to have her friends back too—a group of them had called to do their homework together.

He'd heard mention of a boy, but the conversation had grown too quiet for him to catch any more details.

Dang Dempsey talking about dating. He cursed me. Heaven help him if he had to already deal with boys. He'd wanted to go about another ten to twenty years before that happened.

Suddenly wanted to talk to Jemma about it. See if it was normal and that kind of thing. But more than anything, he just wanted to talk to her.

Even his earlier notion about the benefits of being the only adult around here no longer rang true.

Despite her earlier goal to forget about all things involving Wyatt Langford, Jemma's heart still quickened at the knock on the door.

For two whole seconds before she realized the knock was down low, that slight metallic clink to it.

Instead of heading to the front door, she walked into the kitchen, opened the fridge, and dug out the extra bag of carrots she'd picked up when she'd bought more bundles of wood.

She walked back across the living room, basking in the heat from the roaring fire she'd built all by herself—thank you very much—and pulled on her coat.

Señor Fluffypants had figured out that a visit from Casper meant he'd also get a treat, so he was already by the door, eagerly awaiting the moment when she'd open it and he and his pony friend could chow down.

Jemma swung open the door and, sure enough, the white horse stood on the other side. He whinnied, and Jemma extended a long carrot. His loud crunch filled the air, and Señor Fluffypants pawed at her ankles.

Jemma squatted and gave him a baby carrot, popping one into her mouth as well, because she never did get enough vegetables.

Her bunny eyed the carrot as if he were disappointed before glancing up at the horse.

"Don't get jealous and start wanting to bite off more than you can chew." Jemma waved her arm toward the horse. "He's, like, one hundred times bigger than you."

Properly chastised, Señor Fluffypants bit into his carrot. They stood there, the cold filtering in and trying to beat away the warmth of the fire, the crunch of carrots filling the air.

Casper finished off his carrot, green stem and all, and then whinnied.

"Now you're going and getting greedy on me. That's it for tonight. Go home." She made a shooing motion, gesturing in the direction of Wyatt's house, and clucked her tongue.

The horse trotted off in that direction, just like he'd done on Sunday and Wednesday nights. The first night, she'd texted Wyatt to say she'd sent him on his way, but he hadn't responded to that text, either.

Well, unless texting on Tuesday to say he'd cleaned out her chimney counted.

Still, she wanted an excuse to try again, so after she closed the door, she texted him to say that after having dinner with her and Señor Fluffypants, Casper was headed back home, probably for dessert.

As she walked back toward the couch and her laptop, she kept her eyes on her phone, silently chanting for him to reply.

Her shin slammed into something hard—the coffee table—and she hissed and hobbled over to the couch. She flopped down and rubbed the injury, as if that'd make the throbbing there go away.

Then, because she had issues, her gaze immediately returned to her phone.

No dots.

No one word or emoji reply.

Nothing.

After way too long spent staring at her own flummoxed

reflection, she tossed her phone aside and grabbed her laptop so she could get back to her courses. She'd spent hours in her classroom catching up and completing as much of her assignments as she could. Eventually her eyes had reached the burning point, and her body had nearly attached itself to the fibers of her chair, so she'd decided to consider driving home her break, and then hit it again.

No more stopping until I can see the light at the end of the tunnel.

Just a few more months, and she'd finally have that degree. Once she was sure everything would go through, she'd immediately start applying for jobs in administration.

With any luck, focusing on that would also help with thoughts of frustrating guys and how complicated they were to read.

CHAPTER THIRTEEN

THIS WAS A DISASTER.

Or Wyatt supposed it was going to *be* a disaster, since the madness hadn't even started yet. Why had he thought he could host a birthday party, much less be responsible for the entertainment of a group of tween girls?

It was what Bailey Rae had wanted, though, and Lori had said she could help. Only, last night she'd called to say that after a few days of the boys being sick, she'd gotten sick.

Which meant he was on his own today.

And he didn't have cupcakes or a way to entertain Bailey Rae and her friends, since Lori was supposed to have done most of that too. It'd been so late when he'd found out, and he'd been so tired that he'd decided he'd figure it out in the morning.

But now, thanks to feeding the cows, taking care of the frozen water trough, and a surprise newborn calf, it was almost noon, and he still didn't know how to fix the situation.

Havenly Brew didn't make cupcakes, and what accounted for a local grocery store was more like a convenience store. A tiny convenience store that rarely was convenient, because whenever you went into Jack's Market, you ran into everyone and had to have multiple drawn-out conversations about the weather, how every person in your family was doing, all while trying to track down a loaf of bread that was probably a minute or two away from expiring.

No bakery section, no premade cupcakes.

Just bread and bagels, along with a disproportionate amount of fishing gear, and he was pretty sure that even with frosting, bagels would make for the most pitiful birthday dessert ever.

Which was why most people drove forty-five minutes to the grocery store the next town over once a month or so to stock up on the items Jack's Market didn't have.

Wyatt quickly calculated how long it'd take him to get there and back, and supposing he sped and got lucky enough not to get pulled over, he'd still be rushing through the door as kids were arriving, nothing else prepared.

Maybe Lainey Townsend or her grandma could help me out. They lived in the house about a mile down the road, where they had a tiny petting zoo with animals of about every kind, including a few roving goats and llamas.

A couple of times through the years, they'd watched Bailes when he'd had something last minute, and they'd occasionally shown up with casseroles and pies, so they definitely knew how to bake. But he already felt like he'd never be able to repay them for all they'd already done.

Not to mention Judith had been having some health problems this winter and Lainey was busy juggling that and taking care of the animals, which left him crossing that option off the list. If anything, he should send his daughter over there more to help out with the animals. It'd help them, plus Bailey Rae loved taking care of those animals way more than the ones on the ranch.

An idea popped into his head, one he shouldn't entertain, but the amount of relief that hit him made it impossible to bat away. Possibly because he'd been strong for an entire week, and he couldn't fight it any longer.

Add in that he'd do whatever it took to ensure Bailey Rae had a good birthday, and his mind was made up.

He pulled out his phone, tapped Jemma's number, and listened to it ring and ring. It'd serve him right if she ignored him after he'd cut off communication for the most part.

"Hello?" Her voice calmed him even as it made the blood in his veins pound that much harder and faster.

"You know how you're always having disasters and I rush to help?"

She made an offended noise in the back of her throat. "I wouldn't call them 'disasters,' but sure. You've helped me out of a few binds, I'll give you that."

"Well, I have a disaster on my hands. We're talking Level Ten, more important than anything else in the world." Now he was using his daughter's flair for the extreme. "There are a dozen girls coming over for a birthday party and my sister was supposed to help chaperone and make the cupcakes, but she's sick."

He shoved away his pride. "Help. *Please.*"

"When do you need me?" Jemma asked without missing a beat.

That was a loaded question, one he was only going to apply to this situation. "How soon can you get here?"

Jemma sucked in a deep, fortifying breath before lifting her fist and knocking on the door. She'd almost let Wyatt's call go to voicemail, but curiosity had gotten the best of her. She was glad too, because she wanted to ensure Bailey had a good birthday, in spite of wishing it didn't take a disaster for her neighbor to pick up the phone and give her a ring.

The door swung open, and Wyatt stood on the other side, his sandy-colored hair sticking up in all directions, as if he'd spent a lot of the day raking his hands through it. "Oh, thank goodness you're here. Bailey Rae was asking about the cupcakes, and I was trying to stall to keep her from finding out that her dad had no idea what he's doing. So I told her I didn't want to ruin the surprise and dropped her off at the Townsends to help feed the animals."

His long fingers circled her wrist and he tugged her inside. "I really don't want the surprise to be that the party is a bust."

Jemma's skin hummed at the contact, and when she went to scoot out of the way of the door at the same time Wyatt reached around her to close it, her body bumped into his.

He put his hands up on her hips to steady her, and her lungs forgot how to take in oxygen.

Their eyes met and held for a beat, and she could feel her cheeks warming.

He cleared his throat and took a step back, his arms dropping down to his sides. "Hi. I probably should've started with that."

A flutter worked its way through her body, starting low in her gut and moving up over her heart. "Hi."

"You look nice." His gaze drifted down to take in her bright-pink top and jeans, and a smile tugged his lips when he reached her pink shoes with the glittery bow.

The shoes made her happy, but now she fought the urge to squirm under his scrutiny. "Thanks. You look...stressed."

He barked a laugh, and she threw her hand over her mouth. "I didn't mean...well, I did, but it sort of popped out."

"No use covering up the truth. I did tell you I was having a disaster, didn't I?"

She nodded. "Yes. You made sure to point out that I had a whole lot of disasters first, of course."

"It's my subtle charm—so subtle, you have to search through the fumbling foot-in-mouth moments."

She laughed, sort of wishing his charm was subtler so she wouldn't notice it so much. Then again, the first two times they'd interacted, she'd been sure he was barely civilized. Now she knew too much about how good of a dad he was, that he was kind to his animals, and how he tried to hide his laugh during girly movies, although he never did quite succeed.

Speaking of disaster, the bags of flour on the kitchen counter caught her eye, and she did a double take at the kitchen. Cupboards were flung open and random ingredients were scattered around the room, as if there'd recently been a home invasion.

"Yeah. I'm wondering where to even start." He raised his eyebrows at her expectantly. "So?"

She was onboard with helping, but admittedly short on experience. Individual birthday parties weren't quite like big class parties, where parents signed up to bring treats. "I'd say start by calling the bakery."

His face fell. "You don't know how to bake?"

Her jaw automatically clenched as she tried not to take offense to the incredulous way he'd said it, and he quickly revised it to, "What I meant to say is that the nearest bakery is the next town over, and the girls will be here in a little over an hour. Plus, Bailey's so set on a rainbow theme."

"I'm sure we can figure out how to make cupcakes. I just might need some help. And a cake mix—please tell me you have one, because those bags of flour are scaring me."

He grimaced. "I do at least have some frosting, since

Bailey Rae and I both have a habit of eating it by the spoonful. She also stocks up on sprinkles like they're going out of style, so I've got those as well."

"Okay, I'll find a recipe online." She made sure to add "simple" to her search, and before long she'd found a chocolate cupcake recipe that had amazing reviews. She called out the ingredients, and within a couple of minutes, they were lined up before them, but Wyatt didn't appear to be any calmer.

She set her hand on his forearm and experienced that snap of electricity, the one that had her wanting to touch him way more than she should. This wasn't about her, though—it was about assuring him and keeping him from panicking. "We've got this."

"What about the decorating?"

"That's the easy part."

He furrowed his brow, the doubt clear.

She nudged him aside with her hip so she could stand directly in front of the mixing bowl. "I might not know much about baking, but I use glue and glitter on a regular basis at school—decorating's my wheelhouse."

"Great," he said, flashing her a smile. "I'm gonna get a rep as the guy who threw a glue-eating party."

She gave him a gentle shove, and dang, his biceps were rather solid. "It's an example, but if you don't behave, I might use actual glue on *your* cupcake."

His jaw dropped, and he threw a hand to his chest as if she'd deeply insulted him.

Jemma gave a nonchalant shrug. "Don't worry, nowadays glue is non-toxic."

"Man, they really take all the fun out of things these days."

A giggle slipped out, and she worried she was accidentally

flirting with the guy she'd told herself she was going to stop crushing on. If only he didn't make it so hard to ignore her attraction. Not just the chemistry that sparked and ignited every time she was near him, but how she smiled more, and how they joked back and forth so easily, almost as if it was second nature.

They moved around the kitchen, going between mixing and filling cupcake tins. The temperature rose with all the baking, and it rose more every time Wyatt put his hands on her hips to temporarily move her out of the way. Or when she brushed past him and got a whiff of his cologne mixed with a hint of citrus, sweet grass, and hay.

The timer pinged, and Jemma pulled the cupcakes out of the oven—they'd dipped in the middle instead of being nice and round on top, but she figured they could fix that with extra frosting, and who didn't like extra frosting?

While the cupcakes were cooling, she divided the two containers of frosting into three bowls, and soon they had pink, blue, and purple frosting. She formed a makeshift decorating bag out of a sandwich bag by cutting off the bottom right corner.

Wyatt poked his head over her shoulder as she swirled the pink, blue, and purple mixture on top of the cupcakes.

"The one thing I know about glitter is that there's never too much. I'm guessing that also applies to sprinkles." She poured on a bunch, twisting the container so there were pink hearts and cool colorful rainbow shapes, along with purple crystals.

After she'd decorated the first dozen, she extended the bag of frosting toward Wyatt. "Here, you try decorating one."

"Oh, I don't know if—"

She thrust the bag into his hands and moved aside. "Just squeeze from the top and twist the cupcake as you go."

Wyatt grabbed the bag right in the middle and squeezed with all his might, sending frosting out both ends. A glob dropped onto his forearm and pants, and he gave her an accusing look as she burst into laughter.

"Okay, I guess we need to talk about finesse. You don't have to use all your strength for frosting."

"So you're saying I'm strong?"

She snort-laughed, and he swiped his frosting-coated forearm across her side.

"Ah!" She moved to get him back, but he was using that dang strength to keep her at arm's length. Since she couldn't get to him, she wiped at the frosting and popped the glob on the tip of her finger into her mouth. "Mmm. This is super yummy."

Wyatt took his own taste. They stood there grinning at each other, snapping out of the trance when Bailey waltzed in through the front door. "I'm hom— Ooh, can I help decorate cupcakes?"

"Of course," Jemma said. "I need someone with an artistic eye."

Bailey carefully frosted two cupcakes, and Jemma couldn't help adding, "Much better than your dad. He's a lost cause when it comes to decorating—he uses too much strength and not enough sprinkles."

The next thing she knew, a handful of sprinkles were tossed at her head.

Bailey giggled, and then she and Jemma shared a glance and launched a full-scale attack against Wyatt. Sprinkles flew, frosting was flung, and the counters were soon even messier than when she'd arrived.

Finally they called a truce so they'd have enough supplies to finish the rest of the cupcakes.

A tantalizing swirl of affection corkscrewed through

Jemma when she looked at the cowboy standing next to her, covered in pink, purple, and blue frosting, sprinkles stuck to it and in his hair. She imagined she appeared equally as disheveled, and yet, she couldn't stop smiling. Couldn't stop the longing that came along for the ride.

Bailey glanced at the time and gasped. "People are going to be here in ten minutes. I have to change!" She streaked out of the kitchen and disappeared down the hall.

When Jemma turned back around, Wyatt had a washrag and was taking it to the mess they'd made. She finished up the last few cupcakes, arranged them on a big platter, and then helped with the last of the cleaning.

Ten minutes passed in a blur, and both she and Wyatt glanced at the door when the bell chimed, their eyes both on the wider side.

"I can get it," Jemma said, starting toward the door.

Wyatt caught her hand and gave it a quick squeeze, much like his daughter had done the other day after school. Only, his eyes bored into hers, peering deep down into the very core of her. "Thank you. I'm not sure what I would've done without your help."

"You're welcome," she said, her voice slightly breathless.

Then she turned and practically floated across the room to answer the door.

The party was winding down, and Wyatt glanced at Jemma, the way he'd been doing since she'd shown up at his door and saved him and this party.

As Bailey had opened presents, Jemma had snuck out to her car and returned with poster board she kept "for emergencies." She'd drawn a giant rainbow and asked to use his printer. When the party hit a lull, she'd brought out what she'd been working on and had the girls play Pin the Unicorn on the Rainbow, using one of her silky scarves as a blindfold.

The girls had giggled endlessly, and Bailey Rae had grinned wider than ever, teeth and all, exuding happiness at every turn.

Every time he'd remember something needed done and go to do it, Jemma had been a step ahead of him. They made a good team, the areas they were prepared for vastly different, their strengths complementing each other.

After the last parent came by to pick up their child, he sagged back against the wall, exhaustion hitting him with the adrenaline fading.

Voices drifted from the other room, and he pushed himself off the wall and paused in the archway of the living room. Bailey Rae was seated on the couch talking to Jemma, a serious expression on her face, and he didn't want to intrude.

"You really don't think my teeth look too big? At the beginning of the school year, Jessica B. said they were Bugs Bunny teeth, and for a while I stopped smiling, but I hate not smiling."

Immediately Wyatt bristled, his protective instincts going into overdrive—looked like he needed to have a chat with Jessica B. He'd already suspected someone had said something, but hearing his daughter say it aloud made an ache form in the center of his chest.

He hated that he couldn't prepare her better for the world. For times when people were unkind.

"They're not too big at all! You're beautiful, and I love your perfect smile. It makes me smile every time I see it." Jemma brushed the curly strands of hair that'd fallen into Bailey Rae's eyes off her face. "When I was your age, I thought my ears were too big—a few of the girls in my class teased me about how one always poked out of my hair."

Jemma turned her head to show Bailey Rae, although he thought the way her ear peeked out was adorable. He also smiled at the few remaining sprinkles that stood out against her dark locks. "I heard about this surgery that pins ears back, and I was determined to save up my money and get it done."

Bailey Rae pushed onto her knees and swept back Jemma's hair. "Did you have the surgery? Because they look like normal ears."

"Nope. No surgery. I either grew into them, or it was all in my head. As you can see, occasionally my ear still sticks out of my hair, but I just shrug it off. I like my hair. I like my ears, and I especially like wearing big, dangly, sparkly earrings."

The grin on his daughter's face grew even brighter, making her cheeks stand out. "I like my smile. And I like being happy."

A mixture of relief and gratitude went through him, washing away the ache that'd formed, and he walked into the living room. Both of them glanced up at him as he approached.

Bailey Rae shot up and hugged him around the waist. "Thank you so much, Daddy. It was the best. Party. *Ever.*"

Wyatt was about to tell her to thank Jemma, but before he could, his daughter spun and hugged her. And because he could see the fondness that filled Jemma's expression as she hugged his daughter back, a few of his worries faded.

"I know we already had dessert, but could we watch a movie and relax now?" His daughter flopped back on the couch and dramatically put her wrist to her forehead. "I'm exhausted."

He and Jemma exchanged a smile, and then she pushed to her feet. "I'll let you guys get to relaxing."

Everything in Wyatt screamed *no, don't go yet.*

Bailey Rae grabbed her teacher's hand and basically voiced the same feeling. Jemma glanced at him, a silent question in her big blue eyes.

"Stay," he said. He almost added, *unless you're too tired,* or *unless you need to go,* but selfishly, he didn't want to give her an excuse to leave.

His daughter was already seated on the far side of the couch, and Jemma sat back down in the middle cushion, which left him no choice but to sit right beside her. Not that he would've chosen differently.

He hardly noticed when Bailey Rae started up a familiar movie. All his attention was on how relaxing it was to have Jemma with them for their movie night. How right it felt.

Jemma's blinks became longer and longer, and her posture slackened. Bailey Rae leaned against her side, and Jemma drifted to his, her head coming to rest on his shoulder.

Here I am, the only one awake, and I'm watching a movie with choreographed musical numbers. But he didn't move, because moving might mean losing being this close to Jemma.

As he closed his eyes and basked in the peaceful happiness, he contemplating letting himself go, just a little bit. As long as he focused on friendship, he could keep his expectations real and be able to have Jemma in his life more.

Yeah, he was tired, but as he joined the two women in dreamland, he also decided it was the best idea he'd ever had.

CHAPTER FOURTEEN

THE NAME AT THE TOP of Jemma's inbox Tuesday afternoon made her tummy feel like she'd downed a package of Pop Rocks and followed it up with soda.

She quickly glanced around, confirming she was alone before clicking to read the email, savoring each word and reading it in Wyatt's voice.

> *I don't check my email often, so I just got this. What do you need me to do to help with the play? I'm pretty good at using my overwhelming strength for making messes if that helps.*
>
> *PS, better text your reply so I'll see it today instead of next week after you're cursing my name for not helping you with your disasters.*

Her phone was in her hand, her thumbs moving across the screen as she let herself grin like a smitten Cheshire cat.

First of all, my play is not a disaster. Second of all, how are you at using your perfectly sufficient muscles to swing a hammer?

After a moment or two spent waiting, she refocused on the stack of papers in front of her. Logically, she knew Wyatt was often in the middle of manual labor tasks that didn't allow him to quickly shoot off a text, but her paranoid brain traveled back to those days when he hadn't replied.

No more sitting around waiting on him. She wasn't going to be that girl anymore.

Her phone chimed, and she scrambled to pick it up, making it clear she wasn't quite as cool as she was mentally telling herself to be.

Wyatt's text read, *Downgraded to perfectly sufficient? Really? That's how you want to play this?*

You're the one who said overwhelming, not me, Jemma replied. *I like to call it speaking the truth.*

Of course, she knew if she pulled out her dictionary app and typed in "overwhelming," it would tell her the word was an adjective, one that meant very great in amount or so great as to render resistance useless. Which might describe the way she felt in Wyatt's presence a little too accurately.

Apparently you need another demonstration, Wyatt texted. *When do you need me?*

Saying "right now" probably wouldn't be in the play-it-cool category, but she missed him. Missed the tantalizing joy being around him brought on and how much she laughed whenever they were together. The fact that she'd accidentally fallen asleep on his shoulder Saturday night proved she was growing more and more comfortable around him.

All those lonely feelings she was used to living with were long gone any time she was around Wyatt and Bailey.

Jemma replied, *Saturday is the big set-building day so we can have a full week to practice onstage. Several students and parents will meet in the gym at three.*

Her phone rang, vibrating in her palm, and a combination of disappointment and impatience rose up. Who was calling, and why did they have to do it while she was in the middle of talking to Wyatt? Who knew how long she had before he'd be on to another activity?

Every negative emotion faded when she saw Wyatt was the one calling her. She answered, excitement quickening her pulse and dancing across her skin.

"I know this is going to make me sound like an old man," Wyatt said as soon as she answered, "but I don't like texting. My thumbs are too fat and callused, plus it's just easier to call and have a simple conversation."

"I'll refrain from teasing you," Jemma said, mostly because she'd rather hear his voice than take the watered-down version in her head any day.

To tell the truth, it was a nice change. Most guys she'd dated hated talking on the phone. More than once she'd concluded it would've been much easier to have a quick conversation than a strung-out one that had often left her feeling distant instead of closer.

"Saturday's too far away. How about you eat dinner with Bailey Rae and me tonight? Least I could do to repay you for helping me out with the birthday party."

Without thinking and on automatic courtesy mode, she about said there was no need to repay her, but how could she pass up dinner with Wyatt and Bailey? "I suppose my frozen, microwavable dinner will wait for me one more night. What time, and what do you need me to bring?"

"How's six? And just yourself."

"That's perfect." *You're perfect.*

Whoa there, thoughts. Getting a little carried away.

She'd promised herself she wouldn't repeat her past mistake of thinking she and a guy were heading to somewhere beyond friendship, and she needed to be careful. But that didn't mean she should settle for being lonely when she had the means to change the situation.

"See you then," Wyatt said, and she wished him goodbye.

After outlining tomorrow's lesson, she gathered her stuff and crammed it in the big bag she lugged around. On autopilot, she turned to where she kept Señor Fluffypants's cage, but then she remembered she'd left him home to give him a day off from the constant attention. The kids were great with him, but her bunny had seemed a smidge tired from the hustle and bustle yesterday afternoon.

On her way out of the school, she ran into Camilla, who held the door open for her. "Hey, do you want to grab dinner at the diner? I know it's a bit early, but I'm starving."

"I, um, actually have dinner plans." The giant smile that spread across her face couldn't be helped, in spite of the fact that she was so going to get busted.

Camilla's eyebrows disappeared underneath her dark hair, satisfaction heavy in the curve of her smile. "Let me guess. With one of our town's most eligible single fathers?"

"And his daughter. It's just because I helped him out of a bind over the weekend. He was down a cupcake decorator, and I happen to live nearby and don't have much of a social life."

Camilla tilted her head. "Don't sell yourself short. It has to do with more than that, and you forget that I've been with you at our country dance sessions and in the coffee shop. You're turning into quite the social butterfly."

Funny, it took someone else saying it aloud for her to realize it was true. She was getting to know the townspeople one at a time. She not only knew the regulars at Havenly Brew but had also become a regular herself.

This week's drink was the Macho Mocha Man and came with a straw that had a moustache. Since she hadn't brought her bunny, she'd used the straw all day, and the kids had giggled every time she'd taken a drink. "It's this town. No one here really allows introverting."

"That's right," Camilla said, keeping stride with her as they walked to the parking lot. "No introverting on my watch."

"Honestly, it's nice." It'd helped Jemma with her goals, providing the perfect kickstart she needed to put herself out there more and make the most of this adventure. "And I can see how much everyone cares about the community." Another thing that'd made it easier to push her comfort zones, since they embraced her the same way they embraced each other.

"Speaking of, you should come with me to the basketball game on Friday night. The entire town shows up to support the team, and it's always a good time."

"I'm in." Wow, she hadn't even needed to pause to have an internal pep-talk. *I can't wait to report my progress to Randa—she'll never believe it.*

"Awesome." Camilla paused at her large truck. Most of the people here drove big trucks or SUVs, making her car the runt of the parking lot. "See you tomorrow, Jemma." The principal paused to waggle her eyebrows. "Have fun at your dinner."

"I will," Jemma said, the smile back on her face. While she still needed to be careful about lines and not letting her heart get too carried away, it was nice to have another friend who was cheering for things to go well.

Wyatt tried to tell Jemma he'd take care of the dishes, but she said he had plenty to do as it was, and household tasks always went faster with help.

Bailey Rae had gone to her room to change into her pajamas and get ready for bed, so he decided to use the time to have an uninterrupted conversation and find out more about Jemma.

"So, did you always want to be a teacher?" He handed her the plate he'd rinsed, and she stuck it in the dishwasher.

"When I was younger, I wanted to be a fashion designer."

He glanced at her clothes, perfectly matched and paired, and brighter and fancier than most people around there wore. "I could see that."

"Yeah, but once I was heading to college and needing to get serious about my career, I discovered how hard it is to make it. I'd have to study in New York or Paris, and I didn't want to be so far away from my parents. Plus, I realized I'd need to learn how to make patterns and sew, and I just wanted to *wear* the clothes."

She extended a hand for the next plate. "During my first year of college, I took general education credits, and I had a friend who was in elementary education. She got to make a diorama, and I was immediately like, 'ooh, sign me up!'"

Wyatt laughed. "You're saying it was the glue and glitter."

"Oh, for sure." She laughed and then pivoted to lean back against the counter. "What truly hooked me, though, was the desire to make a difference. I've always loved kids, from their honesty to their optimism. The more I looked into it, the more I knew it was where I belonged.

"As I began my career, I occasionally got frustrated by how hard it was to make the changes without the support from administration. Which is one of the reasons why I started working on my Masters in education. Just a few more months, and I'll be done. I know as a teacher I probably shouldn't say I'm so over taking classes, but I'm so over it. The homework and the hours online, I mean—I'm still good to go on the teaching."

"But you'd like to be in administration."

"That's the big-picture plan, yes. I'm not sure how much room there'd be for that here. I didn't exactly plan this detour to your teeny-tiny town."

She shuttered her features, and he prepared himself for her saying she didn't like it. At first, his ex had called it charming and had idealized the idea of the farm, but once she'd seen the work it took firsthand, the charm had faded, and over the years she'd grown more and more discontent in his "podunk" hometown.

It was fairly common to get married young around these parts, but in retrospect, perhaps they'd rushed down the aisle before they'd been ready. He'd been determined to make it work, but Andrea had hated it here, and he'd hated the idea of moving somewhere where he'd need to get a desk job. Besides, how could he turn his back on everything his father had worked for and let go of land that'd been in his family for generations?

Despite the bumpy ride, his marriage had given him Bailey Rae, and he fully believed in learning from your past, not dwelling in it.

"Wyatt?"

He realized he'd zoned out a bit, his history stirring up his concerns about the current situation and acting as a mortar to build the brick wall between his heart and the woman across from him. Jemma hadn't said anything bad, but she hadn't said she was planning a future here, either.

In fact, it sounded like the opposite. "Sorry. Got lost in my thoughts."

"No worries. It happens to me from time to time too."

"Where were we?" He quickly searched his memory. "Something about you not planning on the detour here."

"Right. Mostly because I didn't know 'here' existed." She

nudged him over and switched places with him, taking over the rinsing and handing him the dishes. "There were layoffs at my old school. It was hard for me to accept that I was fired simply because I was the last hired.

"Not that I wouldn't feel horrible if someone else got laid off," she continued, "but I threw my entire self into teaching while watching a few of my coworkers phone it in. They were probably burned out, but they sprinted out the door with the kids, never planned lessons in advance, and had no control of the classroom.

"One guy, I heard him yelling disparaging things at a kid and…" She clenched the glass in her hand so tightly he worried it'd break, and he gently peeled her fingers away from it. "Anyway, it reaffirmed my decision to get my Masters. But I needed a job and found the online posting for the position at the elementary school. After talking to Camilla over the phone, I felt really good about it.

"Then I saw there was an adorable cottage for rent, and it seemed like fate had finally shined down on me. I needed an adventure, and Haven Lake was offering me one."

"Then you got here and changed your mind?" He'd probably asked it too tightly, the answer mattering way too much to him.

She placed her hand on his forearm, her fingers soapy and wet, and still her touch caused his breath to lodge in his throat. "Not at all. Loneliness got the best of me my first week—as did the snowy roads, as you saw. But now I'm so happy I took a chance and got to meet the people here, even if it's only for a little while."

A fond smile touched her lips. "Everyone's been so nice, and I hardly have to discipline the students, which always makes my job easier. Not to mention it means happier students and parents, and happier me."

Her thumb dragged across his skin, and every nerve ending in his body pricked up. "I like spending time with you and Bailey—that makes me happy too."

So much to dissect in that statement. It sent warmth rushing through him, and yet he wondered how she felt about *him*.

Which was crazy, considering he'd pretty much given up on dating, thinking he was too busy and that most women wouldn't want to deal with the fact that he already had a kid anyway. They were a packaged deal, and even if Jemma only cared about Bailey, he'd understand. She was definitely the sweeter, fun one.

But that "even if it's only for a little while" made him hesitate to make a move. To ask her out.

"I'm all ready for bed," Bailey Rae said. "And before you ask, I used the timer on my toothbrush, so yes, I brushed really, *really* good."

Jemma smiled at him and slowly dropped her hand. His skin tingled where her fingers had been, and he wasn't sure he'd ever fully catch his breath around the woman.

"Would it be okay for Jemma to tuck me in?" His daughter fiddled with the hem of her unicorn pajama shirt. "I know I'm a little too old, especially now that I'm officially nine, but it always makes it easier to say goodbye to the day and fall right asleep."

Jemma's eyes met his and she gave a slight nod, indicating she was willing. Judging from the affection that danced in her eyes, she was more than willing—she wanted it as much as Bailey Rae did.

So he affected a begrudging posture and tone, and said, "Oh, sure, I'll just finish the dishes while you gals keep the party going." He broke, unable to hold the grumpiness, and the two of them giggled before heading down the hallway together.

Bailey's room perfectly reflected her personality, with bright colors, pink fairy lights, and every type of horse picture on the wall, from realistic to cartooned winged ones with horns.

Bailey picked a book off the shelf, one about a girl who discovered a unicorn, naturally. "I read two whole chapters every night. Usually before Dad comes in to say goodnight, but I wanted to show my book to you. It's got this girl named Phoebe who finds a unicorn. The unicorn is really vain, but in a funny way."

The two of them alternated pages until they'd reached her goal, and then Jemma slipped the bookmark inside the pages and tucked Bailey into her very pink bed.

She brushed a hand over the girl's head, resisting the urge to kiss her forehead since she still was her student and she didn't want to cross lines. "Goodnight."

"Goodnight," Bailey said. Jemma was halfway across the room, her fingers on the light switch, when Bailey added, "Dad smiles a lot more when you're here."

Jemma's heart clenched in a tight knot, constricting further with each attempted beat. Hope pulsed through her, tempting her to give in to the notion that it meant Wyatt was crushing right back.

She flicked off the light and then walked down the hall.

Wyatt stood in the center of the kitchen, his back to her. He started the dishwasher, wiped his hands on the towel hanging on the handle of the oven, and turned to face her.

Yearning, attraction, and fear clashed, twisting up her emotions.

What was she doing, playing house and getting so attached? But how could she just shut down her feelings when they were stronger than they'd ever been? She wasn't sure she could, and she didn't want to brush them aside like they didn't matter.

She cleared her too-tight throat. "You have an incredible daughter. The girl radiates joy and kindness."

"I got lucky with her for sure. I've been meaning to thank you for talking to her about her teeth the other day. I tried, but it's not the same coming from me."

That meant he'd probably heard her talking about her ears, and while she'd gotten over the notion that they were too big long ago, the tips of them burned.

"It's crazy to me that gals like you and Bailey Rae wouldn't realize how beautiful they are."

Jemma nearly melted to the floor at the compliment, a puddle of a girl who really liked a boy. Maybe she should take a page from her students and give him a note that said, "Do you like me? Check yes or no."

Talk about awkward. While she was thinking about that, how hard would it be if she started dating Wyatt and things went badly? What if they broke up? Then she'd never be able to come over and enjoy dinner with him and Bailey.

Bailey. I need to think about Bailey's feelings.

Every day at school would be harder for her. Harder for Jemma, too.

One thing was for sure, she couldn't afford to make brash decisions. She needed to think—more than likely, she'd end up overthinking—but at least her brain would still have a chance to overrule her extremely sentimental heart.

She jerked a thumb over her shoulder. "I should go. I have some classwork to take care of."

Wyatt simply nodded.

"Thanks again for dinner. See you on Saturday for set building?"

Her heart thumped faster as he strode toward her. "I'll walk you out."

Of course. He wasn't charging over to kiss her. It was just his gentlemanly sense of duty. She grabbed her coat and zipped it all the way up.

The snow crunched under their feet as they made their way to her car, and instead of opening the door for her, he turned to face her. Moments ago, she was reminding herself to be careful, to think of the possible awkwardness and avoid making impulse decisions.

But now their breaths were coming out in white puffs that mingled in the air between them and he was peering down at her, and all her reasons to not follow her heart faded to the background.

Wyatt tipped up his head. "The stars are extra bright tonight."

She lifted her gaze to the inky, diamond-studded sky. Without the city lights and smog to obscure them, the stars were so much clearer out here, the milky way in full view. "Well, you know how much I like glitter."

His smile kicked up a swarm of butterflies that definitely didn't care about making sensible decisions. "That's why I instructed them to shine brighter tonight. Just for you."

"And because of all that impressive strength of yours, they listened?"

The wattage on his grin turned up a notch. "I'm glad you're no longer insisting my muscles are just perfectly sufficient."

Standing so close to him, his big body blocking the wind and sending a shock of awareness through her, there was no use denying that he was impressive. Not only strength-wise and in handsomeness, but also at making her feel safe, happy, and cared for.

Another thing she couldn't deny—she was a heartbeat away from falling for Wyatt Langford.

CHAPTER FIFTEEN

THE SQUEAK OF SNEAKERS ON the shiny wooden floor greeted Jemma first. As she stepped farther into the gym, several familiar faces grinned, and a handful of people waved.

This was just what she needed to keep her mind off Wyatt Langford.

Not that it would prevent her from thinking about him at all, obviously. But the basketball game meant she could throw herself into cheering and talking to other people. That way, she wouldn't end up texting Wyatt and inviting herself over to his house.

She'd see him tomorrow, and that'd have to be soon enough, because anything more might land her in heart trouble.

Tonight, she'd cheer and hang out with a woman who'd become a close friend. Tomorrow morning, she'd worry about fortifying herself to see the guy she couldn't seem to stop thinking about. She'd accidentally gone and fallen the tiniest bit, but it was a short fall, one she could pop back up to her feet and recover from.

Any more, and...

It's too dangerous. I don't want to crush and burn again.

Having all the parents and students around to build the props would help prevent her from getting caught up in his handsome face, the crinkles that formed around his eyes when he smiled, the way his corded forearms and coarse hair had felt underneath her fingertips…

A pleasant shiver worked its way up her spine. *I'm doing a bang-up job not thinking about him.*

Finally, she regained her focus and spotted a waving Camilla in the crowd.

Jemma started up the bleachers, taking careful steps, since she'd worn her black-and-silver Mary Jane heels. As she'd been getting ready at the cottage, she'd eyed her sneakers, but they didn't match the floral navy top she had on. White and navy were also the school colors, and wasn't that more important than being able to easily bound up bleachers?

People called out greetings as she passed, and Dorothy Hembolt caught her hand and stopped her. "Jemma, dear, have you met Christopher Foster?"

Jemma searched her brain for the face that went to a name she couldn't recall. Dorothy tapped the guy seated in front of her on the shoulder, and he glanced back at the two of them. He was midthirties-ish, had dark hair, and was wearing a polo shirt and khaki pants.

In a lot of ways, he looked like Simon and the kind of guy she used to think of as her type.

"Christopher, you simply have to meet our new teacher. *Miss* Jemma Monroe." There was no missing the emphasis on how unmarried she was, but not one to leave things to chance, Dorothy added, "She's single just like you. And isn't she pretty?"

Christopher beamed up at her. "Nice to—"

"I don't think she's single," the guy to Jemma's left said, and she quickly tried to place him. He looked vaguely familiar, but not familiar enough to be updating people on her dating life. "I heard the ladies at the coffee shop say something about her and Wyatt Langford being an item."

Jemma's jaw dropped. She also realized why the guy looked familiar—Tyrone Willis ran Willis Wheels and Mechanic Shop on Main Street and often popped into Havenly Brew for a pastry and a drink.

"Oh," Dorothy said, so much excitement in one tiny word. "I had no idea."

Before Jemma could say neither did she, and clarify that it wasn't true, the music teacher gave Christopher a consoling pat. "Sorry. Sounds like you're too late."

Her face felt too hot, and her mouth was definitely too dry. "Oh, you're not too... I mean, I'm not..." How to explain this? Although, why should she have to? Evidently, she was going to have a talk with April and those women who sat in the shop all day, adding their theories to the grapevine.

Camilla stepped down the bleachers and grabbed her hand. "Jemma, so glad you could make it." She flashed a bureaucratic smile. "If you'll excuse us, she and I made plans to watch the game together, and it's almost to start."

Wyatt stood just inside the entrance to the gym, scanning the bleachers, same way he'd been doing a moment ago, before he'd witnessed something that'd made every muscle in his body clench. He slowly exhaled through his nose, telling himself to breathe. To act like it didn't bother him that Chris Foster had grinned up at Jemma with what Bailey Rae called "heart eyes."

Was the entire town trying to set Jemma up with *that* guy?

Why not me?

The notion popped into his head before he could stop it. Never before had he wanted to have anything to do with the townsfolk's matchmaking tendencies, but Jemma hadn't been the woman in that equation before.

At least Camilla Alvarez had saved her—Jemma had looked completely overwhelmed by all the attention.

Which meant maybe she didn't agree with their matchmaking efforts, either, and that made him renew his steps. Bailey Rae was at a friend's house. After he'd dropped her off, he'd driven by the school and seen all the cars and had thought about how long it'd been since he'd gone to a basketball game.

Way too long.

In theory, it was supposed to occupy his mind with something besides Jemma, so he wouldn't call and invite her over again.

She's going to leave. Soon.

How many more signs did he need?

Then again, he could either sit away from her and hurt his neck because he was constantly straining to see her, or he could take some initiative and sit by whom he wanted to.

As he charged up the aisle Jemma had been standing in moments ago, the people who'd been talking to her gave him funny looks. It was more than the usual double-takes over the fact that he'd left his ranch and still existed. There was almost a weird smugness to them, as if they were in on a secret. Clearly he was supposed to know the secret, but he didn't have a clue what it was, and when it came to whatever crazy scheme the townsfolk had going on, he'd probably rather not know.

Jemma did the double-take he'd expected from the other

people, and her lips parted a few inches as she gazed up at him from her seated position.

He gestured to the open space next to her. "Mind if I join you guys? Bailey Rae's at a friend's house, and with her occupied elsewhere, I was wondering who was going to talk my ear off all game."

One of Jemma's eyebrows arched higher than the other. "And you chose me?"

He sat down next to her. *I'll choose you every time,* he thought but managed to keep inside. "You're chattier than most."

She gave him a sort of half frown, half pout. "Hey. Admittedly it's not the first time someone's told me that, but usually it sends most people running away, not toward me."

"They're clearly missing out," he said, and the pout morphed into a beautiful smile, one that had his pulse skidding.

Camilla leaned around Jemma and nodded. "Hey, Wyatt. Glad you could join us." There was an extra sparkle in her eye, a self-satisfied lilt to the words.

Apparently, she was in on the same secret everyone else was.

He glanced away and noticed heads of the people surrounding them jerking back to face the gym floor. Not very subtle.

Looks like they've all paired us up. Guess that was to be expected.

If it wasn't also complicated, he'd be all for it.

The starters were announced and rushed to the center of the court, and then the crowd was focused on the players and the game that was about to begin.

Jemma raised her voice over the din. "I can't believe how full these bleachers are. I went to a couple of games in high school, and they only ever pulled out one side of bleachers—and they were sparse."

"Here the entire town gets in on it," Camilla said. "See the pictures along the far wall? Those are the teams who won state championships." She glanced at Wyatt. "See the second-to-last one? The guy in the middle?"

Wyatt shook his head as Jemma squinted at the picture. She looked to him and then back at the picture. Then at him. "You played basketball?"

"Why do you sound so incredulous?"

"I guess I just assumed you were born wearing boots and a cowboy hat, and that doesn't fit the typical basketball-player image."

"Cowboys make great athletes." He leaned his forearms on his knees so he could see if the Smith kid made his shot—nope. "It's all that manual labor. When my dad was having me buck bales, he'd talk game strategy. Sometimes I wondered if Coach put him up to it."

He rarely mentioned his father, but regardless of all the people surrounding them, he felt safe mentioning him to Jemma. "He was always sneaking in life lessons as we were working. He wanted me to be as well prepared for life as possible."

It'd helped get him through his father's unexpected death and was one of the reasons he wanted to instill the same thing in his daughter.

"Sounds like a great dad—sounds like you. In my experience, parents don't hear how good of a job they're doing enough, and you're a really good father, Wyatt."

Validation he didn't realize he needed flowed through his veins. Sometimes he felt like he was bungling it up, his only saving grace that he was the one who'd stayed. He'd be there, no matter what, even if it meant shopping for dresses and learning to frost cupcakes.

The home team scored, and the band burst into a loud celebration song that made it impossible to hear anything but that and the cheering.

When the noise died down, he glanced at Jemma and found her looking back at him. Her hand was on her knee, and his fingers twitched with the urge to take it in his.

Did she lean in, or did he?

Either way, his attention turned to all things Jemma. Her dark, wavy hair, her blue eyes, so full of wonder and tenderness. The kind smile she so freely gave to people whenever they crossed her path. Suddenly he understood the full meaning of the word "magnetic," because she was a magnet, pulling people in.

Pulling *him* in.

"Wait." Two creased formed between her eyebrows as she lowered them. "Why did the refs blow their whistle?"

The question jerked him out of his trance, and luckily he was able to figure out what'd happened and explain the call. She asked a few more questions, and he clarified the rules she was fuzzy on.

He'd drifted closer in order to be heard over the crowd, but even after she stopped asking questions, he couldn't gather enough motivation to move away.

"I wish I could've seen you play," she said.

"I used to dominate, so it was quite a sight."

"Sounds like you were super humble, too."

He laughed, full-out, and a couple of people turned toward him. But he didn't care. Let them talk—they were going to anyway. "It was the first time I felt truly good at something. For a little while, the rest of the world disappeared and it just came down to me, my team, and tearing it up on the court."

He ran his palms down the thighs of his jeans, inhaling sharply when his pinky brushed Jemma's. "I always figured I'd teach my son how to play and go to games the way my dad came to mine—it was about the only time he'd leave the ranch. Then along came Bailey Rae. Of course I realized I could still have that, only with my daughter. But she's completely uninterested. Not a competitive bone in her body. She'll probably be a cheerleader, a decision I'll fully support, for the record."

Jemma observed the girls on the side of the court who were shaking their pompons. "I always wanted to go out for cheerleading, but I chickened out. I was sure I'd get cut."

"One thing I like about Haven Lake is that kids get more of an opportunity to try everything. Sports, extracurriculars. They get a chance to learn and see if it's something they enjoy instead of getting cut and never knowing."

"That would've been nice. And extracurriculars are so good for students. Usually their grades improve, they get into less trouble, and it gives them a built-in friend group." She swept her hair behind her ear and bit her lip. "Sorry. I went into administrator teacher mode. I'd tell you I can shut it off, but the truth is, I can't."

"You're a really good teacher, Jemma." He'd needed to hear her compliment, and he figured she didn't hear it enough. It was true too. He could tell. "I can't believe the difference I've seen in Bailey Rae this past month, and I know a lot of that is because of you."

Jemma ducked her head, a slight blush on her cheeks. "Thank you. That means a lot to me. She—and all my students—mean a lot to me."

They sat back to enjoy the game. Between him and

Camilla, they taught Jemma a lot about basketball, including the boys' names, and by the middle of the second quarter she was cheering along with the crowd. She got so into it, jumping to her feet every time the ball was shot.

Her enthusiasm was catching, and she should've been a cheerleader, because he was cheering louder than he had since high school. Every time she sat down, her knee bounced, or she crossed her leg and that foot went to wiggling. He'd always wondered how elementary teachers kept up with so many kids at once—with Jemma, he suspected they had to keep up with her right back.

The clock ticked down the last three seconds of the quarter, and one of their boys shot from half court.

And made it.

The crowd erupted, everyone who was physically able jumping to their feet. Jemma turned to him, and he wanted to hug her, but his brain insisted he keep lines in place.

Instead, he held up his hand for a high-five. She smacked his palm, then pivoted and did the same to Camilla.

His former classmate then studied him studying Jemma, just like she'd done throughout the first half of the game. This time she went the extra mile, tipping her head toward Jemma, like, *see how awesome she is?*

He gave a conciliatory nod to say of course he did. He didn't know a silent way to convey that unfortunately it didn't change things. He couldn't bring anyone into Bailey Rae's life unless she was going to be there for good. And Jemma had a lot of her life ahead of her. She probably wouldn't want to be tied down, not to the town or to him.

Whoa. Why'd my brain have to go there?

It was getting ahead of itself, something it did too often around Jemma. But tonight was one of his few free nights, so he decided to just let himself enjoy it. While reminding himself not to get too attached.

The extra adrenaline in the air coursed through Jemma as well, and she glanced at Wyatt again. She couldn't seem to stop looking at him. There were these occasional moments where she thought maybe he felt this thing between them too. But they were so fleeting, and he hadn't made a move.

Hadn't she decided a move would be bad, though?

With him this close, she was once again having trouble reminding herself why falling for the cowboy next door was a bad idea.

He opened his mouth, and she held her breath—he'd talked quite a bit tonight, and it only made her want him to say more.

"That last shot was amazing, right?" The man at half court said, the microphone up to his lips. "And it just so happens that our half-court competition is tonight."

He listed off a couple of people who'd asked to take part then said, "I hear Wyatt Langford is in the audience tonight. Do you guys remember the cutthroat state championship game when he made that beautiful three-point shot that se-cured the win?"

The crowd roared, and Jemma gaped at him. "I take it back. You were being humble."

"Not very," he said with a laugh.

People began chanting his name, and the guy with the microphone gestured for him to come on down.

The line of Wyatt's shoulders tightened, his hesitance clear. "This is what I get for attending a town function," he muttered before standing and starting down the bleachers.

People held out their hands as he made his way to the floor, and he smacked them like a rock star at his own concert.

"Was this a setup?" Jemma asked Camilla.

"I don't think anyone knew he'd be here, so I'd say no. But we were in the same graduating class, and he really was a big deal. More three-pointers than anyone else in history—and the record still holds."

Camilla turned to fully face her, and Jemma felt like she should pull up her shoulders for some reason. "Speaking of Mr. Three-Pointer, don't tell me you're going to deny that you guys have crazy chemistry. I sat here and witnessed it myself."

"We're friends," Jemma said, and her friend rolled her eyes.

The movement at center court stole back her attention—she didn't want to miss Wyatt's shot. The two teenagers who'd volunteered for the competition launched the ball, both missing by about a yard or so.

The announcer extended the orange ball to Wyatt, but instead of taking it, he leaned in and whispered something to him.

The guy chuckled and lifted the microphone. "I just got word that our newest town resident and the fill-in for Mrs. Anna Lau's third grade class is also in the audience."

Everything inside Jemma turned to stone.

"Miss Monroe, would you care to join us?"

Heads swiveled her way, making it impossible to give the *no thank you* response caught in her throat.

Especially when they started cheering.

She slowly pushed to her feet and carefully made her way down the bleachers, smiling at everyone who tossed encouraging words her way. They were also chanting her name, which seemed more like a bad omen than a cheer.

She aimed a glare at Wyatt as she approached, and he had the audacity to grin wider. She dipped her head to speak into the microphone. "You guys keep chanting *miss*, Monroe, and I'm pretty sure that's exactly what's about to happen."

The crowd sniggered, and she was too hot and too cold, and yet a sense of acceptance and community also wove through her, leaving her feeling a whole lot at once.

Wyatt smoothed a knuckle down her arm, and everything inside her calmed before going berserk. *Just what I needed. A few more emotions added to the mix.*

"I couldn't help it," he whispered, causing goose bumps to sweep across her skin. "If I have to be at the center of attention, I want you with me."

He probably didn't mean it in the way it sounded, but for tonight they were a team, and that made it a great night. So she'd shoot an air ball and let the crowd laugh at her lack of coordination. Afterward, she could insist Wyatt console her. Bonus, this would make good blackmail material for whenever she had one of her livin'-in-the-country-type disasters and had to call on him for help.

"Who's going first?" the announcer asked.

The notion that bad news should come before good news meant she should, right? She took the ball. Stared at it. Stared at it some more.

It was grippier than she'd expected, and heavier too. The air was another thing that seemed heavier down here, but she was fairly sure that was the suspense and weighted expectations of a hundred plus pairs of eyes.

"Need a few tips?" Wyatt asked.

Swallowing took more effort than usual, and she managed to nod. "Not that they'll help, but yes, please."

He demonstrated shooting and following through with an invisible ball.

Her hands trembled as she lifted the ball, flat in her right palm as she steadied it with her left one.

Wyatt placed his hands on her shoulders and squared her off toward the basket. "Just focus on the white square on the backboard…"

His warm breath hit her neck, and seriously? She was supposed to focus on something besides how close he was?

"Tell you what. If you miss, I'll take you out for ice cream. And if you make it, I'll take you out for ice cream."

Desire swirled into her tornado of emotions. Every nerve ending was on high alert, both from Wyatt and the buzz of the crowd.

Finally, she fired the ball, throwing her entire body into it.

It landed about halfway to the basket, but the arch had been more impressive than any other time she'd shot a basketball.

One of the kids retrieved the ball and threw it to Wyatt. He squared off at the half court line, and she wondered what he'd do if she went to help him and give him a pep talk. Maybe whisper in *his* ear.

Only, they were in front of most of the town, and she'd never be able to play it off as a casual move. Not to mention she rarely made moves. Nope, she waited for the guy, and sometimes it meant waiting forever, only for them to let her down easy.

That same adrenaline from earlier filled the air, and Wyatt took his shot.

Without thinking, Jemma grabbed his hand, needing a lifeline to hold on to as she waited to see if the ball would fall through the white netting.

The ball hit the rim, and Wyatt gave her hand a squeeze, the pulse of it echoing in the beat of her heart.

The big orange ball bounced for an eternity, bump, bump…

Swish.

Hoots and hollers filled the gym, so loud she was sure it shook the rafters.

And Wyatt held on to her hand, his eyes locked on to hers, as if she were the only person in the entire room.

CHAPTER SIXTEEN

T HE ROAR OF THE GAME and celebratory cheering still rang in Jemma's ears as Wyatt walked her out to the parking lot. He started right as she turned to go left, and she bumped into him, her hands coming up to grip his biceps as she worked to remain steady on her heels.

"I'm that way," she said with a giggle, her breath coming out in a frosty white cloud.

Wyatt cupped her elbows, ensuring she stayed upright. "I'm the other way. But I just assumed I'd drive us to the diner for ice cream. I owe you, after all."

"Oh. Right." She hadn't known he'd meant tonight, and her insides gave a little leap over the fact that she didn't have to say goodbye just yet.

Every version of Wyatt was melding together to give her a better whole picture, and this version was extra fun. He seemed at home and more carefree than usual. She had a feeling he didn't take a time out from his busy life very often, and after burning herself out with school and work, she knew how important it was to take a break.

"Then I guess I'll let you lead," she said.

He offered his elbow, and she linked her hand in the crook of it. When she shivered, he tucked her closer in a sort of side hug that made her feel imbalanced in the best sort of way. She essentially glided to his truck, where he helped her inside before circling the hood, climbing inside, and firing up the engine.

The radio played in the background, a twangy tune she never would've considered her style. It used to not be. But sitting across from a real-life cowboy, driving down Main Street so they could hit the small town diner, she glanced around at what she'd originally declared the middle of nowhere and decided she might be a little bit country after all.

Naturally, the diner was full of everyone Wyatt had ever known. He should've thought through his plan better, but he didn't have ice cream at his house, and with the way he couldn't stop staring at Jemma, he wasn't sure he trusted himself to be alone with her without giving in to the temptation to kiss her.

And yet, there was something comforting about the familiarity of a packed diner to celebrate a win. The full tables, din of dozens of conversations and clattering plates, plus the scent of greasy food took him back to high school all over again, when his life had revolved around basketball.

And his girlfriend.

It was before the complications, back when he hadn't known how many of those the universe could throw at you at once.

After a handful of years of not being sure he believed in the kind of romantic love that lasted forever, he hadn't expected to feel the glimmer of it ever again. But tonight, at half court when Jemma had taken his hand, spark after spark had fired through his body until it was more than a glimmer—it was a full-on blaze.

He'd let it cloud his reason, and right now, he didn't want the haze to clear.

In fact, he stepped a tad closer to Jemma, placing his hand on her lower back so it could flood him again.

After ordering milkshakes, they sat at a tiny table, the booths too full to have a chance at getting one to themselves. Again, he told himself that it was good. Being smack dab in the center of the action would keep him in better control. As they waited for their order, several people stopped to chat.

Tyrone Willis gave the two of them a wide grin and then patted Jemma's shoulder and told her she just needed some practice and she'd at least be a decent free-throw shooter. Others stopped to rehash glory moments from the game and talk about their half-court shots, and there was also talk about state championships of yesteryear and, of course, the weather.

"I'm starting to struggle to remember names," Jemma said, concern creasing her brow. "They all know mine too, so it makes me feel that much worse."

"Well, that's partially because you're new, and partially because they announced it at one of the biggest games of the year."

"Still." Her lower lip popped out, and he fought the urge to tap it.

He settled for placing his forearms on the table and creating a more intimate bubble with their bodies. "Gloria, the woman with the pen and pad who took our order, has worked at the diner since she was sixteen."

"And she's now…?"

Wyatt leaned closer. "No one knows. But my dad remembered her serving him in high school, and that was over five decades ago.

"Then you've got Norman Morrison..." He gestured with his chin to the grizzled old man who looked like he'd be able to take on anyone he met in a dark alley. "He's served in two wars, and every evening he comes to the diner, orders the exact same meal—double bacon cheeseburger, no pickles—and takes home three ketchup packets and two containers of cream. Back when they used to have ashtrays, he'd take one of those home."

Jemma blinked, soaking it in as if there'd be a pop quiz later. "I was trying not to listen to gossip while I was in the coffee shop earlier this week, but they were talking about this carpenter dude and how mad his wife is that he didn't get a different job after cutting off his fingers." She bit her thumbnail. "Ever since, I've been dying to know did that really happen, or where they exaggerating?"

Wyatt nodded. "Tony Garcia. Yep. Only has two and a half fingers on one hand now."

Her jaw dropped.

"The accident was last year, though, and he's still a great carpenter. He just readjusted and went on with life like it wasn't a big deal. If you see him and his wife out and about, she'll most likely drag you into a discussion about dangerous jobs, and he'll proudly show off his missing fingers and make jokes about it."

Gloria set their milkshakes in front of them, and Jemma thanked her by name.

"Sure thing, honey," came the gravelly reply.

Jemma attempted to suck her drink out of her straw, but it must've been too thick, because she abandoned it and tipped the glass to her lips. When she brought it back down, she had whip cream on her lower lip and the tip of her nose.

"Oh my gosh, why haven't I had one of these here before? Like, how didn't you tell me to grab one the second I got into town?"

"After seeing you in the snowbank, I had my doubts you could safely drive to places. I didn't want to be responsible."

"Ah!" She crumpled up her napkin and tossed it at him. He caught it, which was inconvenient for her—obviously, she didn't realize she had part of her milkshake on her nose.

"You have a little…" He tapped his own nose, and Jemma's eyes widened. She wiped at the wrong side with her fingertips. Gripping her napkin, he stretched himself over the table and used it to remove the whip cream.

Her cheeks were slightly flushed, but the laugh that came out was more amused than embarrassed. "And now you have a little…"

He looked down to see whip cream on the front of his shirt. He'd leaned too far over his shake when he'd been helping her.

She scooted her drink aside, grabbed more napkins, and dabbed at it. "We're a mess."

He peered down at her, noticing the adorable crinkle that showed up between her eyebrows when she was concentrating, and his insides felt like a mess.

Once they were cleaned up, they finished their milkshakes while they talked about nothing and everything. Every time they had something in common, he'd silently cheer.

And every time she mentioned the city with that hint of longing, he'd volley back to the side of the line where he stuck to friends only.

But as he walked her to his truck again, a nervous guy who'd just finished an awesome sort-of date with a woman, he once again felt like he was back in high school.

Occasionally, Jemma came home from a date feeling like she'd put her best self forward and hadn't made a fool of herself.

As Wyatt walked her to her car, she realized she'd kind of made a fool of herself but had still put her best self forward. Because it was her true self. Better yet, Wyatt hadn't seemed embarrassed to be with her, not even when she'd ended up with whip cream on her nose.

He had this way of teasing her that made it easy to laugh at herself. He didn't make her feel like she was too chatty, either. He let her talk and talk. He always listened intently, and when he talked, she also hung on every word.

The guy was unexpected in so many ways.

"Guessing this is you," Wyatt said. "Call it my incredible powers of deduction, considering I already know what your car looks like and it's the only one left in the parking lot."

It was pretty crazy how the school had gone from bursting to ghost town in the matter of an hour. Then again, she'd seen elementary kids charge out of school at record speeds, the formerly bustling halls empty within minutes.

Jemma turned to smile at her gentleman escort.

Hours of spending time together, and yet she didn't feel ready to say goodbye. Whether in a crowd, at the diner, or just the two of them, she always enjoyed her time with Wyatt. Her heart pitter-pattered, hope tapping its way into the mix.

It'd been such a good date. *Er, hangout thing.* Since it *wasn't* a date, she shouldn't go analyzing it like one. Not that it stopped her from thinking it'd been the best date she'd ever been on.

Or hangout thing, so to speak.

"Well, good night," she said. "When Camilla brought up the ballgame, I uncharacteristically said yes without taking a second to overanalyze or make myself nervous about it, and I'm so glad I did."

"Me too." His grin spread across his face and lit her up inside, like a hundred sparklers that started glowing and fizzing at once.

Then he leaned closer, his arm winding around her—he was going in for a goodbye hug!

Jemma threw her arms around his waist, embracing him tightly. She'd wanted to hug him all night. He was solid and warm and smelled amazing and...

Not hugging her back.

His hand was on the handle of her car door, just the one arm stretched out. Her sluggish brain put it together a few seconds too late. He'd reached around her to open the door.

Heat crawled up her neck and settled into her cheeks as they burned with the embarrassment of a thousand suns. "Oh. I... Wow, thanks so much for opening my door. Obviously, I super appreciate it. Goodbye!"

"Jemma."

She waved, acting like she didn't hear him. The way he'd said her name had been in this letting-down-easy way she couldn't stand to hear right now, not with mortification taking over.

She snapped her seat belt into place and quickly started her car. She gave another wave without looking directly at him—but enough at him that she didn't run him over and complete her humiliation.

What had she been thinking? Calling it a date in her head and launching herself at him while he was being a gentleman?

She'd try to claim it was simply a friendly gesture on her end, but she was sure her squeaky voice and red face would give her away.

The way her heart *thunked, thunked, splatted,* definitely did.

CHAPTER SEVENTEEN

WYATT'S GAZE SOUGHT OUT JEMMA the moment he stepped inside the gymnasium at the elementary school. Onstage, several people milled about open boxes of varying sizes, moving props here and there. The woman he was looking for stood in the middle of the action, pointing people in different directions.

Bailey Rae perked up at his side, bouncing on the balls of her feet. "I'm gonna go find my bow and arrow to show you."

He nodded, and she was off and sprinting up the steps to the stage. She paused to hug Jemma, who smiled and squeezed her back. A moment later, Jemma peered over his daughter's head at him.

Every ounce of oxygen whooshed out of his lungs. It was like he kept forgetting how pretty she was. How much joy seeing her happy face brought him. He'd be sure he fully realized it, then her eyes would lock on to his, and he'd take in the slope of her nose and the way her hair framed her cheekbones and how her grin radiated through her features, and yeah. Pretty inside and out.

Not a newsflash, but it still struck him motionless for a couple of seconds.

Last night, he'd had such a great time. He'd wanted to

hold her hand in the diner and as he walked her to the car, but he'd restrained himself.

Finally, he'd forced himself to open her car door so he could tell her goodbye. Then he'd gone home to mope about the fact that he had to consider what was best instead of being the impulsive kid he'd been in high school.

He hadn't realized she'd assumed he'd been going in for a hug, and the way she'd thrown her arms around him had spun the world off its axis.

Even now, the ground seemed to tilt beneath his feet, his center of gravity changing to the woman up front.

Jemma ducked her head and glanced away, breaking him out of his trance. Clearly she was embarrassed, and as he'd started to do last night before she'd sped away, he wanted to tell her she had nothing to be embarrassed about.

He should probably clarify that he wasn't looking for a relationship right now, though. That they should stick to friends. How did one do that without offending the other person? Especially when it was the opposite of what he selfishly wanted to do?

Bailey Rae stepped out from the velvety blue curtains that'd seen better days—they'd seen better days when *he'd* been in in elementary school—and withdrew a heart-tipped arrow. She notched it into a big white bow.

Right as he opened his mouth to ask if she was supposed to be firing it onstage, his daughter demonstrated how much of a crack shot she was by launching the arrow at Jemma.

The chiding he was about to give Bailey Rae crashed into the warning he meant to call out, but it was too late anyway.

The foam, heart-tipped arrow hit her teacher right in the bum, and as she spun around to find the source of what'd hit her, he clamped his lips so he wouldn't laugh.

"Sorry, Miss Monroe," Bailey Rae called, but the giant,

toothy grin sapped some of the sincerity. His dad senses pricked up, although he wasn't sure what to make of it.

Jemma simply laughed, tossed the arrow back to Bailey Rae, and told her to be more careful.

Wyatt's boots echoed up the steps and across the stage as he crossed over to the woman in charge to receive his instructions. He tipped his hat, hoping to lighten the mood and return things to normal between them. "Howdy, ma'am. Heard there were sets to be built."

"You heard right, cowboy," she said, but she didn't quite meet his eyes. He was sure it was because of how last night had ended. If he'd known Jemma was going to hug him, he absolutely would've hugged her back.

Even if he should know better.

He stretched out his fingers and brushed them down her arm. At the touch of her soft skin, they automatically curled until his hand cupped her elbow. "Put me to work, city girl."

Her gaze lifted, and her smile hit him square in the chest, flooding it with sunshine. The knot he hadn't realized was causing the tightness in his chest loosened. They were okay. He needed them to be okay.

Which, unfortunately, only reiterated everything he already knew.

"The right section of the set is in severe need of a facelift. The fabric's drooping, and I'm afraid it'll come the rest of the way down halfway through the show if we don't do something about it. If you could take care of that, I'd appreciate it."

She was still being oddly formal. Possibly because of their audience.

Since he could stand here all day and still not figure out the inner workings of the female mind, he hefted his toolbox and headed in the direction she'd pointed. He wished his task took him closer to Jemma, but after last night, there'd definitely be enough speculation about them to keep April busy telling anyone who'd listen all about it when they came into her coffee shop.

He was up on the ladder, pounding a nail into the frame of the set, when he spotted his daughter's colorful outfit out of the corner of his eye. Today it was a shirt with glittery silver hearts and a purple, pink, and blue tulle skirt. Since she'd found the skirt online and had done extra chores for two weeks to earn it—all while talking nonstop about it—he knew a ridiculous amount about fabric these days.

He paused and watched as Bailey Rae giggled at whatever the Matthews boy told her, the tip of one of her pink boots turning inward as she shyly brought up a shoulder.

The clack of heels drew his attention downward, to Jemma. She glanced out the "window" that would give her a prime view of the kids. "Aren't they cute?"

He frowned. "'Cute' isn't the word I'd use. She's only nine—and just barely."

"It's just a little crush."

He shook his head. When he glanced back to where the kids had been, they were gone. He tested the bounds of the ladder, stretching taller, but he still didn't see them.

Jemma reached up and twisted a strand of hair around her finger. "Anyway, I just came to see if you need more nails."

"Yes, please." He descended a few ladder steps to grab them, hesitating with his hand hovering over her palm.

The Matthews kid streaked across the stage in large strides.

"Chase, don't you dare jump off the—" Before Jemma could get out the rest of her sentence, he leaped. She threw her free hand over her face, her fingers spread enough she could halfway watch as he hurtled through the air.

The kid's boots landed on the gym floor with a loud thud. Something smacked Wyatt in the rear, and he swung around in time to see Bailey Rae dart behind the curtains with her bow, her quiver wiggling with her rapid movements.

The heart-tipped arrow she'd hit him with had landed at his feet. He had a sneaking suspicion the Matthews kid had been a distraction.

Wyatt had definitely been Cupid's target.

Jemma stifled her laugh the best she could as she eyed the foam-tipped arrow next to the heel of Wyatt's boot. At least she wasn't the only one who'd been shot today—and thank goodness she'd made sure those were *soft* arrows.

"Bailey Rae," Wyatt said, in that low, warning parental tone that made most kids sit up straighter. While there was plenty of storm in his voice, he hadn't quite managed to cover up the hint of amusement.

She popped her head through the set window, her curls forming a blond halo that made her look extra cherubic. "Sorry, Daddy! It was a bet, though, and I couldn't lose a bet."

"Maybe we should put away the bow and arrows for now," Jemma said, gesturing for her to hand them over.

Bailey maneuvered the bow and quiver full of heart-tipped arrows through the window to Jemma. She grinned up at her, and while she'd seen a lot of expressions on Bailey's face, she'd never seen so much mischief in the mix.

Which meant she should take measures to ensure whatever she and Chase had planned didn't get out of control.

"Bailey, can you go work on the Olympus sign?" Jemma turned and raised her voice. "Chase. Mr. Langford needs a volunteer to help him nail up the sagging canvas. Can you come up here and use some of those treehouse-building skills to whip our set into shape?"

"Sure thing, Miss Monroe." The clinging noise of his spurs rang out as he climbed up the stairs and grabbed a hammer. There was a whole lot of mischief in his features, but that wasn't uncommon when it came to Chase.

A month ago, she would've balked at the idea of handing a student a hammer, but his parents had okayed it, saying he'd been building things for years. In fact, they'd told her the more jobs she could give him that would wear him out, the better.

"I'm okay to leave you two alone, right?" she asked Wyatt, the smile on her face undoubtedly moving to smug territory.

He tilted his head as if to say he didn't find it funny but that she didn't need to ask. Which she knew, but it was fun to tease him about his daughter's crush.

She only got one step away before his deep voice drifted over and sent tingly currents skittering across her skin. "Miss Monroe, don't you think it's high time you learned how to hammer? You never know when a skill like that'll come in handy."

Her shoulders tensed, and she spun around on her heel. "Who said I didn't know how?"

She got the head tilt again. He twisted the hammer in his hands around and extended the handle toward her.

Okay, so she didn't have extensive hammering skills, but from what she remembered when halfheartedly building props for the high school production of The *Wizard of Oz*, it was just swing and hit. Like baseball, only the nail was steady.

Not that she'd played baseball very many times, and it'd been at least a decade. She also had struck out all but once, and that hit had been so short the first baseman had caught it before she could get there.

But if it meant Wyatt standing close to her like he'd done when he'd been acting as advisor for her half-court shot, she decided she could use a refresher.

Jemma took the hammer from him. "For the record, I have swung a hammer before. It's just been a while."

"Great. Then you can teach me."

She gave him a mock dirty look, and he grinned.

Although other teachers and parents were making various props, helping students paint signs, and color the butcher paper they'd put in the windows to make it appear sunny or stormy "outside," depending on the scene, Jemma was still in charge. She quickly scanned the area, biting back a snigger when Mrs. Hembolt was seated in a chair next to the kids with the markers, singing out instructions in her loud, soprano voice.

Half the kids seemed happy about it, and some winced, but it was effective at making all of them work faster.

Since everyone was accounted for and busy—even Chase was hammering away—she turned back to Wyatt. "Okay, let's do this."

"The canvas is coming undone right here and needs more securing." Wyatt pointed, while with the other hand, he dug a nail out of the pocket on his shirt.

She took the nail from him, lined it up, and went to tap it in. It sort of caught, but when she removed her fingers so she could swing harder, the nail fell. Ah, yes, now it was all coming back to her, how she'd gotten frustrated at how the nails wouldn't stay in, so she'd given up and had handed the hammer over to one of her classmates.

She bent to get the dropped nail at the same time as Wyatt did, and they knocked heads. They both came up giggling and rubbing their foreheads. "You're as hardheaded as I expected," she joked, and he laughed harder.

"Right back at you." He positioned the nail in place and instructed her to tap it in.

"You trust me not to smash your fingers?"

He simply shrugged.

"*I* don't trust me to do that."

"I've had plenty of smashed fingers in my day."

She carefully tapped it in, and it was easier since she didn't have to hold it at the same time. Once it was for sure lodged in place, Wyatt let it go, and she hit the head of the nail a little harder. It bent slightly, but the fabric stayed place.

"Here, I'm just going to make sure it's flat enough not to catch a kid as they walk by." Wyatt took the hammer and flattened the head of the nail, the tip of his tongue sticking out as he concentrated.

Jemma couldn't help staring, watching his arms flex as he swung the hammer, admiring the amount of concentration he poured into everything. Her emotions were getting the best of her, and she didn't look away in time to avoid being caught. But as Wyatt's gaze met hers, he smiled, the corners of his eyes crinkling, and she got that fresh-from-the-rollercoaster feeling in her gut.

"What else needs to be done?" Mrs. Russell asked, and Jemma jerked her attention away from Wyatt. All around, people were watching them. Some were trying to be surreptitious about it, and some didn't bother.

"Please put the painted decorations off to the side to dry, and I'll make sure to come in early on Monday to put them away before they have any gym classes. As soon as Mr. Langford and I secure this last section, we can fill in the windows and hang decorations, and then we should be about done for the day."

Jemma held out her hand for another nail, and when Wyatt placed it in her palm, a zing of electricity coursed through her. Shouldn't her reactions to being around him—to every little touch—start fading?

If anything, they were growing stronger with each smile, each word, each brush. Each minute, each second.

Twenty minutes later, the set looked super close to how she'd envisioned it. Cloudy background, Mount Olympus visible through one window and a city landscape through the other. It'd take some stretches of the imagination to make it seem like two settings, but they made do with what they had, and the kids were so cute, all eyes would be on them anyway.

A while ago, Wyatt had ducked behind the curtains and he hadn't come back yet. She wanted to go see him—she found she was forever wanting to see him—but they'd already stirred up plenty of gossip.

As if her thoughts had summoned him, he stepped out from behind the curtain, far cuter than The *Wizard of Oz,* who she'd had a crush on back in the day. Well, her classmate who'd played the role, not the actual wizard.

"Hey, the wires were a bit of a mess," Wyatt said, "but I took some electric tape and did a few minor repairs, and I figured you'd want to know how to work the lights and controls."

She lowered her eyebrows. "How'd you know you wouldn't get shocked?"

"Your faith in me is astounding," he said, and she laughed. "I've done some wiring before. Out on the ranch it takes too long to call an electrician, or a mechanic, or a plumber, so I sort of picked up a pinch of everything—just enough to get by."

She'd never met a guy who was so resourceful, willing to dig in and get things done. She walked over to where he was, and as soon as they were behind the curtain, she said, "Just so you know, I have all the faith in you. Honestly, I think you're amazing."

The instant the words were out, she wanted to stuff them back in, not because she didn't mean them, but the raw sensation overtaking her chest insisted she'd left herself too exposed. She refused to take it back, though.

"Thank you, Jemma." That was all he said. But the way he peered at her, as if he could see into her very soul and he liked what he saw, soothed that raw spot and made her heart swell until he filled every single corner of it.

Wyatt positioned Jemma in front of the big box with various switches and pointed over her shoulder. The scent of her vanilla perfume overwhelmed his senses, and he was acutely aware of how close she was. Every time he was around her, he got lost in her blue eyes, in her smile, her infectious laugh.

"Come on, lever," she said when she flicked it and the red-tinged lights didn't turn on. "Don't you want to work for me?"

Amusement tugged the corner of his lips into a grin—on top of everything else, the woman was completely adorable. "Are you talking to the control box?"

She glanced over her shoulder at him. "I talk to everything, just in case it's listening. Can I confess something?"

Everything inside him froze, but he managed to nod.

"I didn't realize it until I came here, but I talk to my bunny a lot. Like, a lot a lot. It helps, regardless of the fact that I'm relatively sure he only loves me for carrots—much like your horse."

Warmth suffused his veins. "Confession: I find that incredibly endearing. And I talk to my cows and horses all the time."

"I know. That first night we met, you were talking to Casper, scolding him in such a funny, affectionate way. It was super cute, actually."

He could feel the flush in his skin. Before right now, he'd say he didn't get embarrassed. And he wasn't so much embarrassed as…spotlighted, he supposed. She saw him. The real him.

Since going too far down that path might lead to trouble, he worked to stick to the lighter side. "I think we only have to worry if our animals start talking back."

"Oh, Señor Fluffypants talks back. There's just a language barrier."

"Because he speaks Spanish?"

"No, he's a bunny, silly. He speaks rabbit."

He huffed out a laugh as he shook his head, and her grin sent more of that intoxicating warmth pumping through him.

She slowly spun to face him, and now she was caged in his arms. As if someone else was in charge of his arm, he lifted it and put his hand on the side of her neck. There was so much he wanted to say, so much he shouldn't, and he wasn't sure which side of him would win the tug of war.

His thumb drifted over her jawline, making a case for letting go, just for a couple of seconds. His gaze locked on her lips, which parted on a shaky breath.

"Jemma? I'm pretty sure—" Camilla stumbled to a stop, her eyes wide, her mouth forming an O. "Oh. Sorry, I—"

"I was just showing Jemma how to work the lights." Wyatt reached over, twisted the end of the wire around the screw, and used his pocket knife to twist it tighter.

The red lights flickered on. "Looks like everything's good

to go now, so I should probably find Bailey Rae and get going."

What he needed to do was get his head straight, which would never happen around Jemma. He'd already tried space, but that hadn't helped.

Still, he didn't want to run from her, because he was getting confused on the lines between neighborly and friendship and…more. So he gave her shoulder a quick squeeze. "I'll talk to you later."

"Later," she said in a soft voice that made him want later to be right now.

"Dang, girl. I felt like I was busting in on a high school couple who'd snuck back here to make out," Camilla said, nudging Jemma with her elbow. "Sorry about that."

Jemma's mind continued to spin, her thoughts whirring out of control. One was much louder than the rest, though: *Would he have kissed me if we hadn't been interrupted?*

Over the past week or so, she'd been thinking she might be alone in wanting to cross lines, but for one delicious moment, she'd sworn he'd been right there with her.

She could still feel the brush of his callused palm, feel the heat that'd corkscrewed through her as his gaze had dropped to her mouth. "Oh, he was just showing me the control board. Like he said."

Skepticism washed over Camilla's features, and she crossed her arms. "Years in administration have made me a human lie detector, and I don't buy that. Not for a second."

Jemma sighed. "Okay, it started out as that. I'm not sure what it ended up being." If only she'd had a few more minutes to find out.

It was a bad idea, letting Wyatt Langford kiss her.

Or was it the best idea ever?

It'd make things complicated, but nothing worth anything was ever easy, right? If he liked her back, that changed everything. It made it safer to let herself fall.

The only problem was, if she did, she didn't think she could ever go back. The easiness between them would be ruined. She was also fairly certain no guy would ever come close to comparing, either, and she was leaving, and…

My heart is in so, so much trouble.

CHAPTER EIGHTEEN

A FTER A SMALL SNOWSTORM THAT night, the sun had come out, and the roads and sidewalks were clear, only a few unmelted piles in sight. In celebration, Jemma decided she'd grab a quick brunch at Havenly Brew. Then she'd do some much-needed grocery shopping. She was contemplating purchasing ingredients for a semi-fancy meal that'd feed more than one, and she wasn't talking about her and Señor Fluffypants.

The bell over the door of the coffee shop let out a happy jingle, and Jemma practically skipped inside, her cute camel-colored boots tapping out a matching rhythm.

Until she spotted the special's chalkboard next to the cash register. A strange sense of foreboding crept across her skin. "The Wymma? What's that?"

"Oh, it's our new special," April said. "It's a blend of smooth, country hot chocolate with a kick of city cinnamon spice. I also sprinkle heart-shaped cinnamon candies and dark chocolate shavings over the whip cream."

Nancy Gardner, who was seated in a circular table off to the side, raised her cup. "I highly recommend it. It's delicious."

A few other people echoed the sentiment.

Jemma's breaths were coming out faster and faster. Country. City. Wyatt. Jemma. She wanted to believe it was some weird coffee drink she'd never heard of, but there was no way it was a coincidence. "And how exactly did you come up with it?"

A sheepish expression overtook April's face. "Well…"

Jemma's skin was flushed; she could feel it in her cheeks. Apparently she was city cinnamon, so it made sense that she was running hot.

The bell over the door jingled, and the other woman most likely in on this embarrassing development strolled in. Camilla froze when she saw Jemma, guilt creeping into her features.

"I knew it! You told?" The hurt in her voice couldn't be helped—they were supposed to be friends.

"Told what?" Camilla asked. Then she leaned closer. "Is there something to tell?"

Jemma exhaled, doing her best to keep her patience. She was starting to understand the downfall of the way word spread in small towns. She gestured toward the special's board and the new drink of the week. "The Wymma?"

Confusion creased Camilla's features for a moment before dawning smoothed them out. Then she grimaced. "It wasn't me. Everyone saw you two at the basketball game and drew their own conclusions."

"Especially after we heard you two also cozied up while you were building sets for the play," April added with a proud nod.

Jemma fought the urge to cover her face with her palm. "So you made a drink with our names squished together?" The question ended on a high-pitched squeak. She was finally breaking through to Wyatt the tiniest bit, but she could tell he was hesitant to cross into more. She'd already attack-hugged him, only to have him freeze in place.

If he saw their drink, would he think she'd asked April to make it? To give him a nudge?

Would he freak out that everyone was suspecting they were more than friends, the way she was starting to freak out?

Camilla placed her hand on Jemma's arm and spoke in a soothing tone. "Relax. She does this all the time, and people always know it's all in good fun."

"Tastes like chocolate-covered cinnamon bears," Nancy said, licking whip cream off her lip. "You simply must try one."

April wrung her hands together. "You both just looked so happy. I decided it was a good reason to celebrate. That the entire town would want to share the happiness of a new couple."

One thing was for sure, Jemma definitely didn't feel happy now. Out of desperation, she pinched her thigh, hoping she'd shoot up in bed and discover this was a nightmare. She could tell Camilla about it, then they'd laugh…

The pinching didn't do anything but sting, confirming this was truly happening.

"Tell you what," April said, grabbing a cup. "On the house, since I used you as half the inspiration. One for you, and one for Camilla."

Before she could argue, April was making the frothy drinks. She also put a chocolate muffin on a plate without her having to ask, then cautiously slid the order across the blue counter to Jemma and Camilla.

Reluctantly, Jemma took a sip of the drink named halfway after her, and she barely stifled a moan. It was amazing—one of April's best concoctions yet.

Maybe I can be won over with delicious food and drinks more easily than previously thought.

Camilla took a sip of her Wymma. "Don't kill me, but it is really good. The flavors pair so nicely." She hooked her arm through Jemma's and propelled her toward a table in the corner.

They passed Lainey Townsend, who was at her computer working as usual. Jemma had run into her a couple of times here and had discovered she lived just down the road from her, at the place with the llamas. Since she worked remotely for some big company, Lainey often used Havenly Brew as her second office, and they'd joked about being as desperate for fast WiFi as caffeine.

But right now, it was all Jemma could do to nod hello.

Lainey seemed pretty into her work anyway, but the drink next to her laptop looked suspiciously like the one in Jemma's hand.

Everyone in town is going to assume the wrong thing. It's probably too late to even attempt damage control.

The scrape of chair legs vaguely registered before Camilla guided her into a chair and took the seat across from her. "Like I said before, it's just lighthearted fun. So why do you look so stressed?"

The agitating tornado of emotions made it hard to pick one out from the rest, and Jemma ran her hand through her hair, trying to sort through the turmoil so she could pinpoint it herself. "Because I don't know how Wyatt feels, and I'm afraid if he sees our names all squished together like that, he'll panic."

"Because you don't think it's what he wants?" Camilla asked, and Jemma's stomach sank. "Or it's not what you want?"

After a beat or two, Jemma shrugged. It was what she

wanted, but the many obstacles still concerned her—and now she had to worry that everyone in town would also be upset if it didn't work out. "It's complicated. Not only am I his daughter's teacher, I don't have a secure future here. As you're well aware, I was hired temporarily."

"I'm sure we can find you a spot somewhere, even if it takes a while. None of us want you to leave."

The word "leave" made her chest squeeze. How had she gotten so attached to everyone in a month? After her first rocky week here, it had seemed especially impossible.

But here she was anyway.

While she was sure Camilla would try, she knew it wouldn't be that easy. Randa had said the same thing and had also called up contacts and helped her scour every district in the city for job openings.

Jemma had thought she'd had a lot to lose then, but now she had even more to lose.

And if she and Wyatt crossed lines, it would be more than she was willing to risk.

Jemma slowed as she neared the fork in the road. Right, toward her cottage? Or left, to Wyatt's ranch?

The steering wheel seemed to turn on its own, as if it knew her heart better than she did.

I need to talk to him anyway. See if I can get ahead of this whole Wymma thing.

She eased the car to a stop in front of the porch, but as she climbed out, she spotted the top of a familiar cowboy hat near the corral. The driveway had turned to mud, but the grassy areas still had a light dusting of snow that made each individual blade stand out.

Wyatt glanced her way as she approached, and his smile was like a beacon in a storm, one that guided her toward him and pushed her worries aside enough that she could smile back.

"Hey," she said, because she was eloquent like that.

"Hey," he said back, probably because he'd never had a chatty problem.

Casper whinnied and came running, and if it wasn't for the wooden beams of the fence he frequently broke out of, he would've plowed right over her.

"Sorry, big guy." She patted her pockets, as if he'd understand that. "I don't have any carrots on me."

The horse stuck his long nose over the fence, and she ran her hand over it and then up to rub circles on his forehead. Surprisingly, he seemed about as happy about the rubdown as when she fed him carrots.

"Have you ever ridden a horse?" Wyatt asked. He was leading a tall, pale-brown pony with charcoal-colored hair. The horse had a saddle on its back, so her cowboy neighbor was obviously getting ready for a ride of his own.

"Do the kind on the merry-go-round count?" she asked, and Wyatt cocked his head. "Don't look at me like it's a common thing. There are city things I bet you haven't done. Like...have you ever gone to the opera?"

"No, and I wouldn't willingly, either."

She laughed. "If I'm being honest, I'd always wanted to go to the opera. But once I went with my friend, I was like, whoa, this is a whole lot of superhigh singing." Mrs. Hembolt would've been in heaven—perhaps a decade or two ago, she would've been the star. "It was in Italian too, so I had no idea what they were saying."

"You're saying there was a language barrier, just like with you and your rabbit."

A giggle burst out of her. She did that so much more around Wyatt. She couldn't even look at him anymore without her heart soaring and silently screaming how very much she liked him. "Much the same, yes. In fact, I'm thinking of auditioning Señor Fluffypants for a musical."

He laughed. "Perfect. Take Casper with you. See if they can find a way to keep him penned."

"What do you think? *The Sound of Music,* or *Footloose?*"

"Not sure if Casper can dance, but if he could make some decent money, I'll get right on teaching him." Wyatt gathered the reins in his hands. "Well, what do you say? You up for a ride?"

"Oh. I was just on my way home from town, and figured I'd stop by and say hi." *And tell you there's a drink named after us because everyone thinks we're a couple to cheer for, and I totally do too, but it also scares me, and I'm afraid it'll scare you even more.*

"You can't come out here to the country and not learn how to ride a horse—especially if you're going to drive your car into ditches. Horses might be your only chance at transportation."

"Hey!" She lightly smacked his arm. "It was only one time, and you're never going to let me live it down, are you?"

He shook his head, mischief dancing in his hazel eyes.

She stuck her hands in her pockets so she wouldn't attack-hug him again, and rocked back on her heels. "I suppose I should try the horse-riding thing." Clearly he'd been on his way somewhere. "Unless you're busy now. I can come back later."

"It'll get too cold for you once the sun sets—I'll just take you along." He ran his hand over the horse's muscular neck. "You don't mind, do you, Dasher?"

The horse whinnied.

Wyatt climbed into the saddle, the leather creaking as he settled in, and then he reached for her hand. Jemma gripped it like a lifeline. She slid her foot into the stirrup as instructed, and Wyatt pulled her on in front of him. He showed her how to turn the horse using the reins and how to pull him to a stop.

Then he told her to point Dasher toward the lone tree across the way.

He nudged the horse forward, making a clicking noise with his tongue, and Jemma gripped on to the reins. She bumped a bit in the saddle until she found the rhythm, her heart picking up speed at the new adventure.

Okay, this is more fun than I thought it'd be. Most likely because of the cowboy behind her and how he'd give soft instructions in her ear, his warm breath hitting her neck and leaving her slightly dizzy.

Still, there was also something about feeling the strength of the horse underneath them, taking long strides that ate up the distance. The sprawl of endless land leading to giant snow-capped mountains. The last rays of sunshine made the snow sparkle, leaving the ground glittery and the clouds and sky a picturesque mix of purple, reddish-orange, and pink.

The cool air nipped at her skin, but it only added to the buzz of a new experience, one that let her focus on the beauty of this place she'd been lucky enough to land in for a while.

"Can we go faster?" she asked, glancing at the cowboy behind her.

He was just as beautiful as the land, something she doubted he'd appreciate her voicing. Normally she wouldn't think of a guy as beautiful, but it was as if he'd been sculpted from the same stuff as the mountains, resolute and captivating, promising excitement to those who dared to go exploring.

"Faster it is. Better hang on." After she gripped the saddle horn, the reins wound around her fist, Wyatt gave a loud "yah," and then they were flying across the field, the cold wind whipping her cheeks.

It was what she imagined flying would feel like, only she had a warm body behind her, making her feel more secure.

Making her feel an overwhelming amalgamation of delight and longing.

They arrived at the field with the tree, where a lot of cows with swollen pregnant bellies also were. Once Wyatt found the cow he was looking for, he reached around Jemma to take the reins. He cut the black cow from the rest of the herd, and Dasher stayed by its side, urging her toward the barn. They kept a slow, measured pace, though, no more galloping.

Wyatt explained the cow showed signs that she'd be having her baby soon, so he wanted her in the barn so he could keep a closer eye on her and keep the baby calf—once it came—warm.

As soon as the mama cow was secured in the barn, Wyatt dismounted and helped Jemma down with a hip-grip move that ratcheted up her heart rate.

While he led Dasher into the corral, Jemma stomped around, trying to keep herself warm. Her nose and cheeks were numb, and her toes were following closely behind.

Wyatt secured the gate as he came back out of the corral, and then he stepped closer to her and rubbed his hands over her arms.

"I'm not built for cold weather," she said as a full-body shiver gripped her.

"Well, let's get you inside, then." He wrapped his arm around her shoulders and started for the house. "I'll even make you a fire so you don't go home and smoke yourself out."

She curled closer to his side, soaking in his warmth. "I have groceries in my trunk. I'd be happy to make dinner."

"I'd be more than happy to eat it."

CHAPTER NINETEEN

WYATT HAD JUST FINISHED STACKING the wood in the fireplace when Lori and Bailey Rae burst through the front door.

Jemma had unloaded her bag of groceries, the sounds of opening drawers and cupboards and clanging pans drifting over to him as she moved around the kitchen.

After she'd offered to make dinner, he'd almost called and asked Lori to keep Bailey Rae a little longer, but his sister had already picked her up, taken her to dance practice, and let her hang out for most of the afternoon.

Good thing he'd resisted, because he needed the reminder that pulling Jemma too far into his life could end in a debris-riddled mess that would not only affect him, but his daughter as well.

Besides, he leaned on his sister too much as it was, considering everything she already had going on.

"Oh, hello again," Lori said, her gaze moving to the woman in his kitchen.

"Jemma!" Bailey Rae rushed over, the pink skirt of her ballet outfit streaming behind her, and threw her arms around their fill-in chef, who squeezed her back with equal zeal.

He soaked it in, letting himself pretend for a moment

that it was a possibility. Him and Jemma and Bailey Rae. Happy. Cozy.

A family.

"Oh, sure," Wyatt teased. "You hug your teacher before you hug your dear old dad." Bailey Rae bounded toward him and he crouched down so she could give him a big hug, the tight bun he still hadn't mastered bumping his chin. "Were you good for Aunt Lori?"

"Dad. I'm *always* good."

Wyatt looked to his sister for confirmation, even though Bailes was a dang good kid, one he didn't have to worry too much about. Save kids who said unkind things to her, and then having to control his own temper. She was doing much better this semester, though, and he had no doubt in his mind that a lot of that was thanks to Jemma.

"Honestly, she helps so much with the boys that I'm thinking of stealing her for longer," Lori said, a silent question or hint in the mix of words.

His knees popped as he straightened—it'd been a long day. "We can schedule something next week."

Lori's arched eyebrows were definitely asking if he was sure, and in case he missed that, she tipped her head toward Jemma.

She had a knife in her hand and was stabbing the top of the square container she'd placed on the counter. "If you're hungry, I'm about to pop one of the only meals I can make in the oven—premade lasagna that I only have to stab and warm up. It's kinda my specialty."

His sister laughed. "Thank you, but we ate already."

Jemma opened the oven and placed the lasagna inside, and he tried not to think about how much he liked having her in his house, moving around like she belonged here.

Careful. That's a dangerous line of thinking.

The oven door closed with a bang that seemed to surprise her, and then she set a timer.

They all wished Lori goodbye, and then Jemma rounded the counter and asked Bailey Rae about her day.

His daughter started backward, telling her about helping Aunt Lori out with her kids and how they'd made corn muffins and soup, and then she mentioned dance practice. She was finally getting the routine down and did Jemma like her skirt and wait one second and she'd grab her toe shoes so Jemma could see them.

Bailey Rae dug into her bag and withdrew the pink hand-me-down slippers with the never-ending ribbon. He'd had to watch a YouTube video just to help her figure out how to tie them. "Did you ever try ballet?" she asked as she handed Jemma the shoes.

"So long ago that I only remember what a plié is and how much they hurt your thighs."

"They totally do!"

Wyatt had been against ballet lessons at first, mostly because what skill would that teach his daughter? Lori was the one who'd told him she needed to have hobbies and to do girly things he might not understand.

It wasn't until her first recital that he'd understood. He'd seen her joy. The way she'd shone onstage. How hard she worked at it, teaching her discipline and endurance in a more fun way than he ever could.

"Can I show you some of my routine?"

Jemma extended the shoes back to Bailey Rae. "Funny, I was about to ask if you would."

His daughter's entire face lit up, and she went to bouncing on the balls of her feet. "I'll get the music going. Daddy, can you move the coffee table?"

As usual, he was a sucker for whatever she wanted. He

slid the coffee table aside and kicked his discarded boots into the corner so she'd have a decent area to show off her skills.

Music that made him cringe blared through the speaker Bailey Rae had sent her music to. The people in town called the fairly new dance teacher "progressive," which was just a fancy way of saying doing ballet to loud, obnoxious pop music.

Not that he was a classical music guy, either. Give him a song heavy with a non-synthesized guitar any day.

Jemma moved next to him to watch the show. Bailey Rae counted in her head, each nod a beat, and then she was off and moving. Up on the tips of her toes, spinning, dipping, twirling. Her skirt flared, and her grin widened.

Music notwithstanding, it was amazing to watch her get lost in the music. To see how far she'd come. And more impressive, how she didn't get dizzy from doing those countless turns. These days, he spun around to check on an animal and almost lost his balance.

The song came to a close, and they clapped as Bailey Rae bowed. Then she held her hand out to Jemma. "Show me what you remember."

"Oh, I, uh…"

Bailey grabbed her hand and tugged, and then both of them were in the center of the room. Jemma glided along with his daughter, laughing and spinning, and he took a step forward, afraid she was going to wreck into the fireplace.

But then she straightened out. She blinked as if she were trying to regain her bearings. After shooting each other a sidelong glance, they both bowed, and he clapped extra loud. Jemma's eyes locked on to his, and he suddenly found it hard to swallow.

Even harder to breathe.

"That was a real fine show," he managed to scrape out.

He cleared his throat. "But it's time for some real music." He grabbed his phone and set his favorite country music playlist to shuffle.

"If you think that's going to stop me from dancing," Jemma said with a laugh, "I'm sorry to tell you it's not going to work. Camilla's been dragging me to country dance aerobics every Thursday night, and I'm getting pretty…decent. Well, that's probably a stretch. But I stopped wrecking into people." She wrinkled her nose, a ridiculously adorable move. "Mostly."

He huffed a laugh, trying to picture his city girl out on the dance floor.

Er, not my city girl. The city girl. Yeah.

"Ooh, show me some moves." Bailey Rae quickly unlaced and kicked off her ballet slippers, the ribbons puddling on the floor.

"This is the scuff kick." Jemma demonstrated, and Bailey Rae followed. "Oh, and there's this one Essie calls the penguin tail."

"She always has the best names for moves," his daughter said.

Jemma did a sort of waddle shuffle and then lifted her leg and smacked her hip. Bailey Rae mimicked the movement, and then they added it to the first bit of choreography.

Jemma looked to him. "Want to join us? I think you'd be a natural at the penguin tail," she said, and his daughter giggled.

"Funny." He lowered himself to the arm of the couch. "But I'd rather stay where I am and watch, thanks."

"Suit yourself." She glanced down at Bailey Rae. "This is the one I always struggle with. The kick ball change makes me want to put my weight on my right foot, but I'm supposed to lean on my left. I have to do it super slow the first few times, but every time Essie speeds it up, I get all turned around again."

He had no idea what half those words meant, but he liked watching the demonstration.

"I think I got it," his daughter said, and then she and Jemma did it together. Slow at first, then faster and faster. Bailes called out those nonsense words a few times, and then Jemma applauded herself.

"That's it. I think I've finally got it. Let's do the entire thing," Jemma said, and his daughter enthusiastically nodded. "Five, six, seven, eight."

They strung the steps together, doing the same moves and completing the routine.

He was still grinning, feeling those same dangerous desires about the three of them together like this all the time, when Bailey spun to face him. "Daddy knows how to country dance. The couple-type dances with lots of spinning."

His grin faded, and he let his forearms fall down to his thighs. "No. I don't know how to do any of that anymore. That sort of knowledge slipped out when you made me memorize the name of every My Little Pony."

Bailey Rae tipped her head, her lips pursed. "Don't make me call you a pants on fire."

The girl was going to be the death of him.

Jemma crossed her arms. "Let's see your moves, cowboy."

With a groan, he reluctantly pushed to his feet and reached out for Bailey Rae's hand.

"Show Jemma. I'm too short, and besides..." She let out a long exhale. "I'm exhausted." She flopped onto the couch, several of her blond curls slipping out of her bun. "My turn to sit and watch."

Time seemed to grind to a halt as he turned to Jemma.

To dance or not to dance? Not that his daughter had left him much wiggle room.

One of his favorite songs came on, tempting him further.

If he was being honest with himself, the idea of dancing with Jemma was tempting enough.

"Don't think I won't boo you guys," Bailey Rae said from her spot on the couch. Evidently she'd turned into the harsh judge on all those talent-type singing and dancing shows.

Wyatt extended a hand to Jemma, and she slipped her much-smaller one into his. He guided her other hand to his shoulder and placed his hand on her lower back, fingers spread wide. "We'll start left. Just let me lead."

"It's not really in my nature, but I'll do my best." The smile she flashed him made his gut tighten.

"Three, two…" He guided her around the room, avoiding the mantle and a sketchbook that'd been left on the floor. As the music picked up speed, he brushed off his rusty moves, reached up and took Jemma's other hand, and then twirled her out before spinning her back to him.

Jemma gripped his upper arms as she peered down at his feet and tried to follow his steps. "You said you were going to teach Casper to dance, and now I'm thinking Casper needs to wait his turn."

He laughed and took one of her hands again, repeated the spin move but then guided her under his arm as she worked to keep up. They got tangled up for a couple of seconds before she dove under his arm, the way he'd been attempting to guide her to do.

The song was coming to a close, so he twirled her back in tight, securing his arm around her lower waist. The air in the room grew thinner as their eyes met. A beautiful grin curved Jemma's lips, making it impossible not to stare at them.

His heart beat a rapid pace against the palm she had on

his chest, and he wondered if she could feel it too. Her cheeks were slightly flushed, and a haze filled her eyes, one he was sure was reflected in his.

The song ended, and Bailey Rae clapped and added an ear-piercing whistle she'd learned herding cows, and the world around them sharpened back into relief.

Wyatt dropped his arms, took a step back, and rubbed his neck.

Jemma reached up and fiddled with her dangly earring. "Thanks for the dance. I should probably go check on the food."

He stood in the center of the living room, not sure what to think or do. Every minute he spent with her made him want to spend more and more, and he was already getting in too deep.

"It's ready," Jemma called as she came around the archway of the kitchen.

Bailey Rae pushed off the couch. "I'm going to go change out of my leotard. I'm much too full to eat another dinner anyway. Call me when it's time for dessert, okay?"

Wyatt cocked an eyebrow. "If you're too full, why doesn't that apply to dessert?"

The shrug was over the top, the sigh extra dramatic. "I'm not sure about the exact science, but it's a thing. Just trust me."

He shook his head, but he was fighting laughter, and Jemma didn't bother fighting hers as she leaned against the archway. "We'll have to study the science behind that in class this week, because I'm not sure how it works, either, but I know it's very, very real."

"See?" Bailey Rae said.

"Great. There's two of them now. Ganged up on in my own house."

The gals grinned at each other, and that thought about Jemma belonging hit him yet again.

"Anyway, you guys enjoy your space." Great, now his daughter was giving him the same type of look his sister had, heavy on the hinting he should take advantage of any time he could get.

She started down the hallway, abruptly backtracked, and took two candles off the bookshelf that was in severe need of dusting. She put them in the middle of the table, unlit. "I won't come out of my room until you knock and tell me there's dessert, I promise cross my heart."

Dang it. She was already seeing them all as a happy family. So much for stopping it before it got out of control.

CHAPTER TWENTY

"SMELLS DELICIOUS," WYATT SAID, GRABBING a couple of plates. What else could he do? Refuse to eat when he was starving? Tell Jemma she should go when she'd brought her dinner over to share?

More than that, he *wanted* to have dinner with her.

Clearly Bailey Rae wanted that as well, but she wanted more than the two of them to share a meal. She was playing Cupid even when she wasn't onstage. First there had been the arrows, and now with the dancing and the candles.

His daughter probably didn't realize the reason they were supposed to be romantic was the soft candlelight, but right now, with his and Jemma's undeniable chemistry firing between them, the air felt smothered with enough romance.

They ate in silence for a few minutes, as if neither one of them knew what to say. It felt more like they had too much to discuss instead of too little, and he worried the minute one of them started, everything would unravel.

A *clink* sounded as Jemma set her fork on her plate. She'd crossed her legs and her foot was bouncing. It seemed more than her usual energetic manner, and immediately the muscles in his shoulders and arms tightened.

Here it comes.

"I, uh, have some news. Or not news but…" The swinging foot picked up speed, and she worried her bottom lip with her teeth.

In that moment, he was sure she was going to tell him she was headed back to the city. Anna Lau's maternity leave was almost up. He'd known it was coming, so why had every organ in his body gone into failure at once?

He wasn't sure how to fortify himself for the blow, but he did the best he could, putting on his best poker face. "What is it?" He was proud of how steady his voice came out.

She licked her lips, and here he was focused on her mouth again. "There's a drink. At Havenly Brew. Named after us."

He took a second to try to put what she'd said together, but her words still didn't make sense. "There's a what now?"

Jemma reached up and wrapped a strand of her shiny dark hair around her finger. "You know how April has her drink of the week, and they all have cutesy names? Well, this week the special is a drink called the Wymma. Country chocolate with a city cinnamon kick. You, Wyatt, plus…"

She blew out a breath. "It's our names smashed together. I didn't tell her to do it, but I figured I should warn you so you're not blindsided when you go in there. If you go in there. But even if you don't, someone will definitely say something to you, and I guess because of the half-court contest and we looked cozy at the play, so everyone just assumed…"

Of course they couldn't just assume. They had to talk about it. Didn't they care that he was trying to keep his daughter from ever being a casualty of his failed relationships again? She'd already been the center of gossip before. People often asked aloud how a mom could leave her child behind, and he understood it was because they were trying to make Bailey Rae feel better about how her life had gone, but it only reminded her that her mom left.

He recalled those first months afterward, when she'd cry out for Andrea. How he'd had to wipe his daughter's tears as she'd asked in her quiet little voice why Mommy had left.

The image of her curled into a ball on her bed, tears streaming down her cheeks, punched him in the chest.

"Your job only entails covering for Anna Lau's maternity leave, correct?" The words burst out of him, and two creases showed up between Jemma's eyebrows.

"Weird subject change, but yeah."

Lead filled his lungs. That was what he was afraid of.

"Are you upset? About the drink?"

"Not at you," he said, but her face dropped anyway.

"Oh." The legs of her chair scraped the floor as she scooted it away from the table, and he placed his hand on her knee.

"It's just if Bailey Rae hears people talking… That's what I'm worried about."

She exhaled and then nodded. "I understand."

He was afraid she didn't, not fully. "It's not that I…" He glanced down at his lap. It wasn't fair to deliver this speech without looking at her, despite making it more difficult to say what he needed to, so he forced his gaze back up. "Jemma, I enjoy spending time with you. But I have to worry about what people say to my daughter. I have to think of her first."

"Of course. I totally understand that."

It'd be so easy to give in to the allure. To let himself go. To try to believe in love again.

Had he not learned his lesson already?

Apparently not.

Women from the city, they simply weren't happy here long-term. She'd just confirmed the fact that she was only here temporarily. How many times did she have to say it until it'd finally sink in?

Even before adding romance to the mix, his daughter was getting too attached, getting all wrapped up in the idea of more.

Bailey Rae's already going to be so devastated when Jemma leaves. If she even thinks there's a possibility of more and it doesn't work…

Maybe he was a wimp for playing it safe, but he'd gone down that route before, and it'd ended badly. He couldn't pick himself up again, and more than that, he couldn't watch his daughter cry or hear her dejectedly ask why everyone always left.

This whole situation was getting way too dangerous for Bailey Rae's heart.

And for his.

Charging on with everything she wanted to say wasn't easy after his last statement. She was relieved he wasn't mad at *her*, but he hadn't said anything encouraging about how he did feel about her.

I enjoy spending time with you could be friends or more. Although she completely understood him thinking of Bailey. The last thing she wanted was to do anything that would hurt her or Wyatt.

"You know I adore Bailey, right?"

He nodded.

She couldn't do it. She couldn't tell him everything, not when he wasn't giving her anything to work with. "Well, I guess I'll help you with these dishes."

Chicken.

"Don't bother with the dishes," he said. "I'll take care of them myself."

Did the same apply to her? "Don't bother confessing that you care about me because it won't change anything?"

She didn't want to disappoint Bailey about the lack of dessert, but she hadn't planned anything, and she got the feeling Wyatt was kicking her out. He was merely too nice to come out and tell her to leave.

"Well, it'll be Monday morning before we know it." She forced herself to her feet, every movement she made feeling like she was underwater, every sound and sensation bigger yet muted. "Guess I'd better go home and make sure I'm prepared."

Wyatt simply nodded again. Like his switch had been set to neutral. All those tender emotions she'd thought she'd seen in his eyes were gone, and he'd been replaced by a bobblehead.

A very handsome bobblehead.

She slipped on her coat, and when she reached for her bag of groceries, Wyatt lifted it before she could get a hold of it.

"I'll walk you out," he said.

Because he was a gentleman first.

No, strike that. He was a dad first. A gentleman second.

He'd make some lucky woman a very good husband one day. The thought made her ache. Made her long for the bravery she'd started the meal with. He'd shown her how to dance, leading and guiding and spinning her and then holding her tightly in his arms, his heart beating against her palm.

Surely she hadn't imagined the connection between them, the one that'd reached deep down into her soul and whispered that she recognized the soul staring back at her.

The cold air filtered through her layers as if they didn't exist, and a whinny carried over. Casper was near the gate, a smear of white in the dark.

Wyatt placed her groceries in the trunk and led her to the driver's side door.

This time she wouldn't lose her mind and fling her arms around him, thinking he was hugging her.

She still had at least a couple weeks in town, so she wasn't sure why every single second took on a desperate edge, like if she didn't gather up the courage to tell him how she felt now, she'd never do it.

Same way she'd waited way too long to confess her feelings for Simon. Months wasted crushing on a guy who hadn't wanted anything more than friendship.

I'm just going to do it. I'm going to confess my feelings and tell Wyatt I want more and see what he says.

If she didn't puke first, that was.

"Wyatt, I have to tell you something." Her heart thudded so loud it echoed through her head, pounding a rapid pulse behind her temples.

"Don't worry about the drink, Jemma. I get it. I'll talk to April and ask her to make a new concoction, one that doesn't make us the center of the gossip."

Man, the guy just kept making it harder and harder. She swallowed past the lump in her throat. "It's not about the drink. Or I guess in a way it is."

His brow furrowed.

"I…" She fidgeted with the ring on her finger, spinning it around and around. *Just say it.* "Over this past month, you and I've had a lot of disasters and a lot of laughs. I can't thank you enough for teaching me how to build a fire, and cleaning my chimney, and for the movie nights and dinners. I'm glad you enjoy spending time with me, because I really enjoy spending time with you too."

His jawline went rigid. Because he was uncomfortable

with emotion? Because he didn't feel the same? Ugh, and they said women were the ones hard to read.

Do it already.

"I like you, Wyatt," she continued, the words naked and raw as they hung in the air between them. "I appreciate the kindness and the friendship, but I think we've got something more going on between us. More than friendship. Maybe we could…" Her heart was going to beat right out of her chest if it didn't go and explode on her first. "Try dating. See what happens."

He closed his eyes as if the words had slammed into him, and everything inside her deflated. Then his lids opened, his eyes boring into hers.

"We know what happens," he said softly. "We get attached, Bailey gets attached, and then we've got a mess on our hands because you're leaving."

She sucked in a sharp inhale. Yes, he made a good point, but this kind of a connection didn't come along every day. Not only did she care deeply about him, she cared about Bailey, and as more than a teacher. She wanted to spend her nights watching movies, eating s'mores, and dancing in the living room. She wanted to hold Wyatt's hand and hug him and, yes, she absolutely wanted to kiss him.

"What if I wasn't?" Her words came out in a whisper, a puff of white air that faded so quickly for how huge of a moment it was for her.

Wyatt swallowed hard. Not reaching for her. Not leaning in. His features were set. Too cold. "Jemma, I can't give you what you want. It's just not going to work out."

The ground swayed; she was sure it did. Pain radiated from her heart. She'd served it up to him on a silver platter, and he'd shoved it away. Just let it tumble to the ground.

Stay strong. If you can't do it for you, do it for Bailey. Who you have to see tomorrow morning. Blinking didn't stop the tears from rising to her eyes.

"I'm sorry," he said, defeat heavy in the words.

Well, at least she could say that this time she'd taken a chance. She'd spoken up. "It's okay," she whispered, despite not feeling okay.

She reached up and ran her hand down his stubbled cheek, her way of saying goodbye to the possibility of them. "Goodnight, Wyatt. Thank you for everything you've done for me. I'll always remember it."

He stood stoic. Quiet. She turned to open her car door, but he beat her to it, and why did he still have to be so nice? Why couldn't he be a jerk so it wouldn't be so hard?

Right before he closed the car door, he looked her straight in the eye, gave her a sad smile, and then said, "Goodbye, Jemma."

She cried all the way home. Which, sure, was only a couple of minutes, but long after she'd washed off her makeup and climbed into a bed to read a book, Señor Fluffypants beside her, the words on the page blurred her eyes, the tears continuing to flow.

CHAPTER TWENTY-ONE

"WHAT HAPPENED?" CAMILLA ASKED AS soon as Jemma walked into the teacher's lounge for coffee Monday morning.

It was more what *hadn't* happened. She couldn't go to Havenly Brew for fear that she'd see the Wymma drink on the chalkboard and cry. Or that someone would ask her about Wyatt and she'd cry.

Or that Wyatt might be in there, possibly just to get coffee and muffins, and likely to tell April to take away the drink. If that was the case, oh, guess what? She'd cry.

Clearly the makeup hadn't hidden the fact that she'd cried herself to sleep, since Camilla continued to stare at her, concern swimming in her brown eyes. "Jemma? Chica?"

Jemma sucked in a deep breath and slowly let it out. It was ridiculous to hurt so much over a guy she hadn't technically dated—yeah, that stung—but she had known him better than she'd known most of the guys she'd dated. "Wyatt doesn't want to be more than friends. I'm not even sure he wants to be that anymore, actually."

Camilla adamantly shook her head. "That can't be true. I saw the way he looked at you. Heck, the entire town's seen the way he looks at you."

"It wasn't enough." *I wasn't enough,* she thought, letting herself sink into the darkness for a weak moment.

Camilla wrapped her arms around her and pulled her into a big consoling hug. "I don't understand."

"It didn't work out. I took a chance, and I crashed and burned." Jemma couldn't help the sniff that came out. She pulled away, wiped underneath her eyes in an attempt to keep her mascara from running down her face, and did her best to reassure herself that eventually, the hurt would fade. "Now, can we please talk about something else, because I need to go in and force myself to be cheery in front of my students."

"Sure. You name it, we talk about it."

"How about…?" Her mind searched for a safe subject, one that might have a chance at bringing her joy. "Shoes."

"Okay." Camilla tapped her lip and then her eyes widened. "Ooh, did you know there's one of those gently used resale shops the town over? They have some fabulous shoes, very fancy brands, half the price."

"That's my favorite kind of price besides free."

"I'm not sure free is a price," Camilla lightly teased with a grin. "Right now, I'm glad we didn't hire you for your math skills."

Jemma snorted a laugh. She could hardly believe she could laugh with her heart all mangled in her chest, no longer beating right. It was like it'd started to beat for Wyatt, and now it didn't remember how to function without him around.

Camilla wrapped and arm around her shoulders and guided her toward the burbling coffee maker and tower of community mugs. "Let's grab you some coffee and get you ready for the day."

Instead of fighting it and telling her new friend she could do it herself, the way she would've when she'd first moved here, she went ahead and gave in, glad to have someone to lean on for a few minutes.

The day had been one of her rougher ones teaching, but tomorrow they'd dig into her Hiding Homophones lesson, and she always dressed up as a detective that day. Sherlock Holmes hat and magnifying glass and everything to help them suss out the words that sounded alike. The kids loved it.

Twenty minutes before the bell was set to ring, Camilla knocked on her open door. "You have a visitor."

Jemma's heart skipped a couple of beats. Had Wyatt changed his mind? Did he miss her as much as she already missed him?

"Class," Camilla continued, "Mrs. Lau wanted to come say hi and let you meet her baby."

Okay, so that *you* was a collective you, and how on earth had her brain jumped to such a far-out conclusion?

They say time healed all wounds, but she was afraid she might not ever get over the dang cowboy who lived next door.

Since she didn't have time for moping, Jemma shoved those fears to the background, stood, and instructed the class to use the hand sanitizer station and form a line.

Three at a time, the students came up to see their previous teacher and her baby boy. The tiny infant had a full head of dark, thick hair and cheeks so big he seemed to have to work to lift them in a smile.

Basically, he was adorable.

The kids asked a lot of questions, and Jemma let Mrs. Lau guide most of the discussion. When it came down to it, this was still her class. Jemma was only borrowing it.

A sharp pang lanced her heart. She'd definitely gotten attached to more than the cowboy.

At the hand on her arm, she glanced down.

Bailey. Gosh, it was hard enough to see her in the classroom and know she'd never fully be part of her life, not in the way she'd started to foolishly hope for.

"Would you like to have a baby someday?" she yell-whispered in that way kids did when they were attempting to be quiet, but they just weren't very good at it. "I'd kind of like a sister or a brother."

Everything inside Jemma froze. Was Bailey saying…?

It hit her then that maybe Wyatt had been right. It was going to be hard enough for Bailey when she left. She wasn't being overly confident. She could tell when she sincerely connected with a student, and she'd instantly had that sort of same soul recognition with the blond, brown-eyed angel staring up at her.

"Oh, I don't know. It's a long way off yet. You need a husband to have a baby." Maybe not precisely true, but for her, that was what it'd take. She wanted a partner and a more conventional family.

"Well, I know where you could find one." Bailey's eyebrows arched so high they disappeared in her mass of curls.

"Why don't you go say hi to the baby?" Jemma nudged her forward, and Bailey started to drag her feet, but then an *aww* came out, leaving her sufficiently distracted.

Once there were only a couple of minutes left before the bell rang, Jemma instructed the kids to grab their coats and backpacks and line up.

"Thanks for taking such great care of my class while I'm gone," Mrs. Lau said as she readjusted the baby blanket, and Jemma couldn't help noticing the green tractors on the fabric, which made it impossible not to think of the guy she was doing her best not to think about. "How are you holding up?"

"I'm loving it. They're a great class."

The baby started to fuss, and Mrs. Lau extended the bundle to Jemma. "Can you hold him for a quick minute?"

She handed the chunk over before Jemma could reply, and then dug in her diaper bag, muttering to herself about a pacifier.

The baby settled down as Jemma swayed from side to side and cooed at him. As she peered into the precious little face, she knew that someday she did want a baby. She wanted everything.

Right now, she couldn't help thinking she'd wanted it with Wyatt, but surely she'd meet someone else who was willing to deal with her quirks and who liked her for her. A guy who'd care if she was warm enough and prepared for winter storms.

Who'd care if she'd ridden a horse before.

Mrs. Lau finally came up with the pacifier and took the baby, right as the bell rang. Jemma thanked her for stopping in and moved over to the door to dismiss the students.

The air was on the warmer side today, bringing in sunshine and a whisper of spring instead of biting cold.

Spring in Haven Lake was probably even more beautiful, miles and miles of land with trees that'd be all leafy green. New grass. Fields of corn or wheat or whatever crops grew around here. Wildflowers—she bet they had those.

I can't wait to see it.

The realization that Mrs. Lau's maternity leave would officially be up in two more weeks hit her. Which meant that if she didn't find another position where she could fill in here, she wouldn't see it. She'd paid two months' rent, so she could always stay till the end of February, but what was the point if she didn't have a job?

Yes, she could do her online classes, but being so close to Wyatt and Bailey, yet so far away…

Her heart caught as she spotted the familiar tan hat in the crowd. Bailey ran over to Wyatt and gave him a hug.

Why was he here?

Well, obviously he was picking up Bailey, but he usually waited in the truck.

He gave a half nod without really looking at Jemma, and that same pain that'd crashed into her last night washed over her again.

And as she watched them walk away, on to their life without her, for the first time in weeks, she couldn't wait to go back to the city.

CHAPTER TWENTY-TWO

HOW PATHETIC WAS HE, REJECTING Jemma and then showing up after school every day for a tiny glance? It hurt every time, so Wyatt wasn't sure why he couldn't stop doing it. He just needed to see that she was okay.

But he'd seen the hurt flicker through her eyes, so he was pretty sure he was doing more damage than good.

By Thursday afternoon, he'd decided he was done. No more thinking about Jemma. Okay, that was also impossible. But no more swinging by.

He was at the coffee shop today. April apologized for naming a drink after him and Jemma. She'd said Camilla had come in and demanded she change it, so the drink of the week was now a mint chocolate latte with a hint of coconut, called Mint to Be.

Which just reminded him of Jemma, anyway.

Because he wasn't indulging in seeing her for a few seconds after school anymore, he decided to get the stupid drink, and dang if it wasn't delicious. That made him wonder how the Wymma had tasted.

He knew what it felt like to *almost* be with Jemma. To be happier. For his skin to hum from her nearness, and how his heart went crazy at the lightest brush of her fingers. How he wished he could go back in time to the night she'd hugged him so he could hold her in his arms and memorize what it felt like so he could torture himself with that as well.

How had she gotten past every one of his barriers so quickly and so easily?

Man, what a sappy sentimental fool he was turning into.

"Everything okay?" April asked, and he wasn't sure he liked the discerning arch of her brow, as if she could figure out what was wrong with him, so why couldn't he?

"Yep. Just fine." He lifted his drink. "This is real good, by the way. Guess I should try the drink of the week more often."

"Thank you. And I think trying new things, being open to possibilities that could make you happier in general, is good for you."

They gawked at each other, neither backing down.

Then the blessed chime of the door broke off their staring contest. Lainey Townsend came in, laptop bag over one shoulder, a leashed goat by her side.

Wait. What? Wyatt did a double take. He'd seen a lot of crazy things in this town, but a leashed, pajama-wearing baby goat in the coffee shop was a new one.

His surprise must've shown, because Lainey said, "He's my service goat."

He lowered his eyebrows. He'd heard about people taking all sorts of animals on planes under the guise of service animals—and he was sure some were legit—but goat was a new one.

Lainey lightly punched his shoulder. "Just kidding, Wyatt. He's just the needy runt of the litter, and the last time I left him at home, he ate half my grandma's afghan as well as one of her hearing aids. I've got to get some work done before I take him to the clinic so Dempsey can give him a checkup, and April was nice enough to agree to let me bring him in for a bit."

April rounded the corner and squatted down in front of the goat. "Look at you, little cutie. Do you eat things you're not supposed to? Huh?"

It bleated and nibbled on the string of her apron.

Under other circumstances, he'd laugh or at least smile, but he couldn't help thinking Jemma should see this, and how much he wanted to tell her about it, and then all he felt was empty.

I've gotta get out of here before I end up having a breakdown where I sit at a table and pour my heart out to a busybody coffee shop owner, my neighbor, and a freaking goat.

He called out a farewell and hightailed it home.

Later that day, after taking care of some of the ranch chores, he walked into the house and glanced at Bailey Rae, seated at the table, homework out in front of her. Her legs were swinging, much like Jemma's did whenever she sat down.

His daughter lifted her head and gave him an exasperated look. She'd been doing that a lot, not telling him why, but he had a sneaking suspicion she was wondering why he was too dense to follow her cupid plan.

He wanted to tell her he was trying to protect her, but he couldn't, because he never wanted her to feel like *she* was responsible for people leaving. For relationships that didn't work out.

Her swinging legs stopped, and she tilted her head. "Hey, Dad?"

Instinctively he could tell he wasn't going to like what came next—something in her tone. So he took a deep breath to steel himself and asked, "What?"

"How 'bout we invite Jemma over for dinner? Or we can

go over there. I'd like to pet Señor Fluffypants without everyone else crowding me. Ooh, and I bet she'd show me all the shoes and purses she has in her closet."

A deep, breath-robbing ache radiated through his chest. "I'm sure she's busy."

"But how can you be sure if you don't call and ask?"

He infused his voice with decisiveness. "I just know."

Bailey frowned at him, as if he must be exceedingly dense, and honestly, he was wondering himself. "How about I call?"

Evidently he hadn't done a good enough job of using his stern dad voice. "How about you do your homework?"

"I can call her and ask about my homework. Good idea." Bailey Rae reached for the phone.

"Bailes, put the phone down. Come unload the dishwasher so I can start dinner."

"I thought you wanted me to do my homework."

She'd never been a bad kid. Sure, every now and again he had to remind her to do her chores or nudge a little, but she hadn't talked back like this before, either. This time he didn't hold back. He gave her the dad glare, no wiggle room. "Sounds like you want to be grounded."

With an epic sigh, she hauled herself out of the chair and sulkily stormed into the kitchen. The plates and cups rattled as she pulled open the dishwasher, and with the way she was slamming down bowls and banging the cupboard doors, he'd be surprised if the dishes and the house survived.

To be honest, he kind of wished he didn't have to be the adult and he could slam a few doors too.

Once the dishwasher was empty, his daughter turned to him. The frustration lingered in her big brown eyes and the set of her jaw, but there was a hint of sorrow that yanked at his heartstrings.

"Why won't you talk to Jemma anymore?" she asked.

He scrubbed a hand over his face. "You're too young to understand."

"Young doesn't have anything to do with understanding. Plus, I'm really smart."

Wyatt exhaled and squatted in front of his daughter. "You are. Smartest girl I know. It's just complicated, baby girl. Jemma doesn't live here."

"I know. She lives next door."

Naturally his daughter couldn't make this easy on him. "She's only in Haven Lake temporarily. She's going to head back to the city soon."

"Maybe she wouldn't, though, if she had a reason to stay."

For a short while maybe, but his life would never be enough to keep her happy long-term. "Once you're an adult, you have a lot of responsibilities. Jemma also wants to work in school administration, and I don't wanna ask her to give up on a job she's been working for and dreaming of. I just need you to understand that she cares about you, and I care about you. Neither of those things will ever change, no matter what happens. Okay?"

His daughter's bottom lip quivered, but she lifted her chin and nodded.

He pulled her into his arms, his heart aching right along with hers. Hugs had been getting shorter as she got older, but this time she fully wrapped her arms around him and squeezed for all she was worth.

Snippets from his daughter's life flashed through his head, of her first steps and her first words. How after Andrea had left, he'd go to drop her off for first grade, and she'd extend her arms for him and cry. It was all he could do to force himself to leave her there, and it took a whole month until she'd stopped crying.

There were years when she'd had to come along with him

everywhere, making work twice as long. But she'd learned what it took to take care of the animals and the land, and when he'd been able to teach her to string and fire the bow he'd had when he was younger, they'd begun connecting more, differing hobbies notwithstanding.

She was his whole world.

He'd do anything to keep her from experiencing heart-break again. He realized that wasn't totally possible, unfortunately, but he'd do everything he could for as long as he could.

Even if it meant experiencing his own heart breaking as Jemma Monroe left town for good.

"You would've been so proud," Jemma said to Randa, who'd called to check in. The tech gods must've felt sorry for her, because FaceTime was actually working, allowing her to see her best friend's face. It did make it a bit harder not to burst into tears, but she'd still take it.

"I got up the courage to tell Wyatt how I felt, and I just put it out there. I told him I wanted to be more than friends." Her voice broke and she gave a super attractive sniff. "Of course, since he didn't feel the same way, I sort of wish I would've kept on being a coward."

Randa gave her a sympathetic look. "Oh, hon." She softened her voice. "At least now you know."

Jemma would like to agree, but part of her would've rather gone on living in Delusionland, where she, Wyatt, and Bailey could keep on acting like a happy family.

The image onscreen wobbled as Randa set her phone on her bathroom counter and pulled her long blond hair into a ponytail. "What exactly did he say?"

The grief she'd barely kept at bay spilled over. "That he couldn't give me what I wanted and that it wasn't going to work out. Basically, he was trying to nicely say he only wanted to be friends. You'd think I'd learn." Fresh pain wrenched her already-beat-up heart. "Maybe I'm destined to only ever be the buddy."

"That's not true. I could hear how much you liked him, though, and I'm sorry it didn't work out."

Señor Fluffypants nudged Jemma's hand, as if he saw she was sad and wanted to comfort her. Most likely he just wanted carrots, but she liked her version better, so she picked him up and snuggled him close. "And now I need a job again."

Randa grabbed her phone, and the screen went a bit jumbly again as she started down the stairs to her apartment. "Do you want me to poke around?"

The downer side wanted to say, *why bother?* They'd already poked around a couple of months ago. "If you hear of anything, let me know. At least I'll have my Masters in May. That should help." Lately she'd been reconsidering how much she wanted a job in administration, mostly when she contemplated not being in the classroom anymore. Regardless, her degree would help her move up a tier when it came to qualifications and being a more desirable candidate.

"It will. For sure. And at least we have something to celebrate—soon you'll be back living here by me so we can hang out."

During her first couple of weeks in Haven Lake, all she could do was compare the country to the city and think of everything she missed. Now she felt the same way but reversed. The idea of never going into the coffee shop, country dancing with Camilla and her co-workers—of not being around when Dorothy burst into her glass-shattering soprano in the middle of a conversation—sliced and stung.

How could she go about her life without so many of the familiar faces she'd grown to love?

Leaving her students was also going to be impossibly hard. She wasn't sure she could say goodbye to Bailey without bursting into tears, and she was supposed to be a grownup, not go around upsetting the children.

But they're not your students. You were just borrowing them for a while.

She sniffed again.

"I wish I could reach through the phone and hug you," Randa said, settling on to the couch in her apartment with a spoon and a carton of ice cream.

"Me too." Jemma did miss her friend something fierce, so she was going to attempt to go the silver-lining route and focus on how soon she'd be back home and this would be a fond memory she occasionally recalled.

Ah, remember how I lived in the country for a couple of months? How the roads weren't plowed and I became half of a drink in the coffee shop and a horse knocked on my door?

How I spent time with a cowboy and his adorable daughter and fell in love.

Misery gushed from the hole in her heart. Maybe she'd skip recalling that last part. And how could she have let herself fall in love?

But she knew she had, her efforts to take it slow fruitless.

This adventure had ended up being as hazardous as her dictionary had warned it'd be.

She just had to get through the Valentine's Day play, and then she could focus on the next step in her tumultuous life.

CHAPTER TWENTY-THREE

S LOW, DEEP BREATHS HELPED JEMMA stay on the edge of hyperventilating instead of giving in to it. She shouldn't be so nervous. The kids were the ones who had to be out on stage. But she'd helped organize the entire event, and soon, most of the townsfolk would pour through the double doors of the gym.

Soon, Wyatt Langford would come through those doors.

No matter how much she fortified herself, it was going to hurt. But at least she had something else to cling on to. Randa had called her earlier today with good news.

Great news, actually, and she knew she'd feel more happiness about it once the curtain closed on this whole production.

"Jemma?"

She spun toward Camilla and threw her arms around her, nearly knocking her tiny friend right over.

The principal's surprise only lasted a second or two, then she hugged her back. "What's this for?"

"Everything."

"All-encompassing. I like it."

Jemma laughed. "For giving me a shot and taking me in and all your help. Most of all, for your friendship."

Camilla's forehead puckered as she pulled back. "Why do you sound like you're saying goodbye?"

"I..." Jemma propped a smile on her lips. "Well, it's not quite goodbye. More of a precursor."

The bafflement in Camilla's expression only grew. "How about you tell me like you'd tell your students, because I'm lost. And a pinch worried."

A shallow sip of oxygen helped clear Jemma's head. "Mrs. Lau is due to come back at the end of the month, right?"

Camilla nodded. "Yes, but with a newborn, she'll probably need a substitute here and there, and I'm working on finding you a spot."

Jemma grabbed her friend's hand. "I appreciate that, Camilla, I do. But a friend back home called me this morning to tell me there's an opening at the district office—the same district I used to teach in. They promoted an administrator I used to work with, and since she's in charge of filling her old spot, she told me that if I want the job, it's mine. They'd have me start training the first week of March so I could help with summer school."

"What did you just say?" another voice asked, one with an edge of bewilderment and dismay.

Jemma spun around to see April holding three stacked gallon buckets filled with pink liquid. Great. Now that she'd overheard, the entire town would soon find out.

She supposed tonight she'd just cut them off at the pass and announce it at the end of the play. Then she'd get it over in one fell swoop.

"But you can't leave," April said. "What about Wyatt?"

That relentless twinge in her chest throbbed to life again. "What about him? He just wants to be friends. He made that very clear."

"*Pfft!*" April set the buckets on the white tablecloth with red and pink hearts. "I don't believe it. He came into the shop the other day and he looked completely miserable."

A sliver of hope rose, but then she remembered it'd only stab her in the heart later. She'd given up a job for a *what-if* before, and she vowed to never do it again. "I can't stay here to become unemployed, all so I can be friends with my neighbor, miserable or not."

Maybe he did care. She wished it was enough, but she'd already flung her entire heart at his feet, and he'd stomped on it. She couldn't just go back to being buddies, even if nights spent with him and Bailey would almost be enough.

Almost.

"But maybe if you told him how you genuinely feel about him," April tried, and Camilla winced. She'd heard the story already, but Jemma supposed the coffee shop owner wouldn't give up until she'd gotten the full scoop as well.

"I did." Jemma was proud at how steady it came out sounding, especially considering the way everything inside of her was crumbling. "I told him I wanted to be more than friends."

"Sometimes guys can be really dense. Are you sure he understood?"

Tears blurred the two women for a moment before Jemma blinked them away. "I'm sure. I poured out my heart, and it wasn't enough."

April shook her head and then pulled Jemma into a hug. "That boy's clearly lost his marbles. I have half a mind to call up his mother and tell her he's being an idiot. Maybe she can fly here and straighten him up."

Jemma could only imagine that weird phone call. April would call; of that, she had no doubt. "That's not necessary. I was just telling Camilla that I have another job lined up. I'll miss you all, but I can't stay here, living so close to him and…" Her voice broke—right when she was being so tough too. "I can't."

Both women gave her understanding smiles.

Jemma wiped at her eyes. "We so don't have time for this. 'The show must go on' and all that. April, need help carrying in punch?"

"That'd be nice."

They went out to the parking lot, grabbed nine more gallons out of her trunk, and set them up behind the table. They took cups and napkins with arrow-shooting cupids out of their wrappers and arranged them on the table.

Then Jemma pulled out her phone checked the time.

In a few minutes, her students would show up, and they'd let in the parents and the rest of the community about twenty minutes after that.

Dorothy Hembolt was on the piano next to the stage, tuning it and playing snippets of the songs. The words automatically went through Jemma's head—at this point, they'd been so seared into her mind she'd be able to sing them until she was Dorothy's age.

A grunt escaped as Jemma hefted the giant crystal punch bowl and set it on the center of the table. April poured the frothy pink punch into the bowl. Jemma was about to ask if it had a special name, but before she got out the question, the side door opened, and Chase and Bailey came inside.

"Look, Miss Monroe!" Chase rushed over, looking dapper in black pants, red suspenders, and a black fedora. He yanked the suspenders away from his body and let them snap back.

"Wow, Chase. I'm so used to the cowboy hat that I almost didn't recognize you!"

He huffed, his whole body getting in on it. "I asked my mom if I could wear it, but she said no, it didn't match the outfit or my part."

"Well, the fedora looks sharp," Jemma said. "If I were Cupid, and I'd gone crazy, I'd want you on my side."

He grinned and turned to Bailey. "Come on, Ba-Rae. Let's go find your bow and arrow and shoot—" His eyes went wide, and he grimaced. "I mean…we're just gonna…look at it. Yeah, that's it."

After taking a second to make sure she wouldn't accidentally laugh like she wanted to, Jemma affected her best teacher voice. "No shooting anyone before the play. Got it?"

He nodded and waved an arm for Bailey to come on already.

But she shook her head and motioned for him to go ahead. With a shrug, he rushed toward the stage.

Jemma made sure Mrs. Hembolt was aware of him—the woman gathered him and the few other students who were streaming in the other door and ushered them backstage—so at least everyone was being supervised.

When Jemma turned around, Bailey was still standing next to her. She was wearing her pink leotard with the flowy skirt, and she had on white wings, a pink glittery heart necklace, and matching earrings.

"Hey, Miss Monroe," she said. The usual cheeriness was missing from her voice and demeanor. Despite the heart regalia, her pink lips formed a somber line, her hanging head making her look more like one of those melancholy weeping angels than the god of love.

Jemma secured the skirt of her red wrap dress to her thighs before squatting. "What's wrong, sweetheart? Are you nervous?"

"A little bit, but that's not what's wrong. I just…" She shrugged her slim shoulders, the feathery wings moving with the motion. "I'm not a very good Cupid."

"I disagree. I've seen you as Cupid, and whenever I watch you up on that stage, I think you were born to play that role."

She let out a sigh that seemed to weigh about a hundred pounds for as long as it went on. "I had all these plans and…" She sighed again, and her lower lip came out in a pout.

Jemma couldn't help but sympathize. Her plans hadn't worked out, either. First when she'd been laid off and ended up here, and then after she'd fallen in love with a guy, with the town, and with the amazing girl in front of her. "I wish I could tell you that plans always work out, but they don't, even when you really, *really* try."

"I did. I tried so hard. And I thought it was working."

I so feel you.

Jemma wasn't sure if the girl was talking about Chase or about her and Wyatt. Maybe she was simply projecting. "You have to decide if it's worth trying harder or looking at things a different way. If other people are involved, sometimes the only thing you can choose is your attitude. How you deal with it."

"But how can I be Cupid if I can't make people fall in love?"

"There are different types of love. Like in the play. It's about kindness and treating each other with respect and love, regardless of how well we know them."

Bailey scuffed her glittery pink boot against the gym floor. "I guess. I just wish I could choose the kind of love."

"Don't we all," Jemma muttered before reining herself in. Her thighs were burning and with the main doors set to open in ten minutes, she needed to get backstage to help Mrs. Hembolt keep everyone under control. "We'd better go get in place."

Jemma straightened and glanced over Bailey's head at April. "You set?"

"All set. Hey, before you go, can you try the punch really quickly? I'm not sure if I need to add more Sprite." She winked at Bailey, who cracked a smile, albeit a weaker than usual one.

Jemma took the plastic cup April extended and tipped it back. The slushy raspberry mixture burst across her tongue and appeased her sweet tooth. "Tastes perfect to me."

"Oh, phew."

Jemma tossed the cup in the large trashcan next to the table. "What's this one called anyway?"

A smile spread across April's face. "Since it's Valentines, I figured it's only fitting to serve up love potion."

Wyatt settled into one of the fold-out chairs, three rows back from the stage. Normally he'd hang near the very back, but Bailey Rae was one of the leads and was putting his archery lessons to good use, so he wanted to catch every second.

If only he could cut out the seconds when he'd have to see Jemma. Even as he craved seeing her, it'd only be torture. That ache would throb over the spot where his heart was, digging its claws in when he saw her and reminding him of the pain.

He kept trying to tell himself it was for the best, so why did it feel so wrong?

Think of Bailey Rae. Think of how much more it'll hurt if we get closer, only for Jemma to leave.

Speaking of, his daughter poked her head out from behind the curtains. She searched the crowd, and when she neared his area, he lifted his hand.

She waved, nice and big, and a few of the people in the

audience chuckled. She twisted to talk to someone standing behind the curtains.

A flash of red dress. Dark hair. Those same black boots he'd shaken his head over the first time he'd seen them. *Jemma.*

Now he wanted to see her face, despite of how much it'd hurt.

Man, what's wrong with me?

He didn't remember being this messed up in the head, even when Andrea had told him she couldn't take it anymore. She'd been distant, both with him and Bailey Rae, so it'd more clicked the last puzzle piece into place. He'd suggested counseling, but she'd shaken her head, a desperate gleam in her eye.

The need to escape had been so strong, it'd choked the room.

He hadn't been all that surprised, but he supposed it was adding to the chaos in his brain.

A white-winged angel—make that Cupid—bound down the steps of the stage, her wings flapping in her self-propelled wind.

He scrunched up his forehead, worry rising up. Bailey Rae had spent hours memorizing her lines, and she'd seemed okay before they'd left the house this evening. Though still slightly annoyed at him for not asking Jemma to come over after she'd suggested it Thursday night. And Friday night.

She'd probably suggest it after the play too.

Bailey Rae streaked past him, a blur of pink and white. She walked over to the table with the punch. April leaned over as his daughter explained something to her, arms swinging.

The coffee shop owner nodded and smiled, and then filled a cup.

Maybe she's just really thirsty…

She gripped the cup, walking carefully down the aisle before stopping right in front of him. "Hey, Daddy. Can you drink this?"

"Why aren't you backstage? Isn't the play about to start?"

"It is." Some of the punch sloshed onto the toe of his boot as she pushed it toward him. "That's why I need you to drink this."

The refreshment table was for people to visit *after* the play, so he felt like everyone was staring at him, wondering why *he* got punch.

"Please just drink it," his daughter said, anxiety rolling off her in waves as she thrust the cup closer to his face and glanced over her shoulder at the stage.

The *please* did him in. He grabbed the cup and tipped it back. When he lowered his head, Bailey Rae gave him a giant grin, one he hadn't seen in a few days.

"Okay, now you have to throw the cup away, because I have a play to put on." With that, she raced up the steps of the stage and disappeared behind the thick blue curtain.

The lights in the gym faded, and the glow from the red bulbs overhead tinged the stage pink. It was impossible not to think of that moment when he'd been showing Jemma how to work the control box. She'd been so close and had smelled so incredible, and he'd leaned in, lost to the pull.

Two more seconds alone, and he would've kissed her.

It was getting harder and harder to convince himself that he shouldn't have. After all, if she was going to leave, he should've kissed her while he'd had the chance.

It'd only make you miss her that much more.

As if that was even possible.

Every reason for staying away was coming undone, making him think maybe he was just being a clueless idiot.

How often did a woman like Jemma come along?

Only once, that was how often. Kind, funny, and smart—as well as willing to put up with him—wasn't an easy combo to find. He'd never find anyone who challenged yet calmed him the way she did.

Jemma stepped onto the stage, microphone in hand, and a spotlight flicked on, emphasizing how gorgeous she was and making the rest of the room disappear.

The realization that he loved her slammed into him, so strongly he couldn't believe he hadn't already known. Perhaps because he'd been in denial since the day she'd told him she wanted to be more than friends.

He peered down at the empty cup in his hands. If he didn't know any better, he'd think the punch had been filled with some kind of truth serum.

CHAPTER TWENTY-FOUR

T HE AUDIENCE LAUGHED AS CUPID hit the wrong
person. Bailey fired again and hit another passerby.

Still not Brody or Sydney, the people she'd originally been aiming for.

Cupid yanked back the bow for another shot.

Like with the other arrows, it hit another one of the students, missing its mark completely.

Bailey's eyes widened with horror, and she gently flung her bow to the ground and stomped a foot. "It's Valentine's Day, and I've lost my aim!" She threw her hands up over her face, exasperation rolling off her in waves—she was such a good little actress that Jemma felt it, and she was sure the audience could as well. "This entire holiday is going to be ruined. What am I going to do?"

"Okay, guys," Jemma whispered to the kids who were backstage in a group next to her, "go out and line up for the musical number."

The kids filtered out onto the stage. They were dressed up in a variety of dressy clothes, and they all looked so cute and nice, and sigh…

Mrs. Hembolt lifted her arms, her conducting baton in one hand, and as she brought it down, the kids began their song—*almost* at the same time, although there were always a few early and a couple stragglers.

They sang a version of "Stupid Cupid" called "Crazy Cupid." Jemma leaned against the archway, pride filling her. She could tell Mrs. Hembolt was trying hard not to sing along and drown out the students.

The song ended, and a couple of kids tried to go the wrong way before Mrs. Hembolt herded them back toward Jemma, who encouraged them to hurry so they could start the next scene.

Bailey remained on stage, along with Chase, the business-man with a proposition for Cupid.

He told her he'd help her complete her mission in ex-change for her allowing him to shoot an arrow at the person he had a crush on.

At the beginning of Jemma's time here, Chase's thick country drawl had made it hard to understand every word he said, but now she could hear through it.

Despite telling herself not to look, it was as if her eyes couldn't help it. They scanned the crowd and landed on Wyatt.

The fissure that'd formed in her heart shuddered and split deeper, the ache from it spreading throughout her entire body. If only she were a rich businessman who could make a deal with Cupid.

Except, she wanted Wyatt to like her for her, not because an arrow had struck him.

He held his head high, happiness radiating from his fea-tures as he watched his daughter's performance. Of course it had to go and make him all the more handsome and loveable.

When Bailey had told her she had an emergency and needed to tell her dad something two minutes before the play was about to start, she'd whispered for her to go ahead, but to hurry. Then she'd turned to retie one of her student's neckties. Since Bailey had come rushing backstage, out of breath but flashing a thumbs up, Jemma had figured the emergency had been taken care of.

Onstage, Cupid reluctantly handed Mr. Businessman the bow.

Just like the god of love, his arrow missed its intended target, and soon the entire stage was filled with kids who'd been hit by Cupid's arrows.

The few students not onstage went out, and they sang another song, a twist on "The Witch Doctor." They called Cupid, and she told them what to do. Which was basically a whole lot of nonsense words. The witch doctor—or Cupid, as it were—definitely got that part right. Love was rather nonsensical.

Otherwise she wouldn't keep crushing on unattainable guys who didn't like her back.

She wouldn't end up falling completely in love with the single-father who lived next door.

But like the people onstage who found themselves spreading love and kindness, she'd found friendship and graciousness and goodwill and so many things that made life great, even when it didn't go as planned.

As the kindness spread throughout the people who'd been shot, the lights glowed brighter, yellow and sunny.

Kids stepped forward to give their parts about kindness and love, quoting people like Martin Luther King Jr., Audrey Hepburn, Ralph Waldo Emerson, the Dalai Lama, Mark Twain, and Anne Frank.

Her third-graders—people in the village—began working together instead of arguing about everything. They sang a happy song about teamwork and showing kindness and love.

As they began the last verse, tears sprang to Jemma's eyes.

She was so proud of them all, but it also hit her that this was her last big production with these amazing kids. That she'd have to say goodbye.

Fingers squeezed her hand, and she turned to see Camilla. "This is the best Valentine's Day play we've ever had."

"I think you're just trying to butter me up."

Camilla laughed. "Maybe *un poquito*, but I'm also telling the truth. Although you haven't been here long, you've made a big impact."

A giant lump formed in her throat, and it seemed to be trying to push out more tears.

"Just so you know, Anna Lau is also in the audience." Camilla gave her hand another squeeze. "She said she wasn't sure she was ready to come back quite yet. I think she'd like to take the rest of the semester off."

Jemma exhaled a shallow, shaky breath. "Camilla, I…I just can't. There are way too many variables and maybes. The district job starts March first. I can't stay here for maybes, and more than that…" Her gaze drifted to the still-beaming father in the third row, the one she'd fallen in love with. "It hurts too much. It's not good for me, and I'm learning from my past mistakes."

Her friend nodded and gave her a sad smile. "I understand. If you're sure."

Was anyone ever sure about anything? Jemma was sure about it being too painful, though. She had to go back home and try to repair her heart. So she gave one sharp nod and managed to blink away her tears.

No more crying.

This was a happy celebration of her time here.

The kids filtered off the stage, except for Cupid and the businessman.

"Well, that didn't go the way I expected, but maybe all

those misses actually hit the people they were supposed to," Bailey said.

"That's what I do," Chase said, adding a swagger, and the audience laughed. He grinned bigger, fueled by the reaction. "I also have to admit something. I need one more arrow."

Cupid's forehead wrinkled. She slowly took her last heart arrow out of her quiver and extended it to him. You could see the longing on her face. While Bailey was an excellent actress, it didn't hurt that she and Chase were friends with real crushes on each other.

At first Jemma had worried it was only one-sided, but this week, it'd become rather clear Chase liked her back. Not only did his eyes search her out the instant he stepped into any room she was in, he also shared his cupcake with her at lunch, and boys didn't go giving up half their dessert for anyone.

Chase took the last arrow, turned the pointy tip of the heart toward Bailey, and slipped it between her side and arm so it looked like it went through.

Bailey threw her hand over her heart. Then she said, "Silly businessman. I already love you."

They clasped hands and turned to the audience, who cheered.

They bowed, and the rest of the kids headed onstage for the last musical number.

Her students sang their little hearts out, and at the end of the song, they bowed while the audience cheered, just as loudly as they had at the basketball game.

Camilla gave Jemma a quick side hug before grabbing the microphone and flipping the switch on the bottom of it. She tapped the top to ensure it was on and walked to the center of the stage. "Wasn't that amazing? Our third graders have worked so hard, and it was so fun to see it all come together. Let's give them another round of applause."

The audience did as asked, and then Camilla said, "So much work goes into school productions, and we couldn't have done it without Mrs. Hembolt, our music teacher."

Dorothy stepped onto the stage and did a dramatic curt-sey bow.

"And Jemma Monroe, who accepted this job filling in for Mrs. Anna Lau. I sort of forgot to mention in the interview that she'd be partially in charge of the play."

Chuckles went through the audience.

"But she took it on and did such a fabulous job. Miss Monroe, can you join me onstage?"

Ordinarily, this kind of thing would only make her a smidge nervous. As she stepped onto the stage, the bright lights making her squint, a swarm of nervous bees buzzed in her belly. It was more than being in front of a crowd. It was *this* crowd and what she was going to say to them.

Jemma's hand trembled as she took the extended micro-phone. "Thank you all so much for coming and supporting our play. Mrs. Hembolt honestly did most of the hard work. But we've had a lot of help from the staff. Thanks to the parents and the community for building props and making signs, helping kids memorize lines, and everything you do to support the school. Huge shoutout to April from Havenly Brew for providing the drinks tonight. And last but not least…"

Her throat tightened to the painful point as she glanced at her students. Bittersweet emotions and memories flickered, making it harder to get through her mini-speech.

"You kiddos did amazing. I'm so, so proud of you."

Tears rose. Not only would she miss them, she was think-ing of how much she enjoyed the myriad personalities and the group dynamic. It allowed her to get to know the kids on a more personal level, and she wondered if she couldn't do more good in the classroom.

In administration, she wouldn't have that same chance to deal with the students on a more individual basis nearly as much. *That ship's sailed. You've got to stay the course, or you'll end up shipwrecked with nowhere to go.*

If she looked at her students any longer, she'd never be able to get out the rest, so she stared directly into the bright lights, embracing the way they blurred everything else into a dark smear.

Deep breath in.

Long breath out.

"Admittedly, when I got the job offer to come fill in for Mrs. Anna Lau's maternity leave, I'd never heard of Haven Lake."

The smile that spread across her face was genuine, but in some ways, it felt like another version of her smiling. "On my first week here, a horse knocked on my door, I got stuck in the snow because I wasn't used to unplowed roads, and a snake came out of one of the ceiling vents in my classroom. Let's just say I was sort of worried I wouldn't survive another week."

The audience chortled, and her gaze accidentally dipped, right to the guy who'd shown up to get his escape-artist horse. The guy who'd dug her out of the snow. The guy who'd taught her to build a fire, cleaned her chimney, and had been part of some of the best nights of her life.

Jemma glanced at the boy who'd helped her with the snake. To the spirited girl at his side, the one she'd loved from the moment she'd slid inside the cab of the pickup truck and they'd started talking outfits. Every single one of her students owned a piece of her heart, but she'd given more of it to Bailey Rae and her daddy. She'd seen the glimpse of what a cozy family could be like. No more loneliness. A sense of fulfillment she hadn't realized she'd been missing.

A hush had fallen over the audience, save for a few rambunctious toddlers, and Jemma shook herself out of her daze. She was in front of a crowd of people.

Don't fall apart now. You can do that later, when you get back to the cottage.

Who was she kidding? It'd happen the instant she climbed into her car.

She cleared her throat. "Now I can't imagine not having the chance to come to this beautiful little town where people are kind and helpful, and accepted me right away, crazy shoes and all." To her dismay, her voice broke, and she exhaled, exhaled, exhaled. "Which is why I'm going to miss you all so much."

Tears burned her eyes and blurred the faces peering up at her. She wished being unable to distinguish features made this easier, but it wasn't. "I'm taking an administration job at the district office back in the city, but I wanted to take this opportunity to thank you all. To tell you how much I'll miss everyone."

Jemma spun to her class, and a warm tear slipped down her cheek. "Especially you guys. Thank you for letting me be your teacher for a while."

"No," Bailey said, stepping toward her, and Jemma knew she was going to lose the grip on her emotions.

"So everyone enjoy the punch and cookies, and thanks again." She thrust the microphone at Camilla's hands and practically sprinted off the stage.

The curtains closed, and the students drifted over to Jemma.

Several of them asked if this was their last chance to say

goodbye, and she stooped to their level and assured them she'd be at school to finish up her last week. Then she encouraged them to go find their parents and get refreshments.

Chase paused in front of her and patted her shoulder. "You're a pretty good teacher. Even if you're scared of snakes."

Jemma half laughed, half sobbed. "Everyone has their weaknesses. Chase, I want you to remember that you're a good kid. You're smart and funny and you care about people, which is so important in this world right now. Make sure to take care of your next teacher as well as you've taken care of me."

"Yes, ma'am," he said, and then he was off and down the stairs, tromp-tromping all the way.

Then Bailey was the only one left, her Cupid wings making her look even more angelic than usual. "Why do you have to go?" she asked, tears filling her big brown eyes.

The dam keeping Jemma from crying cracked as she lost hold of her emotions.

"I was only here temporarily, filling in for Mrs. Lau. Now I have to go back home."

"Can't you be her helper? Or just, like, help all the teachers—I bet they could all use some help."

"I'm sorry, sweetheart, but it doesn't work that way. At one time, I thought maybe…" That train of thought wouldn't help either one of them, so she backtracked. "I have another job lined up, and it starts in two weeks."

"But what if you had a reason to stay? I thought you and my dad…" Bailey's lower lip quivered and she sucked in a shuddered breath. "Don't you like each other?"

Jemma's heart knotted so soundly she wasn't sure it would ever beat right again. "I'm very fond of your father. And of you." She cupped Bailey's cheek and used her thumb to wipe away her tears. "I'll always remember movie nights and s'mores and seeing a brand-new baby cow. I'll never forget my time here." She locked eyes with her. "Never forget you."

Bailey flung her arms around her neck, and Jemma hugged her tightly, taking a moment to soak in the love of this amazing little girl.

"You'd better get out there and grab some punch," Jemma said.

"Why bother?" Defeat hung heavy in her voice, and she was scowling when she pulled back. "It's supposed to be love potion, but it doesn't even work."

Love potion. Perfect for Valentine's Day, yet not so great for hopeful kids and adults who wanted it to work magic. But hey, at least it didn't have part of Jemma's name in it.

She nudged Bailey in the direction the stairs. "I'll see you on Monday."

With a huff, Bailey finally walked off the stage, tromping down the stairs as loudly as Chase had.

After taking a couple of deep breaths that didn't do much to stifle her urge to cry, Jemma quietly crept down the stairs. She went to poke her head out as Camilla stuck her head around the corner, and they nearly bumped heads.

"I was just coming to check on you," Camilla said. Her face dropped as she took in what Jemma was sure were tear-stained cheeks, possibly complete with streaks of runaway mascara.

"I'm fine. If fine means that I'm about to burst into tears." Jemma glanced around the principle at the people milling around the gym. Most of them had a plastic cup of pink punch in their hands as they stood around chatting with one another.

Jemma should probably go out and personally thank everyone, but she spotted a familiar tan hat in the crowd, and she just couldn't face Wyatt right now. "I'm going to go. I can come back in about thirty minutes to clean up if you nee—"

"Don't worry about it." Camilla gave her a consoling smile. "But if you need a friend, you call me."

Jemma swiped at her cheeks. "Okay."

"Actually, I know you won't call, so I'm going to call you."

Jemma laughed and sniffed. "Thank you." She hugged Camilla, who then pointed to the side door.

"It's unlocked. I'll cover you."

Ducking her head, Jemma rushed over to the exit, cursing the loud clacking of her heels. Without meaning to, she glanced toward the crowd as she pulled open the door, a sort of farewell to these quaint events that the entire town showed up for, whether or not they had a kid in the play. Although most of them were most likely related somehow.

Her last look was a mistake.

Steady, hazel eyes were leveled on her. Wyatt didn't smile, didn't make any expression. Just stared.

Her mangled heart tried to beat, but it was more of a splat. She yanked open the door and for once, she blessed the frigid cold. It stung her skin and helped her focus on that instead of the way her heart was cracking, the split spreading deep and wide as she walked away from the guy she loved.

CHAPTER TWENTY-FIVE

WYATT STARED AT THE SIDE door of the gym, unable to look away for several seconds after Jemma had fled out of it.

Fled was the only word for it. Just like he knew she would. Not so much leaving the play but leaving town.

Her words echoed through his head again and again: *I'm taking an administration job at the district office back in the city, but I wanted to take this opportunity to thank you all. To tell you how much I'll miss everyone.*

A gaping, hollow hole had formed in his chest, and it felt emptier and wider after she'd walked out that door. No one would miss her more than he would.

Well, except maybe Bailey Rae.

It was impossible to avoid thinking about Jemma leaving too, since everyone kept talking about what a shame it was to lose such a good teacher and how much they liked having Jemma Monroe in their town.

Later that night, Wyatt might lie in bed and think of all the what-might've-beens, but right now he needed to focus on his daughter. She was inordinately quiet as she stood next to him, not shoving cookie after cookie in her mouth like she typically would, but nibbling on one with a sad expression that echoed through him.

"You were great up there, Miss Cupid," he said. "To know how to aim well enough to miss on purpose takes real skill."

His daughter shrugged, making her wings flutter.

"You were funny too. Did you want me to grab you some punch?"

Bailey Rae sighed, her irritation and sorrow coming through loud and clear. "It's love potion, but it's stupid and defective and ugh."

"Stupid, huh? Are you saying you wanted the drink to turn everyone into love-struck zombies?"

She lowered her cookie and peered up at him, her eyes narrowing. "Did you drink the cup I gave you? You know it won't actually turn you into a zombie, right?"

"I don't know. I'm craving—" he lifted his arms and made claws with his hands while letting his features go blank, "—braaaaaains."

Bailey's eyes remained annoyed slits, no hint of humor, although the people around him were giving him odd looks.

So much for attempting to lighten the mood. "I drank it, and I liked it a lot. You should try some."

Camilla stepped behind the table to help April fill a few more cups. He wanted to ask when Jemma's last day was, but at the same time, he didn't want to know. Part of him wondered why she couldn't get Jemma to stay—they were friends. She was the principal. Surely she could find her a job.

She'd still leave. She always wanted to go into admin. You knew that.

"Miss Bailey Rae, did you get some punch?" April asked.

She turned and scowled at her, a scowl usually only he got to witness—and most of the time, chores or cow or horse manure were involved.

The way April's eyebrows arched made it clear she was surprised.

"Come on, Bailes. Let's go home." He put his hand on her back between her shoulder blades, but she dragged her feet.

"Your love potion doesn't work," his daughter told April, and along with anger, tears were forming. She set her chin and stared at the coffee shop owner like she wanted an explanation.

"It's just supposed to be fun," April said softly. "Believe me, honey, I wished it worked as much as you did."

"Me too," Camilla muttered, and now she was glaring at him.

April added a glare of her own, and then his daughter aimed her scowl at him.

Great. Three women who were upset with him. Just what tonight needed to land this at the top of his crappy-nights list. Wasn't it bad enough that he was losing Jemma?

"Why am *I* getting the dirty looks? Jemma's the one leaving."

"Maybe she wouldn't if you told her how you feel," Camilla said, throwing her arms up in exasperation.

"We can all see it," April added, placing a fist on her hip. "Don't tell me you're too dense to see it. Do I need to hold up a mirror so you can see the love-struck look on your face when anyone mentions Jemma's name?" She glanced around like she'd have a mirror at the ready, and he did his best not to flinch.

"We're going to lose an amazing teacher." Camilla took a step closer. "An amazing friend."

His heart thumped harder in his chest, and he figured there wasn't any reason to hold back the fact that yes, he did like Jemma. "Look, I wish things were different as well, but she wants to go into administration. She loves the city. Those are things she's made clear several times."

"But Daddy," Bailey Rae said, tugging on the sleeve of his shirt, "didn't you hear the part about how much she likes the town and the people here? She said she was going to miss us, but if she stayed, she wouldn't *have* to miss us, and we wouldn't have to miss her."

April began filling more plastic cups with the frothy pink drink, but her movements were sharp and jerky. "Maybe I should make a new drink to name after you. It'd have eggs and the word 'chicken' in the title."

Wyatt cupped his hands over his daughter's ears before leaning closer to April and Camilla. "How dare you two get Bailey Rae's hopes up. I can handle disappointment, but she doesn't need any more of that in her life. That's why I was hesitant to get involved with Jemma in the first place."

"It's obvious that she loves Bailey too," Camilla said, leaning right back. "Jemma took a big risk, laid her heart on the line, and told you she cared about you. You shut her down. That's the reason she's rushing out of here. Mrs. Lau wants to take the rest of the semester off, but Jemma said it'd be too hard to have to see you all the time."

"That won't stop her from leaving someday, and I'd rather her do it now before we're that much more attached. I have to do what's best for my daughter."

Camilla crossed her arms. "Well, she thinks you should tell her how you feel."

"Another thing anyone can see," April muttered, and then she jerked her chin toward his daughter. "Ask her."

Wyatt glanced down. His hands had slipped the tiniest bit, and she peered up at him, a hopeful expression on her face. "How much of that did you hear?" he asked.

"All of it. The thick headband made it so your hands

didn't really cover my ears anyway. So, you just drive over to Jemma's, tell her you love her, and we can fix it. She can stay."

"Did she just mention Jemma?" Mrs. Hembolt appeared beside him. "I was shocked—*shocked, I tell you*—at her announcement. It's so hard to find good teachers these days. I've taught going on forty years, and she's a marvelous teacher, one this town doesn't want to lose. Did you not hear the song the kids sang?" She burst into song, her voice high enough he was surprised the punch bowl didn't shatter.

He couldn't follow all the words, but her voice and dance moves gleaned lots of attention, and soon people were either moving away or moving close. The gist was you should tell people you appreciate them and go out of your way to say you care.

"If anyone has ideas," Mrs. Hembolt said, waving the crowd closer, "we're trying to think of ways to keep Miss Monroe here in town. Most of them involve Wyatt opening his mouth and telling her how he feels about her."

Perfect. Now the entire town was going to tell him he was a fool to let her go. As if he didn't know. But would the townsfolk be there when she left on her own after the charm of small-town life wore off? Would they pick up the pieces? Help put Bailey Rae back together?

"Y'all do what you want. Come on, Bailey Rae. Let's go home." Wyatt grabbed her hand, but his daughter set her feet and refused to move, same way she'd done the first time he'd made an attempt to leave.

"Daddy, don't take this the wrong way, but you aren't the best at feelings. Or talking. But 'specially talking about feelings." Bailey Rae patted his hand. "Maybe you should listen to their ideas."

Frustration thrummed through his veins. He'd tried so hard to keep his daughter from getting too attached, from getting her hopes up. Now, everything was spiraling out of control, and while he loved this town, sometimes having everyone up in your business was exhausting and made him want to be the hermit who never came into town.

His social-butterfly daughter would never stand for it, much the way she was digging in her heels now.

Wyatt crouched down to be eye-to-eye with her. His annoyance faded as he peered into her perfect round face, so full of kindness and love and enough hope to make his breath catch. From her out-of-control blond curls to her big brown eyes to pink cheeks that popped out whenever she smiled, he loved every single inch of her. But the hint of sorrow on the face that brought him so much joy sent razor-sharp agony through his chest.

"Baby girl, I like Jemma. I like her a lot, and I know you do too. But it's not fair for us to ask her to give up her dreams for us."

Bailey Rae set her chin, her pink lips forming a tight line. "It's not fair that she told you how she felt and you didn't tell her."

"She makes a good point," April said, and Camilla, Mrs. Hembolt, and the other people who'd gathered nodded.

Bailey Rae glanced behind him and motioned someone else toward the melee. "Uncle Dempsey, can you help talk my dad into doing something about Jemma? He's just going to let her leave without telling her how much he cares about her."

Dempsey wove through the crowd and joined Wyatt and Bailey Rae's mini-huddle. "You should really do something, dude. I know you got burned, but what do you do when you get bucked off a horse?"

"End up with bruises and bumps," Wyatt said. "Limp for a day or two. Learn my lesson."

His best friend cocked his head in a light rebuke. "You learn and then you get back on and try again. Women like Jemma don't come around every day—especially not here in our little town—and we all want you to be happy. Everyone can see that you've been happier lately. That you care about her."

"That's exactly what I told him," April said. "Well, close enough," she added.

Dempsey put his hand on Wyatt's shoulder. "I'm afraid you'll regret it if you don't at least go and talk to her."

Wyatt tuned everyone else out, because this was about his daughter. And okay, about him, too. He cleared his throat and returned his gaze to Bailey Rae. "For the record, I did talk to her. I told her I couldn't give her what she wanted, which is true. Our home is here. We're not ever going to live in the city, and jobs in administration are extra hard to come by 'round these parts. Besides, life's not—"

"You can only say *life's not fair* about stuff you can't control." Bailey Rae crossed her arms for emphasis. "You're in charge of yourself."

"True. Which is why I don't see the point in telling her I care, only to watch her leave."

"Um, so you don't regret it." His daughter blinked her big eyes at him. "Don't get mad, okay?"

Bailey Rae loved to preface things with that, and it always made him nervous. It was such a trap. How could you promise not to get mad before you knew if you would be?

"I'll do my best," he conceded.

"Chase was always climbing the big tree at the park, but I was too scared. I didn't want to tell him that, because I didn't want him to think I was a scaredy cat, but finally I just told him. So he helped me up." A big, toothy smile spread across her face. "I was still a little scared about how high it was, but then I sat on one of the branches, and it was so cool that it was worth being a little scared. And don't worry, I was careful."

Sure. Careful until she came home with a broken ankle, and he hunted the Matthews kid down.

Then again, how often had he climbed trees at her age? By third grade, he'd been riding horses and herding cows. As tempting as it was, you couldn't live life in a bubble. It might be safer, but you'd miss out on too much.

"Sometimes dreams change." Bailey Rae raised her eyebrows, about to dump another sage wisdom bomb on him, he suspected. "It used to be my dream to be a unicorn, but I can't be one, so I decided I'm going to be a ballerina. Maybe I'll change my mind again."

Wyatt wasn't sure that was quite the same thing, deciding on a different career when one was impossible, but he understood what she was saying.

"Don't ask her to give up her dreams," Bailey Rae continued. "Just tell her you love her. Then she can choose what she wants."

Put that way, it seemed so simple. And of course his daughter had picked up on the fact that he loved Jemma before he'd fully realized it himself. He swallowed, processing everything she'd said and doing his best not to let hope get the best of him. As always, he wanted his daughter to be prepared.

"She still might leave," he said.

"But she might not. You're so much happier with her, Daddy. Isn't it worth a shot to be happy?"

Surprisingly, people had given them space while they talked, although he was sure they'd done plenty of eavesdropping.

The sea of faces surrounding them silently urged him

to try. They practically screamed they were on his team. He didn't delude himself that it was all about him—most of them didn't want to lose Jemma—but that was where they were united anyway.

Wyatt slowly straightened and glanced toward the heart-covered refreshment table. "April, I think I'm going to need another cup of that love potion. Because I'm about to do something crazy."

CHAPTER TWENTY-SIX

J EMMA LOOKED AROUND THE COTTAGE she'd grown so fond of, at the knickknacks and floral wallpaper and furnishings that were clearly done by someone from an older generation.

The tiny house had felt lonely for all of a couple of days before the hominess had taken over, but part of that was her neighbors. The townsfolk. As odd as it seemed, she didn't want to go back to an urban apartment with one bedroom, no matter if it had shiny stainless-steel appliances and a fireplace that snapped on with a simple flip of a switch.

For a lot of her life, she'd felt a bit weak, but after learning to drive in the snow, light a fire, and put on a play, she felt stronger. She knew she could dig in and do hard things, and she was more confident in her ability to be completely independent.

Even if part of her heart still seemed to think it needed Wyatt and Bailey to beat right.

"The heartbreak will fade with time, right, Señor Fluffypants?"

Her bunny nibbled on the carrot she'd set down for him, making a mess she'd need to take the vacuum to. She should start thinking about boxing up her stuff and finding an apartment in the city.

The city, where there wouldn't be miles of green, the stars wouldn't be so easy to see at night, and there'd be no spur-wearing blond kiddo talking with a thick accent and wrangling snakes for her.

She shuddered at that last one.

Okay, maybe she could do without snakes. If only she could focus on the bad, maybe the idea of leaving wouldn't hurt so much.

But then she thought of never getting to see Bailey's bright, multicolored outfits. Never sitting on the couch next to her and Wyatt as they watched a movie and roasted s'mores over the fireplace.

Since her brain clearly hated her, snippets of their time together flickered through her head. The way he'd called her city girl. Riding his horse, his arms around her. At the basketball game and their half-court shots.

Her cheeks burned as she remembered hugging him when he'd dropped her off at her car that night, only to realize he was trying to open her door like the gentleman he was.

That should also make her want to leave, to renew her vow that she wouldn't fall for another guy who only liked her as a friend. But she couldn't imagine ever caring about another guy the way she did Wyatt.

He'd made her head spin and her heart flutter, and around him, she felt like a fun, better version of herself.

"And here I am again," she told her bunny. "My thoughts keep going 'round and 'round and I already made up my mind, so every part of me needs to accept it."

The string that tied her to the cowboy next door wound around her heart, tighter and tighter until it felt as if it would slice the vital organ in half.

"Including you, heart," she whispered, pressing a hand over the spot in her chest that ached, although it didn't do much to appease it.

She picked up her phone, deciding she should call Randa and cry it out, but then the metallic knock came at her door, nice and low.

Dang it, she'd even miss the escape-artist horse who showed up and only truly loved her for her ability to provide him with carrots. Of course, that was why Señor Fluffypants loved her too.

Maybe that's where I go wrong. I should offer my next suitor carrots.

Hi, I'm Jemma Monroe. Have some carrots. In time, you'll love me, you'll see.

She snort-laughed of the image of digging carrots out of her pocket on her date. Only, thinking about how Wyatt wouldn't be the guy at the other end of those orange vegetables sent another wave of sadness crashing over her.

Yep, she definitely needed to get out of this town, the sooner the better.

Just got to put it all behind me, she mentally declared as she opened the fridge door.

She grabbed two carrots in case it was Casper's last visit and walked back across her living room. Señor Fluffypants was already waiting by the door, eager for his carrot, despite the fact that he hadn't finished the one she'd given him a few minutes ago.

The door swung open with a creak, and cold air rushed in, making her regret not grabbing her coat. The long white-and-black horse nose poked into the room, and she extended the carrot.

Then nearly dropped it when she noticed there was a cowboy astride Casper.

Casper's teeth gripped the end of the carrot, and he tugged it out of her hand before she could drop it.

Jemma blinked up at Wyatt, thinking maybe she was hallucinating. Or dreaming. She wasn't sure which was better.

"Evenin', miss." Wyatt tipped his hat and then dismounted, his hazel eyes boring into her. "I heard you had a thick-headed neighbor who's been bottling up his feelings, trying to keep himself from falling for you."

She licked her lips and opened her mouth, but instead of words, a squeaky, unintelligible noise came out.

His booted steps echoed across the wooden porch as he came closer. His familiar sweet-hay mixed with citrus and musk scent hit her, leaving her fairly certain this wasn't, in fact, a dream.

Everything was too visceral. Too impactful.

"The problem is," Wyatt continued, "try as he might, he went and fell for you anyway."

Finally, her mouth began to work. "And he sends you to tell me? Seems a bit cowardly on his part."

One corner of his mouth twisted up. "I heard he was just gonna send his horse at first. He was afraid you might slam the door on him."

She wrapped her hand around the edge of the cottage door. "I haven't ruled it out yet."

Wyatt reached out and cupped her cheek, his hand warm despite the chilly air. Now she'd never have the willpower to close the door, not that she would've before. "Truth is, I was scared. While I was trying to protect Bailey Rae, she wasn't the only one I was trying to protect."

Her heart beat double time, throwing itself against the wall of her chest as if it wanted to be closer to the guy standing across from her. Her skin buzzed, and her thoughts turned into a delicious, happy mess.

"I'd never ask you to give up your dreams. If you want that administrator job, I'd still like to try to make us work. Long distance will be hard, but if it means I get to be with you…" He brushed his callused thumb across her cheekbone. "I'll do whatever it takes, Jemma."

"To be clear, since I've misunderstood before, you're saying you want to be more than friends."

He nodded. "I'm saying…" He exhaled and locked eyes with her. "I'm in love with you, Jemma Monroe. You came into my life and changed it for the better. You make me happy. You make my daughter happy. We both adore you. And I'm completely—" he took one step closer, "—and totally—" his next step made the tips of his boots hit her stockinged feet, "—in love with you."

Tears filled her eyes for what seemed like the hundredth time today, and her heart expanded to the bursting point. "I don't want to go back to the city. I tried to tell myself I did, but after working in the school here, with such amazing administrators, I feel like I can make more of a difference in the classroom. And of course I love you and Bailey. I tried to stop myself from falling, and look where it got me."

"In the middle of nowhere, with a stubborn cowboy who almost let you go without a fight?"

She didn't know whether to shake her head or nod. She'd come here to shake up her life and have an adventure, and she'd done that and then some. "In the middle of where I belong, with a cowboy who literally rode into my cottage on a white horse."

"I did try to keep Casper outside."

She placed her hands on his sides. "I think you're missing the point."

"Oh, no. I'm just waiting for permission to sweep you off your feet."

"Pretty sure you've done that already, but I'm all for it."

He leaned in, his lips a breath away from hers, and every inch of her soared and tingled, head to toe.

"Wait," she said, and he froze in place. She almost scolded her mouth for forcing out the word because she was so sick of waiting to kiss this man. But she needed to say one more thing, just so there wouldn't be any question. "I love you too, Wyatt Langford."

His mouth crashed down on hers, a mixture of soft and scruff, and she wrapped her arms around his waist. He drew her closer, his hand sliding behind her neck as he angled her head, parted her lips with his, and deepened the kiss.

They broke apart for a moment to grin at each other like the in-love fools they were. He kissed her again, softly, deeply, urgently, tenderly. It was the most perfect kiss in all of history.

Then he slipped his arm behind her knees and lifted her into his arms, making good on the promise to sweep her off her feet.

EPILOGUE

I N ONE MORE WEEK, SCHOOL would be letting out for the summer. Wyatt couldn't wait for his girls to be home more. Anna Lau had decided she wanted to be a stay-at-home mom full-time, so there was a permanent third-grade teacher position open. One he hoped Jemma would take.

Over the past three months, they'd alternated their time between her rented cottage and the ranch, although most nights, he, Jemma, and Bailey Rae had dinner together here. Saturday nights were still reserved for movies and s'mores.

He finished changing the oil in his tractor and checked his watch again, anxious for Bailey Rae to arrive. Jemma drove her home a lot of days, but today he'd asked Lori to pick his daughter up early.

His sister's silver van came down the road and, within a minute or so, she pulled up in front of his house.

Wyatt greeted his sister and opened the door for Bailey Rae. "Ready to play Cupid one last time?"

His daughter beamed at him. "You know it."

Wyatt waved to his nephew and poked his head in to say hi to his niece, who was happily burbling away in her car seat. Lori snagged a bouquet of pink-and-red roses off the passenger seat. Once he'd taken them from her, she extended a drink carrier from Havenly Brew. "Three Wymmas. Country chocolate and city cinnamon, all in one delicious, not-very springlike drink. April had them waiting and ready to go."

"I'll have to call her and thank her again, especially if this works."

Lori grinned. "I'm sure it's going to."

Part of him was sure, but part of him felt like the first time he'd put himself out there. Like maybe Jemma would look around at this life and decide she'd had enough of the country and wanted to return to the city.

They'd taken a few weekend trips to Denver over the past few months. He'd met Jemma's parents and Randa, who'd also come for a visit about a month ago so she could see Haven Lake for herself. The two of them had talked about restaurants, shops, and shows, and there hadn't been as much longing in Jemma's voice, but she'd talked about them fondly enough that it picked at his old scars.

He had no doubts that she loved him or Bailey Rae. They were a family, and now he just wanted to make it official.

"Call me when she says yes," Lori said, and he appreciated her certainty.

His nerves did jumping jacks in his gut as he and Bailey Rae set up the table with red-and-pink candles—lit this time, since he'd be watching them. His daughter set the roses in the vase, and for a moment, he wondered if it was weird that it looked like Valentine's Day had thrown up in here at the end of May.

But the school play had changed everything, and the next day—which had officially been Valentine's Day—had been their first official day together.

"She's here," Bailey Rae said, letting the curtains fall over the window. "Are you sure I shouldn't go in my room for the beginning? I don't mind."

When he'd told his daughter about his plans and they discussed all the details, she'd offered to go to Lori's or the Townsends' so he and Jemma could have some privacy. He'd gone back and forth because he knew children weren't traditionally involved in this part. But it'd been a long time since they'd done things the traditional way, so he'd figured, why start now?

Wyatt walked over and gave his daughter's shoulder an affectionate pat. "I want you to be here. More than that, I'm sure Jemma would want you here."

Bailey Rae nodded over and over, and he had a feeling he wasn't the only nervous one.

Heeled footsteps sounded on the porch steps—Jemma didn't care that high heels didn't really go with ranching. Not that she went out to the field with them, but...

Focus, Wyatt.

The quick knock was followed by her walking in. "Hey, guys, I'm..." Her gaze moved to the table. She turned to him and Bailey Rae. "What's going on? It's a little early for dinner."

"That's why I just got drinks."

"Drinks by candlelight." Jemma stepped forward and kissed him. "And you say you're not fancy." She grinned at Bailey Rae. "Hey, sweetheart. How was your day?"

"Good." Bailey grabbed one of the cardboard cups and extended it to Jemma. "Now take a sip of your drink."

Jemma's eyebrows scrunched together, but she accepted the proffered cup. After taking a pull from the straw, she pressed her lips together. "Chocolate and..." She took another sip. "Cinnamon. Is this what I think it is?"

Bailey Rae was creating the distraction, just like they'd talked about, keeping Jemma's focus on her. "Yep. The Wymma is back. Limited time only."

"That's so weird," Jemma said with a tilt of her head. "I mean, I guess April serves coffee year 'round, but with the hot chocolate part of it, the Wymma seems like such a winter drink."

"Sometimes things you think will only last the winter actually last much longer," Bailey Rae said, giving him a sidelong glance to make sure he was ready. He was down on one knee, box in hand. "Right, Dad?"

"Right," he said, and Jemma glanced at him.

Did a double take.

Then her jaw dropped.

Wyatt opened up the ring box, revealing the engagement ring his daughter had helped him pick out. "Jemma Monroe, you know I love you. These past few months have been the best months of my life. From the first moment you stormed into my life, I knew I'd never be the same."

"Technically," she said, "your horse and *then* you stormed into my life."

He grinned and shook his head. "I had a whole speech prepared. Are you gonna let me finish it?"

"For sure. I just might correct some of the parts."

He laughed, the love he felt for Jemma coursing through him and making his heart swell. Not only did she constantly challenge him and help him through good days and bad, he enjoyed their back-and-forth teasing, knowing love was behind that too.

He cleared his throat so he could get on with his speech. "Jemma, I love that you never stop learning. That you're smart and kind and you make me laugh. You make me happier than I ever thought would be possible. Bailey Rae and I were hoping you'd join our family in a more permanent capacity. The forever happily ever after kind."

Unshed tears made her eyes glisten. She reached out and squeezed Bailey Rae's hand, and then she stepped forward so she was standing right in front of him. "I just signed a contract to teach third grade next year, so I'll definitely be around."

"Is that a yes?"

She smiled and bit her lower lip, glee radiating off her. "Of course it's a yes."

He slipped the diamond ring on her finger before standing and pulling her into his arms. She hugged him back, embracing him tightly and healing every last part of him. "I can't wait to get started on our forever happily ever after."

"Me neither," he said.

They shared a kiss, and then they both turned to Bailey Rae.

Jemma opened her arms, and Bailey lunged at her, arms equally as wide. They hugged and talked over one another about dresses and flowers and how summer would be the perfect time to get married if they could put everything together that quickly.

Jemma gestured for him to come and get in on the hugging action. He happily did as requested, holding them tight.

"After the wedding, can I call you Mom?" Bailey Rae asked.

Jemma smoothed Bailey Rae's hair off her forehead and kissed her. "As far as I'm concerned, you can start calling me Mom now."

In that moment, Wyatt recalled the times Jemma had been over with them, and how nice it'd be to be a family. With his biggest wish coming true, he realized how wise his daughter had been when she'd said some things were worth the risk.

And love was at the very top of that list.

THE END

ACKNOWLEDGMENTS

Since this book is all about a small town cowboy, I guess I should thank my parents for raising me as a farm girl. I loved growing up in a tight-knit community with so many people who cared and took me in…even if they did know a little too much about every move I made.

With every book, the people who always sacrifice and support me the most are the members of my family. To my husband and my kids, thank you for being so supportive, even if I switch books and plotlines partway through conversations without telling you. And extra thanks to Brody for helping me with some of the classroom scenes, and for letting me borrow your name. I also named a few other characters after my daughters. Bailey Rae's sense of fashion came from Sydney at that age, and Kylie really would be the first to step up and look at an animal or creature in class. She's also my very own Rory Gilmore IRL.

I also put my sisters Randa and April in here—well, used their names. Thanks to Randa for sharing her experiences as a grade school teacher, including the snake story, my husband for adding another teacher perspective, and to April for letting me make her a gossip, even though she's far from one.

Thanks to the entire staff at Hallmark Publishing. To my editor, Stacey Donovan: thank you for taking a chance on me, working with me, and getting my voice. It's been a pleasure. Thanks also to Rhonda and Teresa for your input, and to the cover designer and formatters, and everyone else on the Hallmark team who helps my book get into readers' hands.

Shout out to my agent of awesomeness, Nicole Resciniti. You're a rock star, and I can't thank you enough for all you've done for my career. Thank you for your guidance and perseverance and for comforting me when my world's on fire. Xoxo.

Gina L. Maxwell and Rebecca Yarros, I adore you. Thank you for always being there to talk plotlines and answer editing questions and to make me laugh when I need it most. I love our very structured Monday morning video meetings and how we can attend in our yoga pants. I don't even have words for how grateful I am to have you both in my life.

Last, but certainly not least, thank you to my readers for supporting my books and sending me messages that keep me going. Find me on Facebook, where you can tag along on my adventures, including burning my dinners, experiencing lots of mom fails, and managing to generate a whole lot of awkwardness.

And thank you, dear reader, for picking up this book. You help make dreams come true.

CLASSIC ITALIAN LASAGNA
A Hallmark Original Recipe

In *Country Hearts*, Jemma tells Wyatt, "If you're hungry, I'm about to pop one of the only meals I can make in the oven—premade lasagna that I only have to stab and warm up. It's kinda my specialty." But anyone can make our easy homemade version, and it's so delicious, it might become *your* specialty. It'll convince everyone that you know your way around a kitchen. (It freezes well, too!)

Yield: 12 servings
Prep Time: 30 minutes
Cook Time: 2½ hours
Total Time: 3 hours

INGREDIENTS
- 12 lasagna noodles, no-bake or cooked al dente, drained
- 3 cups shredded mozzarella cheese

- 1 tablespoon grated Parmesan cheese

Italian Meat Sauce:
- 1 (1-pound 3-ounce) package sweet Italian sausage, bulk or links, casing removed
- 1-pound ground chuck
- 1 tablespoons olive oil
- 2 tablespoons minced garlic
- 1 teaspoon Italian seasoning blend
- ¼ teaspoon crushed red pepper flakes
- 2 cans (28-ounce each) crushed tomatoes with tomato juice
- 1 can (15-ounce) tomato sauce
- 1 can (14½-ounce) chicken broth
- 2 sprigs fresh basil (optional)
- 1 teaspoon kosher salt
- ½ teaspoon sugar
- ½ teaspoon black pepper

Ricotta Mixture:
- 3 cups ricotta cheese
- ½ cup grated Parmesan cheese
- ¼ cup finely chopped Italian parsley
- 2 tablespoons finely chopped fresh basil
- 1 large egg, beaten

DIRECTIONS

1. To prepare Italian meat sauce: in a large casserole pot or Dutch oven, brown Italian sausage and ground chuck over medium heat, breaking apart meat with a wooden spoon, until no longer pink. Remove from heat and drain excess fat.

2. Return meat to pot; add olive oil, garlic, Italian seasoning and crushed red pepper; cook over medium

heat for 2 minutes, stirring frequently. Add crushed tomatoes, tomato sauce, chicken broth, fresh basil, salt, sugar and black pepper; bring to a boil, reduce heat and simmer for 1 to 1½ hours, stirring occasionally, until meat sauce has thickened. Taste and adjust seasoning; set aside to cool.

3. To prepare ricotta mixture: in a large bowl, thoroughly mix ricotta, Parmesan cheese, parsley, basil and egg; set aside.

4. To assemble lasagna: preheat oven to 375 degrees F. Spread 2 cups Italian meat sauce in the bottom of a large 11-by-14-inch baking dish. Layer 4 lasagna noodles over sauce. Spread one-half of the ricotta mixture evenly over noodles. Top with 1 cup shredded mozzarella cheese and 2 cups Italian meat sauce. Repeat with a second layer of 4 lasagna noodles, the remaining ricotta mixture, 1 cup shredded mozzarella cheese and 2 cups Italian meat sauce. Top with 4 lasagna noodles, remaining Italian meat sauce and 1 cup shredded mozzarella cheese.

5. Bake lasagna for 45 minutes, or until golden and bubbly. (Cover top loosely with foil if cheese is browning too fast.) Remove from oven. Let lasagna rest for 20 minutes before slicing.

6. To serve: using a serrated knife, slice lasagna into 12 portions. Top evenly with grated Parmesan cheese.

For quick and easy lasagna noodle prep: arrange lasagna noodles in a baking dish, slowly pour boiling water over noodles, cover with foil or film wrap and let soak for 20 minutes or until pliable.

Thanks so much for reading *Country Hearts*. We hope you enjoyed it!

You might like these other books from Hallmark Publishing:

A Country Wedding
Love on Location
The Secret Ingredient
Moonlight in Vermont
Beach Wedding Weekend
Love at the Shore

For information about our new releases and exclusive offers, sign up for our free newsletter at hallmarkchannel.com/hallmark-publishing-newsletter

You can also connect with us here:

Facebook.com/HallmarkPublishing

Twitter.com/HallmarkPublish

ABOUT THE AUTHOR

Cindi Madsen is a *USA Today* bestselling author of contemporary romance and young adult novels. She sits at her computer every chance she gets, plotting, revising, and falling in love with her characters. She has way too many shoes, but can always find a reason to buy a pretty new pair, especially if they're sparkly, colorful, or super tall. She loves music and dancing and wishes summer lasted all year long. She lives in Colorado (where summer is most definitely NOT all year long) with her husband, three children, an overly dramatic tomcat, and an adorable one-eyed kitty named Agent Fury.